Dear Reader,

What is your ultimate fantasy? How about visiting an exotic locale and having your heart swept away by a handsome stranger? Workaholic Frankie Jensen has no such fantasy—she doesn't have time for men! So when she finds herself stranded in paradise with no money, no ID and no patience, she's more than wary when a Good Samaritan in the form of a gorgeous beach bum comes to her rescue. Before long, she's living every woman's fantasy, but when her old life comes calling, will she leave her heart in paradise?

I'm so pleased to see *Club Cupid* reissued with a great new package and bundled with a special novella by Joanne Rock. Many readers have written to say they believe *Club Cupid* is the most, *ahem,* "romantic" of my books. I hope you agree, and I hope this humorous story restores your belief in true love!

Please visit my Web site, www.stephaniebond.com, and say hello. And the next time your vacation plans go awry, your plane is delayed, or your car breaks down, keep an eye out for a handsome stranger—*you* just might be stranded in paradise!

Until we meet again,

Stephanie Bond

Stephanie Bond
Joanne Rock

Strangers in Paradise

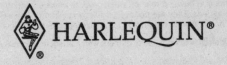
HARLEQUIN®

TORONTO • NEW YORK • LONDON
AMSTERDAM • PARIS • SYDNEY • HAMBURG
STOCKHOLM • ATHENS • TOKYO • MILAN • MADRID
PRAGUE • WARSAW • BUDAPEST • AUCKLAND

ISBN 0-373-83632-5

STRANGERS IN PARADISE

Copyright © 2004 by Harlequin Books S.A.

The publisher acknowledges the copyright holders of the individual works as follows:

CLUB CUPID
Copyright © 1999 by Stephanie Hauck

VALENTINE VIXEN
Copyright © 2004 by Joanne Rock

This edition published by arrangement with Harlequin Books S.A.

® and TM are trademarks of the publisher. Trademarks indicated with ® are registered in the United States Patent and Trademark Office, the Canadian Trade Marks Office and in other countries.

Visit us at www.eHarlequin.com

Printed in U.S.A.

CONTENTS

CLUB CUPID
Stephanie Bond

1

FRANKIE JENSEN JERKED her head vigorously to shoo away the enormous green fly buzzing under the brim of her straw hat. "Oscar, don't *tell* me the new compiler doesn't work," she warned, gripping the receiver of the pay telephone with one hand and juggling a portfolio of documents in the other.

He sighed. "Relax, Frankie—"

"That could delay the project by another eight weeks!" She straightened her sunglasses, then slapped at the fly with a rolled-up flowchart and missed, cursing silently. All these damn insects!

"But Frankie—"

"Which would be career suicide for *both* of us."

"I know, Frankie—"

"Call the president of the software company if you have to, but get that compiler working before I get back to Cincinnati."

"Uh, Frankie—"

"What?" she snapped.

"How's the cruise going?"

Frankie sighed and considered telling Oscar the truth—that her cousin's wedding had been a roaring bore, that she'd been worried sick about missing work, then just plain sick from the constant rocking of the ship—but she didn't want to prolong the conversation. "The cruise is fine." Except for the fact that the Valentine's Day package passengers had paired off like Noah's animals...present company excluded.

"I miss you," he said softly, obviously heedful of office eavesdroppers. "I wish you'd let me go with you on the cruise."

The inopportune sentimentality ruffled her. The one good thing about the trip was that it gave Frankie time to mull over her co-worker's gentle pressure to take their friendship a step further. "Oscar, you know it was impossible for both of us to be gone during this project."

"You're right." He agreed so readily that her frustration climbed a notch. "Where are you now?"

She glanced around at strolling sight-seers and street vendors, an explosion of primary colors and exotic odors—and insects. She swatted at the fly again. "Key West."

"Well, try not to worry about things here. Enjoy yourself, and have a drink for me."

"I'll call you at the next port."

"Promise?"

She fought the urge to sigh. "Goodbye, Oscar." She jammed the phone down, then looked around at the smiling tourists walking arm in arm. Frankie grimaced. Only four more days of Club Cupid. Then she'd be back home supervising the rollout of the inventory prototype. After an entire year of putting the team together, training everyone and agonizing through the system analysis and design, she was stuck on a creaky love boat during the most important phase of the project.

Frankie carefully tidied the papers she'd removed from the portfolio, smoothing the furled edges of the flowchart, trying to squash her burgeoning frustration.

She had a promotion riding on the successful presentation of the prototype—it had to be right.

After slipping the folder into the pocket of her black, soft-sided briefcase, she zipped the top and snapped down a covering flap for extra security. The packet of papers she carried—initial design, data flows and countless pages of handwritten notes from numerous meetings—were irreplaceable. She'd kept them with her during the entire cruise and had even stashed the briefcase under a pew during the wedding ceremony.

From another compartment, she withdrew a long menthol cigarette and smoked it down to the filter within two minutes, looking over her shoulder the entire time. She could just picture running into her cousin who'd promptly tattle to her parents. A ridiculous thing for a woman of thirty-two to be worried about, she knew, but she didn't want or need a run-in with her fretful mother—or her overbearing father. Frankie made a face as she stubbed out the cigarette against the side of a metal trash can, then tossed the butt inside.

She'd quit smoking after the project ended.

After slinging the bag over her shoulder, she checked her watch. The ship sailed at two o'clock, so she had thirty minutes to find souvenirs for her folks.

Frankie pushed the hat back on her head. The sidewalks were packed, the crowd spilling into the narrow street, oozing between parked compacts and delivery vans. Bicycles appeared to be the favored mode of transportation. A calypso band played on the roof of a single-story building across the street, the singers' gyrations hemmed in by an ornate wrought-iron railing, their shakers and bongos providing a beat to which the pedestrians' feet kept time.

If the temperature was one degree, it was one hundred and one. The sun blazed down and the air hung heavy, pungent with the sweet smells of perspiration and incense. The collar of Frankie's knit shirt clung to her sticky neck despite her having captured her long red wiry hair beneath the straw hat. She took a deep breath and entered the disjointed stream of lookers, buyers and sellers, focusing on making it to the leather-goods stand a few yards away.

"Pretty, pretty," a mahogany-skinned man crowed, thrusting a strand of beads in her face. She blinked, then smiled and shook her head.

"Handmade sandals!" another man shouted, waving two pairs of canvas shoes. Frankie glanced down at her white feet shod in ancient penny loafers. They looked a little dorky, but they were soft and comfortable. Maybe her mother would appreciate a pair of the cloth shoes, since she stood all day at the restaurant.

Frankie edged closer to the stand, then pointed to the pair she wanted. But as she twisted to reach into her briefcase, a vicious jerk on her shoulder pulled her to the ground. She felt the strap of her briefcase being ripped off her arm. Disbelief rolled over her as her back hit the sidewalk hard, knocking the breath out of her.

She grunted and blinked, tilting her head to look at the retreating purse snatcher from her point of view on the pavement. Only a glimpse of his khaki-green T-shirt was visible as he fought his way through the crowd. Unsuspecting people in his path yelped as he pushed them aside, reminding Frankie that she too had a voice. "Help!" she screamed, struggling to get to her feet with the help of the sandal man. "He stole my purse!"

Outrage spurred her forward and she took off in the

direction of the thug, yelling at the top of her lungs and desperately trying to keep him in view. The nimble thief scrambled across the hood of a parked car, darted across the street to the tune of screeching brakes and sprinted down the other side. Despite her best efforts, Frankie followed at a much slower pace, still pointing and yelling, and while many people stopped to look, no one seemed willing to join the chase.

Nearly a block later, the purse snatcher long gone, Frankie stopped, her chest ready to explode from exertion. She yanked off her crooked sunglasses, then held her knees, gasping for breath. Panic sprouted low in her stomach and billowed into her quivering lungs. Quickly she took mental stock of her losses: wallet, cash, traveler's checks, identification, credit cards, family pictures...and the project documentation. Hot tears of frustration filled her eyes. Frankie shoved a hand through her hair, wryly noting she'd lost her hat, too.

People passed her on all sides, but no one gave her more than a curious glance. In the distance behind her, she heard the growing whine of a siren. With relief, Frankie turned and spotted a policewoman on a motorcycle threading her way through the crowd. Frankie waved her arms and began yelling before the stout woman wearing Terminator sunglasses had even rolled to a stop. Hurriedly, she described the thief and her purse, then pointed in the direction he had gone. The woman nodded curtly, told Frankie to stay put and sped off.

Frankie glanced at her watch and swore, her apprehension growing. The ship sailed in fifteen minutes, but she *couldn't* leave without the papers. A passerby handed her the misshapen, trampled hat. She smoothed the torn straw, then twisted her hair and tucked it underneath with shaking hands.

The papers simply could not be lost. Her career flashed before her eyes. She'd taken a job with Ohio Roadmakers right out of college. Developing computer systems for a paving and construction company hadn't ranked high on her creativity list at the time, but the starting salary had been generous. She'd settled in, worked hard and progressed through several promotions in the past decade. When the inventory project had been approved, Frankie had been delighted to accept the high-visibility assignment. And now...

The green fly was back. She slapped at it viciously with both hands, her anger focused on squashing that infuriating bug, as if the act would solve her immediate problems. Arms flailing wildly, she suddenly realized how foolish she must look and stopped. But no one paid her any mind. Most of the people strolling past seemed to be bound for Rum King's, a semiopen sidewalk bar a few steps away where, the sign boasted, the first drink cost only twenty-five cents.

Frankie took a deep, calming breath and rolled her wrist to check the time again. Three minutes left. Should she make a run for the dock and beg the captain not to sail? Or wait for the police officer to return and gamble that the ship would be delayed? Or perhaps her cousin Emily would miss her and hold the ship? Frankie sighed. Fat chance... Emily had eyes only for her new husband, addle-brained Albert—they probably hadn't come up for air yet. The thought triggered images on which she instantly decided she'd rather not dwell.

She turned in the direction of the dock, then stopped. If the police officer returned with her purse, she needed to be here. And right now its contents were more important than the last leg of a cruise she hadn't wanted to take in the first place. She brightened a degree. If her bag was recovered, it would be a blessing in disguise because she could fly home early with a good excuse.

Her mind made up, Frankie leaned against a No Panhandling street sign and waited. A few minutes later, she heard the ship's horn blasting in the distance as it moved away from the dock. Party music crescendoed as the locals bid farewell in the rollicking style of the islands. After a couple of minutes, the aged ship crawled into view as it wallowed into the Atlantic Ocean.

Lifting her hand in a rueful send-off wave, Frankie felt a brief stab of remorse—Emily would have to pack up Frankie's cabin and take care of her luggage once Frankie contacted the ship. Her meditating, poemreading, touchy-feely cousin would probably worry about her being stranded in Key West, but right now Frankie felt more free than she had since the rusty ship had drawn anchor in Miami.

She'd dreaded spending Valentine's Day alone amongst a boatful of lovestruck couples. Some realities were simply too painful to face—single, with no outstanding prospects at her age...and Oscar didn't count. *Ouch.*

Frankie worked her mouth from side to side. Her job fulfilled her...really it did. Which was why she had to find that darn briefcase.

Apprehension washed over her anew and she muttered a quick prayer under her breath, promising to stop being such a control freak if her prayers were granted. Biting down hard on her bottom lip, Frankie chastised herself—she had no business keeping all those documents to herself in the first place. Throughout the project, she had released only bits and pieces to the team members on an as-needed basis, but she alone had the complete system documentation and minutes of off-site meetings. She hadn't even kept it on her hard drive at work. In the beginning she had rationalized assembling the private portfolio with the thought that, as project manager, she needed one master set of documents which were always up-to-date. But somewhere along the line, she'd grown possessive of "the Bible" as Oscar had affectionately dubbed the collection of papers. Once their boss caught wind of her stingy—and costly—shortsightedness, she'd be fired for sure.

Where the heck was the police officer? After another thirty minutes had expired, between the heat and the anxiety, Frankie felt close to expiring herself. Key West was so tiny, the officer could have canvassed the entire island by now.

Tingling with rising panic and feeling dangerously close to tears, Frankie looked around, her gaze settling on Rum King's. Fashioned like a Tiki hut, the entire front of the little bar served as a door, open to foot traffic, creating a breezeway to a small patio barely visible on the far side.

She swallowed, thinking how good a drink would feel on her dry throat. Although the bar didn't at all resemble her parents' diner, little details of such establishments—music, clusters of tables and chairs, the laughter of other patrons—had always given her a comforting feeling of belonging when she traveled. Frankie walked toward the bar, her steps quickening. If she stood near the doorway, she'd be able to see the police officer when she returned with her purse.

RANDY TATE SPOTTED the pale little woman as soon as she entered the room. Between the big, crooked hat with the curly dark red hair sticking out, the large sunglasses and her dusty, preppie outfit, she looked completely ridiculous. He shook his head and continued wiping the bar with a damp cloth.

Sizing her up beneath his lashes, he tried to guess her drink of choice. Surprise darted through him when she removed the glasses and revealed a heart-shaped face, dirt-smudged, but younger than he'd first imagined, and very pretty, even with her eyebrows drawn in a frown. She seemed nervous, looking out into the street every few seconds as she made her way toward where he stood behind the bar. A tourist, obviously. Probably on parole from an uptight corporate job. Had she become separated from a cruising companion? Imagining a customer's story had become a favorite pastime. Most tourists' lives were similar to his own rat-race existence before coming to the island, and were easy to figure out.

Dry martini with an olive, he guessed as she walked tentatively closer. No, she wasn't that jaded. And she had arresting, clear blue eyes. Long Island iced tea? Her figure was pleasing, with fabulous, well-turned legs, even if they were as white as milk. He clicked his cheek in sudden decision. Definitely mineral water, with a twist of lemon.

Tweety, a caged blue macaw, squawked as the woman stepped up to the bar. "First drink is a quarter," the bird said clearly, then squawked again, twitching his brilliantly colored head.

"He's right," Randy said, smiling at her surprised expression. "Tweety learned the phrase ten years ago and we haven't been able to raise the price because of it. What'll it be?" he asked, stuffing the cloth he'd used through a belt loop on his ragged cutoffs. Damn, but she was a cute little freckled thing.

But her eyes suddenly clouded. "Twenty-five cents?" Her voice rolled out low and husky, and he immediately liked the sound of her. Suddenly she disappeared from sight. Randy frowned, then leaned over the bar to find her bent at the waist, removing the dimes from her penny loafers. "Nice ass," he muttered under his breath.

"Nice ass," seconded Tweety, much louder.

The woman straightened abruptly, and shot a suspicious glance at the bird.

"Sorry—Tweety has no manners whatsoever," Randy said, shrugging.

She pushed the two dimes toward him, then dug deep in the front pockets of her stiff, khaki shorts. One pocket produced three pennies, the other, one. Triumphantly, she counted out the lint-covered coins and added them to the dime lineup.

"I'll have to owe you a penny," she said, her bottom lip quivering slightly.

Confused, Randy shrugged, loath to ask questions. He was not the stereotypical bartender with a sympathetic ear. In fact, he'd shed the entire White Knight gig ten years ago when he bid goodbye to the Atlanta skyline from a southbound 747. "Sure, lady. What'll it be?" Maybe she was a loon—at the last second he switched back to his first guess: martini.

"What'll it be? What'll it be?" sang Tweety in his high-pitched voice.

"Cappuccino," she said, climbing onto a stool to his right.

Randy blinked, then pursed his lips and scratched

his bare stomach. Was she serious? With both hands, he leaned on the counter and slowly looked all around. Parrot, bar stools, ceiling fans, sand on the floor, island music...yeah, the place still looked like a beach bar to him. And Miss White and Uptight was so fascinated with something he couldn't see out in the street, she hadn't even noticed his reaction.

"Uh, sorry," he said wryly. "Our cappuccino machine is on the blink."

"Oh?" she said, turning to him and frowning deeper. "How about just plain hazelnut coffee, with sugar, cream and a little cinnamon?" She glanced back to the street.

He laughed in disbelief and cocked his head. "Lady, I think you have me confused with Juan Valdez. How about a rum runner?"

Disappointment washed over her face, and for an instant he could swear she was going to cry. "No coffee?"

Randy sighed. The woman was obviously unstable. "I might have a jar of instant in the medicine cabinet." For his own hangovers, he didn't add. "I can doctor it with a little Kahlúa."

At last she smiled, revealing high dimples that triggered a stir in his loins.

"Coming right up." He exited through a tiny door to his left that led to a bathroom he didn't have to share with his clientele. When he realized he was whistling under his breath, he stopped and laughed. Nothing made his day like a pretty woman. Except this pretty woman seemed a little off her rocker. Still, if he played his cards right...

Flings with vacationers were relatively safe—no strings and no awkward attachments to untangle. And a fresh crop of female tourists who appeared ripe for the picking arrived daily, although lately he preferred windsurfing to brief affairs.

But with a little soap and water, Red would be tempting...

In his musings, he knocked over nearly every bottle in the medicine cabinet, sending the entire mess crashing into the sink. At last he came up with a small jar of coffee and returned to the bar, feeling foolishly victorious. But his celebration was cut short when he saw her, head down on folded arms, her shoulders shaking from silent sobs.

Randy rolled his eyes heavenward. *Don't ask, man. Don't get involved. Involvement means responsibility.* Then he glanced back to Red and sighed mightily. Bonkers he could deal with—but the lost-puppy routine broke him up. Long-dormant protective feelings stirred in his chest, but he willed them away with a healthy oath. Then, resolved to act as if nothing was amiss, Randy cocked his head and donned his best island smile.

2

FRANKIE HADN'T MEANT to cry, but for once in her life tears seemed like the only option. She'd invested nearly every waking hour in her career, only to have it threatened by her own stupidity and a petty thief. Surely no one would begrudge her a momentary crying jag.

"Boo-hoo," Tweety mocked, stopping her in midsob. "Boo-hoo!"

She sniffed and lifted her head to discover the half-dressed bartender had returned. He grinned, revealing white teeth, and held up a coffee jar. "Hey, come on, I tried to hurry."

The man's voice rumbled out in a lazy stream, his words running together like a too-big ice-cream sundae. A tiny gold hoop earring gleamed against his tanned skin. His sun-streaked shaggy brown hair hung nearly to his shoulders, the wavy mass in dire need of a trim. The lines of his face were strong and lean and brown, pleasingly balanced by a large nose and square chin. His muscular shoulders were wide and bowed slightly forward. A blue tattoo of a swirl design embellished his right biceps, reminding her of the lollipops she'd loved as a child. The man was one-hundred-percent polar from her *type*, but if she hadn't been so miserable, Frankie would have stopped to appreciate his considerable good looks anyway.

Instead, she hiccuped and offered him a small smile. The guy probably thought she was nuts. "S-sorry."

"No problem," he said cheerfully, handing her a paper napkin sporting a parrot and the bar's name. Frankie blew her nose noisily and when she glanced up, he had disappeared. To her left behind a wall she heard clanging noises and a faucet being turned on. "I don't have a stove to heat the water," he said above the noise. "But the tap gets pretty darn hot."

She nodded absently to the vacant spot where he'd been standing, briefly piqued that he seemed unnerved by her tears which, to Frankie, were such a novelty. "The tap's fine." She eyed the parrot dubiously, then, remembering the police officer, turned and scanned the street for what seemed like the hundredth time. Still no sign of the woman.

The bartender might be able to help her, but she hated to involve a stranger and admit how vulnerable and stupid she'd been. Besides, judging by his unkempt appearance, this guy didn't look to be very trustworthy himself. However, she could at least ply him for information. "Is the police department nearby?"

The clanging sounds stilled, then the barkeeper stuck his head around the corner. "The police department?"

She nodded, trying to look casual.

His eyes narrowed and he looked as if he might quiz her. Then he seemed to change his mind. "Uh, yeah, the office is over about four streets, near the corner of Angela and Simonton." He set a yellow stoneware cup on the counter, wiped a metal spoon on the leg of his jean shorts, stirred the impromptu cup of coffee and pushed it toward her.

Following his movements, Frankie cautiously lifted the cup for a drink, hoping the water was hot enough and the alcohol strong enough to banish whatever germs lurked from the unsanitary preparation. "Thanks."

The man inclined his head, and Frankie realized that his eyes, which she'd assumed were brown, were actually a light gold. All the darkness around them—his black lashes and thick eyebrows—had thrown her. He gave the bar another swipe with his cloth. "If that's all, I need to take care of some things."

She paused, then decided he was a stranger and it didn't matter what he thought of her. "Would you happen to have a cigarette?"

His mouth tightened as he reached beneath the counter and pulled out an open pack of some generic brand, then tossed them onto the counter. "Those things'll kill you."

"I know," she assured him, reaching for the pack. "But I'm not hooked. How about a light?"

Frowning, he produced a book of matches displaying the establishment's name. "Anything else?"

"That's all." Frankie watched him saunter from behind the bar. She guessed his age to be in the mid- to late-thirties range. He wore threadbare navy canvas tennis shoes and his faded cutoffs hung precariously low on narrow hips, revealing a glimpse of neon orange swim trunks.

Impressive—he was a bartender *and* a beach bum. And he wasn't even old enough to have reached his midlife crisis.

Although the long bar where she sat was nearly deserted, clumps of people had spaced themselves out in happy little groups at tall tables on the perimeter of the

open room and on the outside patio. A trio of scantily
clad co-eds gave the bartender their orders between co-
quettish looks, and despite the obvious age difference,
or probably because of it, he appeared to be enjoying
the exchange.

Frankie looked back to her coffee and lit a cigarette,
then took a long, stale draw. Imagine—she'd been worried the disreputable-looking guy would want to become involved in her dilemma. Glancing at her watch,
she gulped the warmish coffee, and the Kahlúa burned
the back of her throat. Oh, well, at least she knew the
police station lay within walking distance. If the officer
hadn't returned by the time she finished her coffee,
she'd walk there to see if the thug had been appre-
hended.

Frankie tried to think positively—the alternative
was too overwhelming. Her folks would be devastated
if she were fired from her job. She stopped, stunned
that her parents' reaction would be uppermost in her
mind. Inhaling deeply, she pursed her lips, recalling
for perhaps the thousandth time the argument she and
her parents had shared when she enrolled in her first
semester of college.

"I won't have it!" her father had shouted, shaking his
finger at her. *"You can study law, medicine, computers—
anything except the restaurant business."*

They'd been working in the diner at the time, and
her father had turned to several of his regular customers and expressed his disbelief. *"Francis and I have
worked in the restaurant for twenty years to send Frankie to
the finest schools, and what does she want to do?"* He'd
thrown up his hands in disgust. *"Run a lousy restaurant."*

The whole scene had been excruciatingly embarrassing, but her mother had stepped in to referee and they had all compromised...on computers. The high-paying corporate job she'd landed after graduation had always been a source of pride for her parents, and while she'd bought into the work ethic, the politics and the money of the position herself, she realized now that she'd made a success of the job for her parents, and in spite of herself.

She took another drag of the terrible cigarette and blew the smoke straight up in the air. Feeling sorry for herself was a waste of time—she excelled at her job and she enjoyed the daily challenges. She'd live through this so-called vacation and get back behind her desk where she belonged. As for the missing briefcase... well, she'd simply handle that problem one step at a time.

"Boo-hoo," Tweety sang. "Boo-hoo."

Frankie lifted her chin. "Speak for yourself, you big canary."

"Nice ass," he squawked, undaunted, then joined in the chorus of a Jimmy Buffett song booming over the speakers in the rafters.

She caught a glimpse of herself in the mirror behind the bar and gasped. Dirty face, disheveled clothes—no wonder the guy took off. He was probably as wary of her appearance as she was of his. As she dabbed at her face with a napkin dipped in an abandoned glass of water, she smiled ruefully. No one seemed to notice when she had screamed for help earlier, and even in her current state, no one asked questions.

So much for chivalry in Key West.

"Okay."

Frankie jumped at the bartender's voice behind her and exhaled smoke in a short puff. When she turned, he stood with one hand leaning on the stool next to her, his eyebrows raised expectantly. "You mean the coffee?" she asked. "It's fine."

He shook his head. "No, I mean okay, what gives? Why do you need the police?"

Frankie took a long drink of the bitter coffee. "A man stole my purse."

His eyes widened and he reached toward her, but fell short of touching her arm. "Are you hurt?"

She shook her head firmly, tingling unexpectedly at his concern.

"Did you lose all your cash?"

She nodded, taking another quick drag to fight the tears welling in her eyes again.

Jamming his hands on his lean hips, he said, "For Pete's sake, why didn't you say something before now?"

"For Pete's sake," Tweety parroted.

"I was waiting for the police officer to return," she explained, hating how he made her feel foolish. "She told me to stay put, but she's been gone for nearly an hour."

"Heavyset woman?"

Frankie nodded.

"That'd be Officer Ulrich. She might have caught the guy and taken him down to the station."

"That's why I asked for directions."

The bartender looked all around the establishment, as if sizing up her options. "Are you alone?"

Frankie studied the ashes on the butt of the cigarette and considered the question in a larger context, then mentally kicked herself and dropped the sooty mess into the nearly empty glass of water. "I am now—I missed my cruise ship."

He pursed his lips, crossed his arms and took a half step backward. "Well, like I said, the police station is only a few streets over."

Frankie stood and dusted off the front of her shorts. "Thanks for the coffee. I don't have enough for a tip."

"No problem."

"Then I guess I'll be going."

He nodded, then shifted restlessly. "You shouldn't have any problem finding it—the station, I mean."

"Thanks." She turned to leave.

"It's next to an airbrush T-shirt shop."

Frankie looked back. "Thanks...again."

He twisted the cloth in his hands. "If you get lost, just ask anyone."

"Okay...thanks."

"Wait."

She turned back expectantly.

He walked toward her, tossing the cloth on a table he passed. "Uh, why don't you let me give you a ride?"

"That's not necessary—"

"I was getting ready to leave anyway, and I'd feel better knowing you got your purse back. Besides, it might help to walk in with a local."

Frankie assessed him from head to toe, aware of the finger of apprehension nudging her. Something about the man emanated more danger than the petty thief who had accosted her earlier. Every sermon her mother had ever delivered about accepting rides from strangers reverberated in her head. "I don't think—"

"I'm Randy Tate," he said, reading her mind. He extended a long-fingered, bronzed hand.

"Um, Frankie Jensen," she said, giving his hand the briefest of shakes.

He grinned. "Nice name. Give me a minute to tell Kate I'm leaving."

Frankie's mind raced as he approached a curvaceous blond waitress. She read about situations like this in the papers all the time. She had just told the man she was vacationing alone and had no identification... practically an invitation for him to commit a violent crime against her.

Glancing around for an ally, she spotted a neatly groomed, middle-aged man sitting alone a few steps away, writing in a journal. A half-empty pitcher of a pale yellow frozen drink sat in front of him.

"Excuse me, sir," Frankie said, keeping one eye on the questionable Mr. Tate.

The gentleman looked up and smiled at her, his silver eyebrows furrowed with curiosity. "Yes?" He spoke with a pleasing English accent.

"My name is Frankie Jensen, and—"

"A pleasure to meet you, Miss Jensen. I am Parker Grimes."

Frankie nodded briefly, anxious to skip the small talk. "Mr. Grimes, I'm in a bit of a bind, and the bartender, Mr. Tate, has offered his assistance in helping me find the police station—"

"How nice of the young man." Parker smiled with approval.

"Oh, yes," Frankie said hurriedly. "But I just met him and I wanted someone to know that I was leaving with him, in case—" She stopped, suddenly feeling foolish.

"In case your body washes up on shore?" the man asked, nodding.

She felt herself blush. "Well—"

"Say no more, Miss Jensen." He glanced toward the

bartender and made a thoughtful noise with his cheek. "He does look a bit disreputable, doesn't he?" Then he gave her a comforting wink. "Don't worry—if you should turn up missing, I'll recount this conversation."

"Ready?" The disreputable-looking topic of their discussion stepped up beside Frankie and pulled a single key from his back pocket. "Hey, Parker."

"Hello, Randy."

Frankie glanced back to Parker, but the man was once again absorbed in his journal. Feeling duped, she frowned wryly and followed Randy into the blistering heat. From out of nowhere he withdrew wraparound-style sunglasses and tucked the ends of the flexible frames around his ears. He turned a corner and led her down a short alley to a weedy, makeshift parking lot for bikes, mopeds and motorcycles. She experienced only mild surprise when he stopped and threw one leg over the seat of a seasoned black Harley-Davidson Sportster.

Frankie bit the inside of her cheek. Stranger, tattoo, motorcycle... If her mother could see her now, she'd have a stroke.

Randy rolled the bike forward to release the kickstand, then walked the vehicle backward out of its spot. Twisting, he flipped down the passenger foot pegs. "Climb on."

Eyeing the motorcycle dubiously, Frankie wet her lips. "There's nothing to hang on to."

Randy's grin made her breath catch. "There's me."

To distract herself from the disturbing option, she asked, "Where's your helmet?"

His mouth twitched. "A head injury would be more merciful than lung cancer. Are you coming or not?"

Rigidly, Frankie climbed on, careful not to touch

him, finally settling onto the hot leather seat, then feeling all around for a handhold. At last she curled her fingers under the edge of the seat. "I'm ready," she announced, squaring her shoulders and staring straight ahead.

He sat holding the handlebars loosely, his shoulders rounded. "First time on a bike?" Frankie caught his look of amusement in the side mirror.

She was tempted to lie, but decided against it and nodded.

"Well, try to relax, and move with me. You'll throw off my balance with that stiff little backbone."

"Okay," she murmured primly, easing her posture a fraction of an inch.

"And you'd better hang on to that hat if you're fond of it."

Frankie loosened one hand from her death grip on the seat and gingerly lifted it to the top of her head. "Okay."

He inserted the key and depressed an innocuous-looking button. When the engine roared to life, her heart vaulted into her throat. With no warning, the bike lurched forward. Frankie abandoned her hold on both the seat and the hat and rammed her body up next to his, circling his waist with both arms.

With her chin resting on his shoulder and her eyes squeezed shut, Frankie felt rather than heard his laughter as he maneuvered the motorcycle around the side of the building and into the street. His back felt solid and safe. She inhaled the odor of strong soap mingled with mild perspiration on his neck. His wayward hair tickled her cheek.

Above the rumbling hum of the engine, the noises of the island descended upon them: pounding music, shouting vendors, creeping traffic. Frankie opened one eye, then the other, but carefully kept her head down as he threaded through side streets and alleys. Relief in the form of a cooling breeze rushed over her arms and legs, and Frankie's heart raced with adrenaline.

"Relax," Randy shouted over his shoulder, shifting his body as if to encourage her.

Embarrassment bolted through her, and she forced her limbs, her torso, to soften. Her thighs cradled his intimately, white against brown. Her breasts—such as they were—were pressed up against his warm shoulder blades. Foreign sensations, which she couldn't justly blame on the bike, vibrated through her body, and her skin sang with heightened awareness.

The sensory overload on top of keen anxiety over her missing bag left her drained and barely able to hold on, even though they were moving at a leisurely pace. Frankie slid her hands over his hard, flat stomach, fumbling, searching for a firm hold, finally twining her trembling fingers together above his waistband. The Kahlúa was working on her empty stomach, and she felt light-headed. Her boneless body moved in sync with his, swaying around tight turns, then upright coming out of the curves.

If she blocked out the deep purr of the engine beneath her, she could easily imagine herself on her beloved and neglected sailboat, moving rhythmically with the water to maximize the boat's speed. The entire experience was delightfully erotic, and Frankie had never felt so aroused fully clothed. For a few seconds, Cincinnati and her pressing job seemed like an uncomfortable recollection. She bought into the illusion, trying to prolong the feeling.

They slowed for a stop sign and he put down his

feet, supporting their weight and the bike's. Frankie eased her hold around his waist, feeling self-conscious, but when she inched back he reached down and patted her knee.

"Better stay close."

Before she had time to register the unsettling intimacy of his touch, they were off again.

Careful to keep her head low and her hat safe, Frankie peeked over Randy's shoulder to take advantage of the brief tour. Key West seemed dressed for company. Tall and narrow, the buildings resembled colorful shoe boxes. Every house looked freshly outfitted in soothing yellows, greens and blues. Many were bed-and-breakfast inns, some were retail stores. Fanciful black iron adorned the structures like onyx jewelry, highlighting gates, porches and doors. Climbing vines, hanging baskets and exotic trees with multicolored blooms framed tiny lush yards. The chamber of commerce was to be commended. In a word, Key West was inviting.

If one had time to indulge in idleness, she reminded herself as Randy signaled left and slowed. He turned his head to the right, grazing his cheek against her nose. "We're here."

She looked up to see the unremarkable entrance of the police department, and sat erect while he pulled the motorcycle in front at an angle, then shut off the engine. Appalled at her reluctance to pull away from her Good Samaritan, Frankie did so nonetheless and pinched herself hard on the back of her hand as she dismounted. He was, after all, a perfect stranger.

Randy pushed down the kickstand, then reached up to remove his sunglasses, the swirl tattoo rippling on his bronze arm.

Correction—an *im*perfect stranger.

3

RANDY TOOK HIS TIME climbing off the bike. It was a good thing Red had been riding on the back instead of the other way around, else she would've probably noticed how her groping hands and yielding body had affected him on their ten-minute trip.

He scratched his temple. Hell, had it been that long since he'd had breakfast with a woman?

"You don't have to stay—I'll be fine from here." She adjusted the absurd hat she'd managed to somehow hold on to so that it sat more crooked than ever.

She was right, he decided. This little episode could mushroom into something messy. He'd simply find another tourist to scratch the itch she'd provoked. Besides, Red had given him an out.

He opened his mouth to say "so long" when he noticed the slight furrow of her eyebrows and the tight set of her mouth. She was worried and scared and on unfamiliar terrain. How could he leave her? Those unbidden protective feelings sprouted in his chest again. *Damn.* "I'll stick around for a little while," he offered, much to his chagrin.

The corners of her mouth lifted just a whisper. "If you insist." Then she turned and marched through the front door.

Randy sighed as he followed, cursing himself under his breath. What a softie he was today.

Officer Ulrich wasn't around, but she'd radioed in

that the purse snatcher had eluded her. On her way back, she'd been summoned to apprehend a shoplifter. Red nearly hyperventilated at the bleak news, but recovered enough to fill out a report, giving a pretty detailed description of the thief. Then she mumbled something about being fired as she signed the paper with a shaky pen.

"Relax," a young officer said in his molasses-slow dialect. "Your purse might turn up somewhere."

But she looked terrified. As she called to cancel her credit cards and traveler's checks, Randy watched and listened with growing dread. *Complications...involvement...*

Next, she called someone named Oscar and asked him to wire her money immediately, all the while assuring the man that she was unharmed and would fax a copy of some design sheet as soon as things settled down.

Difficulties...strings...

The dispatcher wired her cruise ship and arranged a pickup in two days on another ship. Frankie agreed, saying she couldn't extend her trip much longer, regardless of whether or not her bag was recovered.

Problems...responsibility—

Randy's head snapped up. Two days? Hmm. The officer was probably right about her purse turning up, and then... He scanned Red's dusty bod with renewed appreciation.

Long legs...tangled sheets...

Things were looking up.

THINGS COULDN'T GET much worse.

Frankie's mind moved sluggishly, slowed by the waves of fear consuming her. Oscar needed one of the early design sheets, which was stored on a compact disc, which was in the portfolio in her stolen bag, which was God only knew where. Her fingers twitched for a cigarette.

"Where can we reach you, Miss Jensen?" the young officer asked, his habit of pausing between each drawled word grating on Frankie's nerves.

Randy's arm appeared next to hers. He stood behind her, leaning into the counter that supported her weak-kneed frame. "My couch is a little lumpy, but available," he murmured, for her ears only.

She jerked back and narrowed her eyes at him, but he appeared innocent of wicked thoughts.

He raised his hands in defense. "It's just a friendly offer."

"Thanks anyway," Frankie said warily. "Officer, can you suggest a hotel?"

The young policeman shook his head, expressing obvious concern. "You'll be lucky to find a vacancy this time of year, ma'am."

Her hopes sank—much like her purse, she noted dejectedly, which was probably at this moment sinking into the depths of either of the two bodies of water surrounding the island.

Looking back to the bartender, Frankie asked, "A cancellation, perhaps?"

Randy's wink was so comforting, she could have believed that he invented the gesture. "Don't worry," he said. "I have a couple of friends who own B&B's." He scribbled a number on a piece of paper and handed it to the officer. "Page me, Rick, if the bag turns up."

Rick scoffed. "You never answer that thing, Randy."

"I will today."

Frankie wanted to protest because she didn't plan to

spend the rest of the day with him, but as much as she hated to admit it, she needed his help, and, for once, it was good to have someone to turn to in a crisis. "Do you know everyone on the island?" she asked as he held the door open for her.

He shrugged. "I suppose I've served most everyone on the island a drink at one time or another."

Disgruntled, she said, "Everyone here seems to move in slow motion."

Randy's laugh was low and suggestive as he leaned toward her. "I can move as fast as you want."

She stiffened. "This isn't funny, Mr. Tate."

To her surprise, his smile dimmed and he touched her arm gently, sending currents throughout her body. "Listen, Red, I'm sorry about your cash, but at least the guy can't get very far on canceled credit cards. Cheer up."

With horror, Frankie realized her mouth was quivering, and dropped her gaze. "It's not the cash."

"The cruise?"

Her laugh was dry. "Hardly."

"What, then?"

Frankie cleared her throat and looked up. "You wouldn't understand."

One dark eyebrow arrowed up, then he crossed his powerful arms. "Try me."

The gentle seriousness in his voice shook her. She studied his face in the glaring sun for a full minute, noting for the first time the slight creases in his wide forehead, the crow's-feet framing his eyes, the hint of silver at his temples. Was it possible this barkeeper was more than he appeared to be?

"My bag held a portfolio of irreplaceable papers and compact discs. I have to get it back."

"What kind of papers?"

"Documentation for a computer project I'm heading up."

He looked perplexed. "You're on a cruise and you're worried about your job?"

Frankie scoffed. "That silly Valentine's cruise wasn't my idea. My cousin asked me to be her bridesmaid, and I had no choice, even though the timing couldn't have been worse."

"Chained to your desk, huh?"

She lifted her chin. "My career is the most important thing in my life."

"Too bad. But if it's any consolation, you're the best-looking computer nerd I've ever met."

Frankie felt herself blush, but held her ground. "My job depends on recovering that portfolio."

Frowning, Randy scratched his jaw. "Is this some kind of top-secret project?"

"No."

"Then there has to be copies of this documentation somewhere, right?"

She winced and shook her head.

"Is that typical?"

She winced and shook her head again.

"Ouch." He exhaled noisily, then shrugged. "Oh, well, in Key West when things get tough, the tough go to the beach. How about it?"

Frankie swallowed at his abrupt personality change. So much for the multifaceted theory. "The beach? Isn't it a little late?"

He grinned. "Like you said, we move slowly down here. Late afternoon and early evening are the best times to miss the tourists—no offense. Do you swim?"

"Y-yeah."

"Great." Randy unfolded his sunglasses and walked toward his bike. "Let's go."

Her mind raced. She couldn't just sit around getting a suntan while her entire career evaporated. Maybe if she could find a computer with basic software, she could re-create from memory the design document Oscar needed. It was worth a shot. "Do you have a computer?"

He stuck his tongue into his cheek and gave her an amused smirk. "No."

Fighting her disappointment, Frankie asked, "Public library? A school perhaps? Somewhere I can gain access to a computer for a few hours?"

But he simply shook his head. "Not this late in the day. And not tomorrow, either—nothing is open on Saturday except the retail shops." He straddled the bike and looked up. "Come on, there's nothing more you can do here."

Frankie considered the wisdom of parting company with the good-intentioned beach bum. "I have to pick up my money."

"We'll stop along the way."

He extended his hand to help her on, and Frankie hesitated. "But I have to find a place to stay—"

"I'll make sure you get a place to stay." He sighed, his shoulders dropping. "Listen, Red, a little R and R would do you a world of good. Look around—you're stranded in paradise. Have a little fun."

She wavered.

"We'll make a few stops along the way to look for your bag," he added. "The guy might have ditched it in a Dumpster."

Feeling like Alice in Wonderland hovering above the rabbit hole, Frankie relented. He was right—camping out at the police station wouldn't help her recover her bag any faster. And she hadn't had a vacation in the year since the project started. Maybe the sun and sand would do her some good. Besides, his Dumpster theory was a slim, but reasonable, possibility. She smiled and took his hand. "Okay."

His warm grin was reward enough—settling into their body-hugging riding position was purely a bonus. They stopped at a floral shop that doubled as the wiring office and woke up the napping shop owner, but her money hadn't yet arrived. The man yawned and wrote down Randy's pager number, promising to notify them if the wire came before he closed.

Par for the day's course, Frankie thought wryly. Next, they drove down four different alleys where Randy hoisted himself up and poked around in commercial trash bins, but didn't find the briefcase.

"Sorry," he said after restarting the engine and turning to her. "Don't worry—it'll show up."

A compulsion to believe him welled in her chest. This man had a powerful effect on her, lending a sense of security while triggering every defense mechanism in her body. Alarms pealed in her ears, yet she was touched he'd go to so much trouble for a stranger. "Thanks for looking."

"The ride to the beach will be longer, so hang on tight."

"But I don't have a suit."

He grinned. "I have to make a stop along the way— we'll pick up a suit for you there."

Her arguments exhausted, Frankie gave in and tried to put her spiraling career out of her mind. The ride was cool and flirty and just plain fun, she decided as laughter bubbled up in her chest. Randy had tied her hat to the seat, leaving her hair to whip around her face and neck with abandon. She didn't want to think too much about the pleasure of pressing herself up against her Good Samaritan, a man she barely knew, but who'd already hinted he found her desirable.

A memory surfaced, reminding her of a time in college she'd found herself attracted to a James Dean type, a dropout who hung around the student center to pick up girls. He'd flirted with her outrageously, constantly asking for a date. She'd been tempted, but frankly, the guy's reckless style had frightened her a bit. With Randy Tate she didn't fear for her safety, but she definitely felt as if she were walking a balance beam with responsibility on one side and hedonism on the other. The vertigo was absolutely heady.

All too soon, they were on the coast and he slowed, wheeling into the driveway of a large house encircled by a stone wall. The pale stucco structure resembled a hotel, the jungle-thick landscaping picture-perfect.

"Good friend of mine," he yelled over the rumble of the motorcycle as he wheeled into a long crowded driveway as large as a parking lot. "I need to pick up his liquor order for the week, and I'll find you a suit."

When he shut off the engine, Frankie could clearly hear music on the other side of the vegetation. She climbed off the bike and squinted into the blazing sun.

"You're a natural," he said, nodding to the bike. He knelt and untied a canvas sports bag. "You were in perfect sync with me."

Frankie patted her wild hair, tingling at his offhand compliment.

He stood and wiped his hands on his back pockets, then tossed her a knowing smile. "When a person moves that well with a bike, it's a safe bet they're good at other things, too."

Desire sparked low in her stomach, burning away any clever retort she might have conjured up.

His eyes danced. "Like windsurfing, for instance."

Her tongue finally recovered. "Is it similar to sailing?"

"You sail? Excellent." His grin was full-fledged as he moved toward a stone path beside the house. "Red, this could be an interesting couple of days."

Her heart pounded at the innuendo in his voice. A beach fling hadn't been in her plans, but two days in the company of a gorgeous man would definitely take her mind off the bedlam that awaited her in Cincinnati. *And tantamount to attempting a back-flip aerial on that balance beam*, her conscience whispered.

The sounds of music and voices grew louder as Frankie followed Randy to the house. He stopped at an ornate iron gate and gave her an awkward little smile. "Would you mind keeping an eye on the bike?"

"Oh," Frankie said, faintly disappointed. "No problem." She reminded herself he was here on business, then leaned against a waist-high stacked-stone fence and watched him move down the footworn path. An alarming feeling of loss filled her chest when he disappeared, leaving only the movement of giant plant leaves in his wake.

Who was this man who affected her in spite of her better judgment? A carefree barkeeper with whom she had nothing in common. He obviously thought she was overreacting to her missing briefcase—the man probably couldn't comprehend the stress of a corporate job, where dozens, even hundreds, of people depended on you. She sighed, walked back to the motorcycle and freed her hat from the seat to protect her face from the rays of the merciless sun.

Frankie scanned the massive house, the well-planned tropical landscaping and the impressive oceanic backdrop. The picture represented more money than she would earn in a lifetime. Randy had some wealthy customers. The sounds of shouts and laughter alternately rose and ebbed with the roar of the ocean, and she experienced a sense of wonder that for many people this paradise was part of a daily routine. She couldn't imagine not having to be somewhere at certain times most of the day, every day.

She glanced at her watch and frowned when she realized twenty-five minutes had passed during her musings about how the other half lived. Her forearms were turning a light pink and her underwear felt damp and clammy. She frowned and looked around for shade, but all the vegetation lay on the other side of the gate. Craning her neck in the direction Randy had gone, she wondered what could be taking him so long. She really needed to visit the bathroom.

Ten minutes later, she lifted the latch on the gate and stepped into the immaculate yard area. After a glance over her shoulder at the motorcycle, Frankie took a few tentative steps down the stone path, exhaling in relief when she stepped beneath the lush canopy of trees that met above the narrow walkway. She stood still for a moment, allowing the coolness to bathe her scalding skin. The voices and music were much louder now, and she could see snatches of sand and water through the trees and undergrowth. In fact, she could hear Randy's voice relatively close by and decided to walk farther down the path. She saw him standing by a shoulder-high wooden privacy fence, talking to a balding man on the other side of the partition and making notes on a small pad.

The other gentleman noticed her and raised a hand in greeting. Randy turned around, then grimaced in apology. "I'm almost finished," he called to her.

"Join us." The man gestured, smiling in welcome. "I'm Tom Hartelman."

Frankie approached them, feeling a bit sheepish. "Frankie Jensen. I walked down to find some shade," she said, rubbing her fiery arms.

"Randy," the man chided. "Bring your friend in for a cool drink."

"Well, I—"

"Look at her, man. She's frying."

"Actually," Frankie said with a wry smile, "I was hoping I could visit a bathroom."

Randy frowned slightly. "Frankie—"

"Why, of course, my dear," the gentleman said. "Come right in and meet some of Randy's friends."

"Frankie," Randy said as he held the handle of the wooden gate. "Can you wait? My friends are a little different—"

"Relax," she murmured, indignant. "I can hold my own amongst your rich friends."

His mouth twisted in amusement, and when the older man opened the gate, Randy swept his bronze arm wide in acquiescence.

Frankie gave him a tight smile, then stepped across the threshold onto the pale, glittery sand. She felt him fall in close behind her. In fact, his body slammed into hers when she stopped short at the contented scene. Some people were sunning in chaises, some were playing volleyball, some were relaxing in the shade with tropical drinks. There were both genders, all shapes and sizes and skin tones, with one universal theme.

Clothing appeared to be optional.

4

RANDY STEPPED around Frankie and watched her carefully. Her lips parted ever so slightly and her blue eyes rounded. He counted to nine before she swung her gaze to him, her eyebrows high, her expression one of puritan disapproval.

Suddenly contrite, he shrugged, palms up. "I tried to warn you."

She glanced to his friend Tom who, very much at ease with his big nude body, extended his hand. Frankie shook his hand woodenly, and once again Randy felt protective of her, suddenly embarrassed that he had exposed her to the more liberal side of the Keys. When Tom walked off in search of a drink, Randy touched her arm lightly. "Relax, Red, we don't have to stay and you don't have to take off your clothes if it makes you uncomfortable."

She turned back to him, her pale face flushed. Straightening her shoulders in an unconvincing show of bravado, she said in a low tone, "Listen, Buster—my name is Frankie. And taking off my clothes doesn't make me uncomfortable unless I happen to be standing around in public."

Trying his best to smother a smile, Randy asked, "Buster?"

"Would you please show me to the bathroom?" she

asked pleasantly. "Then I'll call a cab and be out of your way."

There it was—that little-lost-puppy routine that tugged at his heart every time. She really was adorable...and completely irresistible. And he knew if she left, he'd spend the rest of the day and all night worrying about her. "Hey," he said, reaching to grasp her arm gently but firmly. "You're not in my way. Stay with me and I'll find you a bathing suit. Then we'll go farther up the beach and try to salvage this rotten day, okay?"

She blinked and seemed to relax slightly. A confetti of freckles paraded across her nose and under golden eyelashes. He could feel her pulse beating beneath his fingers.

"If the waves are calm, I'll teach you to windsurf," he coaxed, aware of his own pulse kicking up.

After a few seconds of silence, the corners of her mouth rose, barely. Then she narrowed her eyes. "Do you promise to keep your trunks on?"

Relieved, Randy grinned. "I have to—too much wind drag reduces speed."

He was rewarded with a wry laugh as she shook her head slowly. "Okay, I'll go. *If* you can find me a suit."

"Wait right here," he said, holding up his index finger. Then he turned toward the beach, his steps hurried.

Frankie crossed her arms and shrank back against the fence self-consciously, watching him walk out among the nude sunbathers. Beneath her lashes, she scrutinized the nudists, some part of her appalled at their lack of modesty, some part of her awed by their lack of self-consciousness, some part of her titillated by their candor. Contrary to her first panicky impression, no orgies were being conducted on the beach blankets. In fact, other than random hand-holding, she saw nothing that could be remotely construed as sexual activity.

Randy, she noted, seemed completely at ease with the environment. He lifted his hand in greeting to more than one person and yelled to others. He stopped by a large blanket where three women and four men lay on their backs side by side. The brunette on the end wore headphones, but removed them when she saw Randy and sat up.

Frankie inhaled sharply at the size of the woman's bare breasts—high and firm, and void of any tan lines. She frowned down at her own slight curves, then glanced back, unable to take her eyes off Randy and his friend. Undoubtedly an old girlfriend, she guessed, surprised that the thought would be so disquieting.

Which was ridiculous, she decided, since a man with his looks on an island where women lay around buck naked would probably fall somewhere short of sainthood. Besides, it wasn't any business of hers anyway.

The couple talked for a minute, then Randy jerked a thumb toward her and the woman glanced in her direction. Frankie hesitated. Should she wave? Join them? Somehow she'd reached her thirties without learning proper nude-beach protocol.

The woman nodded and reached into a bag, withdrawing what appeared to be a handful of white shoe-strings and handed it to Randy. He smiled, then walked toward Frankie looking triumphant.

"One unworn bathing suit, compliments of my friend Sheely," he announced as he stepped up, dangling the garment in the air. "See? It still has the price tag."

Frankie swallowed hard. The shiny garment looked incongruous in his large hand. The top was huge, the bottom was practically nonexistent. And if anything could possibly make her skin look whiter, it was the color white. "I don't think Sh-Sheely and I have the same...uh—"

"Taste?" he supplied, his voice teasing.

She smiled wryly. "Something like that."

"Well, try it on," he urged. "The changing house and bathroom are over there." The red tile roof of a building on the fringe of the garden was barely visible through the trees.

Frankie sighed and picked up the bikini with forefinger and thumb, holding it in front of her as she veered off on a more narrow path that snaked in the general direction of the changing house. Oh, well, in two days she'd be on her way home and these people would forget they'd ever seen her. What did she care if she looked ghastly?

The changing bungalow was nicer than her Cincinnati apartment. Textured glass made up the entire top half of the building. Thick rugs lay on terra-cotta tile floors, with heavy rattan furniture clustered around a sleek big-screen TV, which was black and silent at the moment. A pool table sat against a wall, the balls racked and ready for breaking. Alternative entertainment for rainy days, she supposed. As to the numerous comfy-looking couches on the perimeter of the room, she blushed to think about their intended use.

Unoccupied, the only sound in the building was the swish of overhead fans and light reggae music from hidden speakers. On the other side of a long bar flanked by leather bar stools lay a stainless-steel kitchen that rivaled the one in her parents' restaurant.

There were two changing rooms, unmarked as to which was the men's and which was the women's. She chose one and entered a combination bathroom and lounge, with sinks and open showers and more couches. Not much privacy, she decided, then conceded that nudists were less demure than the population at large.

Her eyes widened at her rumpled, windblown, dusty reflection in the full-length mirror. She didn't even faintly resemble Frankie Jensen, the professional, fastidious systems analyst.

Glancing over her shoulder every few seconds, she showered quickly, grateful for the abundance of thick blue towels. She borrowed a wide-tooth comb from a selection on a marble vanity and detangled her wet hair as much as possible. After stalling for so long, and worrying that Randy might come looking for her, she reluctantly reached for the borrowed suit and pulled it on, then turned around slowly to look in the mirror.

"Oh my God," she muttered. Always pale, her skin looked so bleached it was difficult to tell where she ended and the white suit began. The double-D top swallowed her single-B chest, the excess extending up to her collarbones and down to her navel. The bottoms, in comparison, consisted of a white eye patch held together by two strands of dental floss. There was no back that she could find.

Soft footsteps sounded behind her, and before she could cover herself, the oil-slick, busty Sheely strode in, looking like a bronze goddess freed from her pedestal. "Oh, you must be Frankie," she said, flashing a brilliant smile. "I'm Sheely. Does it fit?"

Frankie stood speechless, flashing back to a similar nightmare in sixth-grade gym class. The woman was wearing only a navel ring, not that her stunning body needed any ornamentation at all. Frankie looked up to the ceiling, burning with embarrassment, trying desperately to think of something to say.

But apparently Sheely needed no encouragement. She unabashedly perused Frankie's body, gently turning her this way and that. "The top's a little big, but the bottoms look great—do you use the stair climber?"

Twisting to see for herself, Frankie said, "No, but I run every other day."

The woman nodded her head of dark hair. "Randy's an ass man."

Frankie blinked at Sheely, her earlier suspicion about the two of them confirmed.

"Why don't you just skip the top?" Sheely asked, shrugging her lovely shoulders.

"Well, I..." Frankie stopped, feeling a blush at the roots of her hair. "This is new for me."

The woman's smile was understanding. "Didn't Randy say you're here on vacation for a couple of days?"

Frankie nodded. "Sort of."

"Don't worry—have fun," she said, waving off Frankie's concern. "You'll probably never see any of us again."

And with a flip of her shiny tresses, Sheely left.

"Thanks," Frankie called weakly. The woman might be right, she noted with a frown. But big or not, the top was staying. And little or not, so were the bottoms.

She was about to reveal various freckles that heretofore only her doctor had seen. Desperate, she wrapped a huge blue towel around her waist, sarong-style, then pulled on her wrinkled brown blouse, leaving it unbuttoned for some semblance of nonchalance. With the addition of her hat, sunglasses and penny loafers, only her ankles and arms remained exposed. She stepped back to the mirror for the full effect. A little better.

Frankie folded and stuffed her underwear inside her shorts, then draped them over her arm and marched outside.

Her shred of confidence shriveled when every head turned in her direction. Sheely offered her a fluttery wave, and Frankie smiled tightly. She stared straight ahead and strove to keep her gaze shoulder level, scanning the crowd until she located Randy—which was easy since he was the only man wearing swimming trunks. He'd shed the shabby cutoffs and standing in the sun, his body was simply sensational. Not overly muscled, not an inch of flab. She tried not to stare at him, but told herself it was better than looking elsewhere on this beach. Her heart started pounding and for a minute she thought she might be having a panic attack. She inhaled deeply with each step.

"Over here, Red," he said easily, raising his hand. As she approached, he lowered his sunglasses and looked her up and down, a smile tugging the corners of his mouth. He stepped away from a circle of naked men, then leaned toward her and whispered, "Are you in there somewhere?"

"Yes," she managed to say with dignity.

"I do have sunscreen," he said, his mouth twitching.

"Randy," an older man with a thick head of blond hair admonished. "Introduce your new friend."

"Maybe later, Phil," he responded, taking her arm. "I think we'd better go before Red has a heatstroke."

To her relief, he bid the group goodbye, then steered her toward the ocean and to the left. Sometime while she was changing, he had acquired a small cooler which he held high as they picked their way among several sunbathers. She followed him past the volleyball game in progress, which, frankly, looked painful to her. After walking around several sand dunes, he stopped under crisscrossing palm trees, set down the cooler and spread out a large blue towel identical to the one she wore.

The sand crackled beneath her shoes and the sun's rays reflected off the ashy surface in sheets of heat that were nearly visible. She could still hear the sounds from the house, and occasionally, a nude swimmer would walk in her line of vision to dive into the waves, but for all practical purposes, they were alone.

"Sorry to take you away from your friends," she said, breaking the silence.

"No big deal. There'll be other parties. Tom's quite the entertainer."

"What's the occasion?"

He shrugged, lowering himself to the towel. "Valentine's Day, I suppose. Seemed like a lot of out-of-town couples. It's the weekend for romance," he added in a mocking voice.

Still standing, she averted her gaze to the horizon, changing the subject. "The view is spectacular."

"This beach is nicer than the areas open to tourists," Randy said. "Tom lets me keep my wind surfboard in one of his storage units." He pointed vaguely to the right, but Frankie could see only sand, water and trees. She looked back to him and wondered briefly if Randy took advantage of his rich friend. He couldn't make much as a bartender.

He smiled up at her, his gold earring catching the sun, and unzipped the canvas bag. "You can put your clothes in here for now."

Frankie dropped her shorts and underwear into the bag, not sure what to do next.

"Feel free to take off your shoes," he added with a teasing grin.

She frowned down at her feet. The loafers did look pretty silly on the beach. Where she'd removed the dimes, two shiny dark circles of leather had been exposed. She slipped her feet out of the shoes, glad she'd touched up the bright pink nail polish on her toes while camped out in her cabin on the ship. The memory brought back the reason she was stuck on this island in the first place and renewed a sick feeling in the pit of her stomach.

"Now the towel," Randy said, his mouth twitching.

Frankie hesitated, but could feel the sweat trickling down her thighs.

"For Pete's sake," he said, raising one hand in the air. "It's a thousand degrees out here."

She toyed with the waist of the makeshift skirt, still anxious about revealing so much skin. Sheely's image loomed large in her mind.

"One quick motion," he encouraged. "Like a Band-Aid."

Frankie laughed nervously, loosened the towel and pulled it off, then spread it on the sand next to his while keeping her gaze lowered. The brown blouse fell only to her waist, offering little coverage. Her face flamed as she sat down, adjusted her hat, then chanced a glance at him. His smile had vanished, and his dark sunglasses revealed nothing. Seconds passed with only the sound of the wind and the caws of seabirds around them.

"Gee, Red," he finally said in a husky voice. "You

could have left some leg for the rest of the female population."

Her skin tingled under his blatant admiration...or maybe it was exposure to the sun. Frankie wavered between feeling flattered and feeling foolish. Was he coming on to her? Was that the reason he'd bothered to help her in the first place?

He cleared his throat. "Better apply sunscreen pronto," he said, rummaging in the bag.

"I don't tan well," Frankie agreed as she twisted her hair into a thick roll and tucked it beneath her hat.

"I've got SPF eight, fifteen, and liquid corduroy," he said, holding up various bottles.

She laughed and reached for the last bottle, then poured a generous amount in her hand and slathered it on every inch of her legs and feet, conscious of his eyes on her while he did the same. His nearness transformed the act of rubbing the cool lotion into her warm skin from an innocent precaution to sensual flirtation. Her skin prickled from heightened awareness as she fought to push the implication of their attraction from her mind. Randy Tate was a tempting distraction from her immediate problems, but she couldn't afford to lose her mental edge in the middle of a crisis. A tiny shift in wind behind her alerted Frankie that he'd leaned close.

"Hmm, never been jealous of lotion before," he said in her ear.

Her back stiffened and a shiver went down her spine.

"Want me to do your back?"

"Uh—n-no, that's all right," she said, leaning forward to shrug out of her blouse. She avoided his gaze and rubbed the sunscreen over her arms, shoulders, face, chest, stomach and as much of her back as she could reach with spine-twisting contortions.

He remained silent until she finished, then said, "You missed a spot."

She looked down and over her shoulder. "Where?"

He took the bottle from her and squirted a gob of the creamy white stuff in his hand, then leaned back on one elbow. Frankie swallowed and closed her eyes, her body tense in anticipation of his touch.

"Here," he said, a split second before rubbing a tiny area between her shoulder blades. His hands were hot, his fingertips as rough as pumice, but the lotion felt cool and slippery. Goose bumps raised along her forearms. How long had it been since a man had touched her?

"And here," he said, his voice an octave lower. His fingers traveled lower, to the small of her back where they covered one square inch of flesh with agonizing slowness. She bit her lower lip and fought the urge to roll her shoulders.

"And here," he said in a whisper she barely heard above the wind blowing in from the sea. His fingers traced a curvy line down her lower back to the top of the string that laughingly stood between her and nakedness.

Her breasts grew taut in response to his caress, the hair on the nape of her neck rising like a hundred tiny fingers. A stab of wanting struck low, and she willed a measure of sanity to return. Giving in to her incredible attraction toward a practical stranger while on a beach—it was simply too cliché. Not that she hadn't fantasized...

Randy's exploring fingers left her skin abruptly and he stood. "Ready for a swim?"

Startled out of her musings, Frankie glanced up. The telltale ridge of his desire strained at the clingy orange nylon of his trunks. She swallowed, grateful he'd suspended the erotic moment, yet vaguely disappointed. "A swim sounds great."

He grinned and playfully pulled her to her feet, then tugged her to the water's edge. Finding his enthusiasm contagious, Frankie laughed into the wind. Randy arrowed his hands, then made a perfect, shallow dive into the gentle waves and surfaced several feet out, his hair slick, his skin shining. "Come on in, Red!"

Frankie hesitated. This man was hazardous, without the courtesy of a warning buoy. Her heart thumped wildly as she watched him tread water, waiting for her. She inhaled deeply, feeling nervous and scared as she waded into the shallows, squishing damp, coarse sand between her toes.

"Don't think about it—just dive in!"

With the expansive horizon at his back and surrounded by azure water, the devilishly handsome Randy Tate might have been a postcard enticing her to indulge in an island fantasy. Frankie bit her bottom lip hard, sensing more was at stake here than a sunburn.

She might be an accomplished swimmer, but her sexy companion made her feel as if she was getting in way over her head.

5

RANDY SLUNG salty water out of his eyes and perused the slender beauty standing at the water's edge. Minus the hat, her long curly hair whipped around her head like a red-gold sunburst. Fantastically pale, her skin glowed like a seashell, translucent and fragile-looking against the harsh backdrop of sea, sand and wind. She dipped a pink-tipped toe into the water, stalling. The borrowed bikini top bagged around her slight curves and the minuscule bottoms gave him a gut-clutching view of her slim hips and unending legs. He marveled at how quickly he had warmed to the little freckled fish out of water. Too quickly and too warm, he decided, squirming.

She took two tentative steps into the clear shallows, then raised her arms and dived gracefully toward him. She winnowed through the water and surfaced a few feet away, her head back, her hair slick and dripping. She let out a gasp. Then, grimacing, she rubbed her eyes with the palms of her hands.

"Sorry," he said sympathetically. "I'm used to the ocean water."

She bobbed, treading water, then turned toward him, blinking rapidly.

Randy sucked in a breath between clenched teeth and nearly went under. The woman was an absolute stunner. Her smoothed-back hair revealed a deep widow's peak and threw her delicate features into relief—incredibly blue eyes framed with glistening gold lashes, high cheekbones, chiseled nose and full lips over a neatly pointed chin.

A tentative smile lifted her face as she extended her arms, pushing at the water's surface. "I feel so buoyant."

"One advantage of saltwater," he affirmed absently, then lay back to float and devour her beneath hooded eyelids.

She bounced up and down with the rolling waves, a smile playing on her lips. Like him, she was a water dog. He could tell by the glaze of sheer pleasure that slid over her expression, softening her eyes and relaxing her shapely shoulders. "Wonderful," she murmured, tipping her face up to the warmth of the late-afternoon sun. "I have to admit this beats February weather in Cincinnati."

"You're from Ohio?" he asked, trying not to stare at the bikini top billowing loosely in the water.

Eyes closed, she nodded. "Uh-huh. Born and raised."

The lines of her profile would inspire a sculptor, he was certain. A beat of desire drummed in his loins, low and prophetic. But he ground his teeth, suddenly determined to avoid the physical encounter he'd been so keen on initiating mere moments ago. He had the feeling that vulnerability was foreign for Frankie Jensen, and the fact that she had put her trust in him during a crisis was an honor he couldn't breach. *Dammit*.

"Ever been to Ohio?" she asked, seemingly unaware of his struggle.

Glad for the distraction, Randy said, "I've been to Riverfront Stadium a few times." He hadn't thought of his and his brother's weekend baseball excursions in years. Those days seemed like a lifetime ago.

She opened her eyes and glanced his way with a laugh. "Don't tell me Key-Westers go to Ohio for vacation?"

"Conchs."

"Hmm?"

"The locals are called Conchs."

"Like a conch shell?"

Randy nodded. "Yeah, except a conch is the animal that once inhabited the shell—it's kind of like a clam, and a favorite food around here."

She nodded as if she were familiar with the cuisine. "Okay, so do Conchs go to Ohio for vacation?"

He shrugged. "People who settle in Key West typically get comfortable. I haven't left since I arrived." Randy immediately regretted opening a door to questions.

Frankie shifted to her back and floated, her arms out to the sides, her toes poking out of the foam in front of her. "When was that?"

The glass-clear water revealed every inch of her long, slender body. He swallowed hard and pretended to concentrate on a group of swimmers throwing a water Frisbee several hundred yards away. "A long time ago."

"So you're a Conch now?" she teased, her tone offhand.

"The natives tolerate me, I suppose." Anxious to shift the subject away from himself, he asked, "Do you sail often?"

Frankie shook her head. "Not anymore."

"Did something happen?"

"Yeah." She laughed. "I joined the rat race."

Been there. "Don't you ever take time to relax?"

Her shoulders lifted in a little shrug. "The project I've been working on has kept me pretty tied up."

Tied up? Randy wasn't sure why everything the woman said seemed sexually charged. Her hair floated in the water behind her, beckoning him. Between her tempting body and her unsettling references to the corporate treadmill he himself had escaped by the skin of his teeth, his body temperature had definitely risen a few degrees. He dunked his head under the cool water, exhaled, then resurfaced and shook off the moisture. "You know what they say about all work and no play," he chided gently.

"Makes Jill a successful executive," she finished in a knowing tone.

Sympathy knifed through him for the woman's misguided goals. Once he too had believed that a double-breasted suit, schmoozy lunches and long hours lined the path to success and self-fulfillment. Indeed, he had risen fairly quickly to become the youngest vice president in a thriving Atlanta savings and loan. Eager and naive, he hadn't questioned suspicious practices until it was too late.

He peeked at Red and experienced a compelling urge to save her from herself. Yet he wondered if he would have listened to well-intentioned warnings when he'd been in the throes of his burgeoning investment career.

Money had flowed like water. The market was bullish and investors plentiful—until Black Monday. The S&L had slammed its doors and the next two years were a nightmarish blur of dealing with bankrupted customers, cooperating with state and federal banking agencies and testifying against his former bosses.

Afterward, Randolph Evan Tate III had liquidated his home, car and what was left of his own investments, packed one suitcase and hopped the train to Hartsfield Airport. In search of not only a new life, but a new *way* of life, he'd asked for a one-way ticket to a perpetually sunny destination. When the clerk suggested Key West, he'd agreed. Within a few days of arriving, Randolph had died, and Randy was born. He'd never looked back...until now.

"I'm the youngest project manager in my company," Red continued, interrupting his thoughts.

Her voice sounded near. Randy glanced over to find she'd drifted closer to him, her head still back, her arms paddling slowly. If he spoke, she'd realize they were on a collision course, so he inexplicably remained silent. Ten seconds until contact.

"Not to mention the only woman," she added.

He told himself to move out of the way. For some reason, this woman stirred sensations and memories best left dormant. Five seconds.

"The only woman, in this day and age, imagine that," she remarked idly.

Her silken leg brushed his beneath the water, sending awareness through his body. She floundered in surprise and Randy impulsively scooped his arm around her back, kicking hard to keep them both afloat. "Easy," he murmured against her hair, inhaling sharply at the overwhelming desire to pull her close.

"S-sorry," she gasped, shrinking from his touch.

Sobered by his intense reaction to her, Randy released her gently. "Are you about ready for a bite to eat, Red?"

She straightened her shoulders, then the corners of her mouth drooped. "Do we have to leave?"

Amused, he smiled. For someone who'd been so reluctant to join him, she seemed to have acclimated quickly. Nodding toward shore, he said, "I brought a snack in the cooler. I have a couple of hours before I'm expected back at the bar."

Her fetching mouth worked side to side. "I *am* a little hungry, but the water feels so good."

"We'll take another swim later, after the sun goes down a bit," he promised as he headed in with a lazy backstroke, ridiculously reluctant to disappoint her. "I'd hate to see you fried on your first day."

"The sun doesn't seem that hot," she said, following him nonetheless with a leisurely overhand crawl.

"The strength of the sun can be deceiving. Here you can get a sunburn in the shade." In fact, he was feeling a little light-headed from heat and hunger himself—at least he *hoped* those were the reasons behind his sudden dizziness.

"Would you check your pager?" she asked behind him.

He nodded, then stood and waded ashore, feeling uncomfortably vulnerable. Since when had he let a woman get to him? Never. He wasn't so desperate for a woman that the thought of not bedding Frankie Jensen should have him this unsettled. She was a virtual stranger, for Pete's sake. Worry niggled at the base of his brain. Then one glance over his shoulder stopped him dead in his tracks.

Frankie waded slowly toward him in direct sunlight, the waves foaming around her lean calves. Sundappled water sluiced from her hair and fingertips, and the ill-fitting white bikini had become completely transparent—so transparent, in fact, it seemed evident she was indeed a natural redhead. The moisture in his mouth evaporated. Randy attempted to take a step backward and tripped instead, sitting down hard in the pale sand.

Frankie tilted her head to shake the water out of her ears and smiled at Randy's clumsiness. Her steps faltered, however, when he pushed himself to his feet and brushed the sand from his hands. With his back to the sun, the man looked almost ethereal with his wide, bronze shoulders outlined and the light bouncing off the sun-bleached highlights of his wet hair. The gold earring and the dark shadow on his square jaw made him look like a pirate. Her heart jumped into her throat in raw appreciation while panic gripped her stomach. What was she thinking? Romping on the beach with a man so exotic, so unified with nature that the presence of the neon orange swim trunks—or any covering at all—struck her as absurd.

As casually as her shaking hands would allow, she pulled her hair over one shoulder and gently squeezed out the briny water. "How about your pager?" she asked without looking up. When her gaze wandered over her skimpy bikini, she froze—the wet, see-through fabric had adhered to her breasts and privates in a way that left no detail to the imagination. Frankie gasped, then jerked up her head, grateful Randy had turned his back. Had he seen her? Of course he'd seen her! Mortified, she crossed her arms in front of her and shuffled past him to drop to her knees on one of the towels beneath the bowed palms, her back to him.

The low rumble of his chuckle reached her. "You have nothing to be ashamed of, Red."

Her face burned with ridiculous pleasure as she yanked her wrinkled shirt from the gym bag. "Please don't call me that."

"Okay," he said, his voice cordial as he leaned over and withdrew his pager. He made a regretful noise. "No word yet. Sorry, Re—I mean, Frankie."

She pulled her shirt around her hurriedly and planted her rear end on the large blue towel, her earlier frustration flooding back. "How can I be sure the police are really working on my case?"

He picked up her hat and plopped it on her head before she could react, and lowered himself to the neighboring towel. "Because," he said with a wink, "we take crime against tourists seriously around here—especially crime against pretty tourists."

His gold-colored eyes sparkled, the dark frame of his lashes and eyebrows providing such a striking contrast, the intensity of his gaze unnerved her. Frankie glanced away, her skin tingly and tight from salty residue. She removed the dilapidated hat and fingercombed her hair, kinked and separated from the moisture. Her stomach ached, partly from anxiety over the lost briefcase, partly from hunger, partly from emotions kicked up by the near stranger next to her. "Where did you move from?" she asked, steering the situation back to safe conversation.

He lifted the lid of the cooler. "Atlanta."

His deep voice sounded guarded, piquing her interest. Had he left a bad relationship? A bad marriage? Aware of the collision course, she derailed her train of thought. "I went to Atlanta twice for training last year."

"Nice place," he said, noncommittal.

"I didn't sight-see," she confessed, smiling in fond memory. "But I *did* visit a different restaurant every night."

He laughed as he withdrew a nugget of ice and

rubbed it on the back of his neck. "No offense, but you don't look like much of an eater."

Mesmerized, Frankie followed his tanned hand as his warm skin consumed the bit of ice. The temperature in their patch of shade shot up. "W-well, there's more to a restaurant than the menu, you know."

He lifted one eyebrow. "Like?"

Like a gorgeous man sitting across the table. "Like atmosphere and ambience."

He grinned. "You mean smart-ass birds and staticky speakers?"

Relaxing an iota, she smiled. "Sort of."

"A restaurant would have to be extraordinarily bad to fail in Atlanta," he acknowledged. "Even with a tavern every few feet in the Highlands, the Friday-night wait used to be three hours."

"Do you miss it?"

He hesitated, then scoffed and reached into the cooler again. "All that traffic—are you kidding?"

Realizing she'd hit a nerve, she proceeded slowly. "Where is your family?"

A look of affection crossed his face as he removed a frosty bottle of beer. "There's just me and my younger brother. He's a missionary in India."

She tried to contain her surprise, but at the sound of his belly laugh, she knew she had failed.

"That's the typical reaction," he said. The corded muscles in his forearm flexed as he twisted off the cap. He extended the bottle toward her.

She shook her head. "I don't drink beer."

"Maybe I should introduce you to my brother."

Frankie bristled primly. "I never acquired a taste for it, that's all."

He shrugged. "Too bad—this is good stuff, brewed

locally." Rummaging in the cooler once more, he withdrew a bottle of water and handed it to her.

"So your brother is a missionary." She brought the bottle to her mouth and drank deeply. The wind had picked up a bit, carrying sand and teasing the ends of his drying hair. Her unspoken words hung in the air between them. *And you're a bartender.*

"That's right," he said cheerfully, as if he'd read her mind. "I corrupt souls, and he saves them. Fork?" He handed her a tiny two-prong utensil, then pulled a white net sack out of the cooler, heavy with shiny redshelled delicacies.

"Crab legs?" she murmured in delight. "I'm impressed. All we're missing is drawn butter."

In answer, he lifted a small plastic container. "A few minutes in the sun, and we'll have warm, drawn butter for dipping."

Amazed, she shook her head as he leaned to the side, stretching to set the bowl on a smooth rock in the sun, just outside their little island of shade. Frankie inhaled the fresh air and stared up into swaying palm fronds. She couldn't believe how her life had changed in the last few hours. By all rights, she should be insane with worry over losing those documents, but Randy Tate, Good Samaritan and self-proclaimed Conch, was having a decidedly calming effect on her.

"I think I'll have a beer after all," she ventured. For Oscar, she thought guiltily, who'd asked her to have a drink for him. Of course, he might not appreciate the fact that she was having his drink with a half-naked sun god.

Her companion nodded, then decapitated a second iced bottle and handed it to her. Frankie sniffed the musky aroma, then lifted the bottle to her mouth tentatively under his amused gaze. The cold liquid splashed down her throat smoothly, the full bloom of the nutty bittersweet taste flowering on her tongue only after she swallowed. Her grimace elicited a laugh from Randy as he situated the bag of crab legs between them.

"The last drink will taste much better than the first," he promised with an easy grin. He cracked a fat crab leg in several places with his strong fingers, and offered her the succulent prize.

Her mouth already watering, Frankie separated the broken shell and used the miniature utensil to pull out a chunk of white meat as thick as her thumb. Unwilling to wait for the butter, she plunged the morsel into her mouth, moaning with pleasure. "This is wonderful," she said thickly.

Randy's eyes danced as he forked a piece into his mouth. "Nothing better than long, tasty legs." His hungry gaze flicked over her gams, and Frankie swallowed the second bite without chewing.

To keep from replying, she took another drink from the mahogany-colored bottle. He was right—the beer tasted better this time.

"Who's Oscar?"

She blinked. "Hmm?"

Randy tossed a spent crab leg aside and cracked another. "The guy you called to wire you money. Boyfriend?"

Frankie swallowed and attempted an offhand laugh. "O-Oscar? Not really."

"Good. Otherwise I'd have to question your judgment."

She bristled. "Why?"

A few strands of shiny pecan-colored hair fell over

his ear as he passed her a crab leg, then retrieved the bowl of butter. He seemed to take his time removing the lid with his wide, blunt-tipped fingers, and she unwittingly followed every move. "Because," he said with a lazy grin, "the man would have to be downright stupid to let you go on a cruise by yourself."

For a few seconds, Frankie basked in the heat of his compliment, experiencing a rush of pure feminine satisfaction. Then a stubborn sense of loyalty seized her. "As a matter of fact, Oscar wanted to come with me, but I convinced him we both couldn't be spared from the project."

He laughed. "And good old Oscar went along with that?"

Frankie frowned. "Of course. He's a responsible man."

"Can't get up the nerve to tell him you're not interested?"

Her acute anger triggered a flash of reality, during which she looked at the situation through Randy Tate's eyes: she was a stranded, half-dressed tourist, seemingly ripe for the picking for a hungry islander with long, able arms. She wasn't afraid of him, but she knew an opportunist when she saw one. Frankie lifted her chin. "Maybe you shouldn't assume so much where I'm concerned, Mr. Tate."

"No need to be so formal," he said smoothly, dipping a chunk of white meat in the butter. "Especially since I've seen your..."

She glowered.

"Freckles," he finished neatly, then devoured the morsel with the most innocent expression.

Frankie pulled her shirt closer around her and flipped the edge of the towel over her legs.

His laugh rolled out pleasantly as he extended the butter toward her. "Too late for modesty, don't you think?"

"I don't appreciate being laughed at."

"I'm laughing *with* you," he said, relegating the butter to a level spot on the towels between them when she made no move to take it.

"Except I'm not laughing."

"Sad but true," he noted, undaunted. "Nothing personal, Red, but you seem unhappy."

Frankie blinked. "Unhappy? Th-that's the most ridiculous thing I've ever heard," she stammered, not about to succumb to his amateur psychoanalysis. "I mean, I'm not entirely happy at the moment, but who would be under the circumstances?" *Picnicking with an outrageously handsome man on a tropical beach.* She gestured wildly. "Believe me, when my job isn't in jeopardy and I'm not stranded thousands of miles from home, I'm happy." She donned what she hoped was a convincing smile. "*I* have every reason to be happy, thank you very much."

"Careful," he said, wagging a crab leg at her. "You protest too much."

Her composure faltered. "And you talk too much."

"Occupational hazard," he said with glib familiarity, then he winked. "I'll sit here and try to think of something better to do with my mouth."

Frankie's throat constricted. His utterly cool disposition unnerved her, and she wondered how he'd achieved his level of nonchalance. Realizing that her quick temper played into his hands, Frankie decided to turn the tables with something she sensed Randy Tate didn't like—questions. "Were you a bartender in Atlanta, too?"

As she suspected, his demeanor changed. Randy averted his gaze and busied himself cracking more legs for them. "No."

When he didn't expound, she pushed her advantage. "Missionary?"

At least he laughed this time. "No."

"Independently wealthy?"

Another laugh. "Hardly."

She tipped up the beer, this time savoring the taste. "If you don't tell me, I'm going to think you were involved in something illegal." When his hands stilled suddenly, Frankie experienced a stab of alarm. Had she misjudged him—was he a criminal? A fugitive? She tensed, remembering she was supposed to go for the eyes and the gonads if he pounced.

But Randy simply handed her another red shell, his gaze a bit sardonic. "Illegal? Depends on who you ask, I suppose."

Edgy, Frankie tucked a stray strand of hair behind her ear. "I'm asking *you*." He bit into a piece of crab, and chewed it thoughtfully. She finished her beer, her gaze riveted on her mysterious companion.

"I was an investment broker."

Frankie skimmed the man before her, taking in his shaggy hair, earring, tattoo and sun-bronzed chest, then burst out laughing. "Right," she said, tossing another shell on the small pile they'd accumulated. "You said that with such a straight face, you must be an actor."

One side of his mouth climbed in a sheepish smile. "You're pretty good, Red."

Frankie held up her hand to refuse another piece of crab, then fingered the neck of the beer bottle. The label of washed-up actor fit Randy Tate's image perfectly, so why did his revelation leave her with a vague sense of disappointment? Because she had projected a level of complexity onto this man out of some misplaced romanticism? "Were you in anything I might have seen?"

"No," he said, laughing and shaking his head. "My work was confined to Atlanta."

Maybe he had no talent, hence the sarcasm about some people thinking he made his living illegally. "You weren't rich and famous?" she teased.

"Comfortable and infamous," he corrected.

"So what brought you to Key West?"

He lifted his bottle for a slow drain, but kept his unsettling gaze on her. Unable to look away, Frankie's skin tingled and her breasts tightened. This man had a way of making her feel as though the liquid he pulled down his throat was a preview of the way he would deplete her own reserves, given the chance. After setting the bottle aside, Randy leaned toward her, slowly...deliberately, then grinned devilishly. "I heard the island was full of damsels in distress."

He invaded her space and her senses as easily as the wind blew, lifting the ends of her hair and his. Frankie's heart pounded as she debated her next move. Advance? Retreat? Surrender?

Randy seemed poised, waiting for a signal, his eyes questioning. Arrogance, she could resist, but quiet chivalry...heaven help her. She eased forward almost involuntarily until only a cool breeze separated their parted mouths. Randy's gold eyes turned molten, but for a split second she had the strangest feeling he might pull away.

Then he inhaled, consuming the air between them, and drew her lips to his.

6

HALF OF HIM wanted her to surrender, half of him wanted her to bolt. From the troubled look in her wide blue eyes, it appeared that Frankie was considering both options when he captured her lips with his. When her mouth moved under his tentatively, sending his body roaring to life, Randy wished like hell she had resisted him, had given him a reason to resist her.

Instead, the prim, leggy beauty acted as if a switch had been engaged that directed her movements. The tip of her velvety tongue flicked against the sensitive roof of his mouth, sending shudders down to his knotted stomach. He cupped his hand behind her head, splaying his fingers in her hair, squashing the soft curls to leverage for better access to her mouth.

Their kiss deepened, each dipping and delving into sweet crevices with a sense of discovery and wonder. Frankie groaned and Randy heard the faint chink of her bottle falling to the sand. He clasped his other arm around her warm shoulders, easing her back to the towel. He followed, reveling in the length of her body touching his.

Since their swim he'd been telling himself to let this one go. Frankie Jensen wasn't the typical single female tourist looking for a romp with a local boy. She emanated seriousness and old-fashioned integrity—certainly not the type to take a romantic liaison lightly.

Randy instinctively knew she'd let few men compromise her single-minded dedication to her career. Almost no one had time or energy for unbridled ambition *and* unbridled sex. He remembered well the long purposeful days and the long lonely nights. Into the kiss, Randy poured all the want and frustration from those days that this woman resurrected. *Just a kiss*, he promised himself.

When his lungs demanded air, he lifted his head and gazed at her—another mistake. The brilliant blue of her eyes matched the deep hue of the water and sky flanking them. Her dark red hair fanned around her head, seemingly alive from the slices of sun falling through the moving palm leaves onto the fiery strands. She lay arched beneath him, her chin up, her mouth parted. The sensible brown shirt lay open, as if in invitation. One of the tiny straps on the ill-fitting bathing-suit top had fallen over a shapely, creamy white shoulder, revealing the swell of her breast and the barest hint of a plump areola. He felt dizzy with the raw desire that pulsed through him. Her name hovered on his tongue, but he was afraid to speak, afraid to shatter the moment.

Without conscious thought, he moved, stroking his raging erection against her thigh. He braced for her objection, and welcomed it. But when her eyes fluttered closed and a raspy moan of need escaped her mouth, he gritted his teeth against a surge of passion, then, admitting defeat, lowered his mouth to the silky contours of her collarbone.

Angling her body under his, he lowered himself between her long legs, kneading the firm muscle at the back of her thigh beneath her rounded hip. He lapped at her pearly skin and nipped at pale freckles, kissing a trail down to her half-covered breast. Heady with longing, he pulled aside the thin fabric with his teeth, gratified when a rock-hard pink nipple popped into view.

A torrent of heat gripped his loins as he pulled the salty tip into his mouth and bathed it with his fevered tongue. She drove her fingers through his hair, pressing him closer. A moan tore from her mouth, sending a vibration through her chest that he felt against his cheek.

So absorbed was he in his sensual ministrations that when Frankie tensed beneath him, he thought she was merely straining into him. Then she shifted and pulled her hands from his hair, struggling to sit up. He fought his first instinct to pull her back to him.

"Randy," she said, breathing raggedly. "Your beeper...is going off."

He raised his head and bit his tongue against the disappointment sluicing through his body. Frankie looked...relieved? With a heavy sigh, he smoothed his hair back from his forehead, rolled over and reached for the offending mechanism.

Frankie sat up, dragging herself backward with weak arms. She gulped for air to clear her fuzzy head, wincing at the pain zipping through her temples at the sudden shift from horizontal to vertical. A breeze swirled around her, cooling her uncovered breast, budding the nipple still wet from Randy's tongue. Mortification over her behavior flooded her. She yanked up the bikini top and secured the minuscule ties, then buttoned her shirt for good measure, despite her shaking hands. Thankfully the sand dune had ensured their privacy, although anyone could have stumbled across them.

As Randy bent over the pager, she stared at his broad back and the mop of shaggy, sun-streaked hair. A stranger, in a strange place. What was she thinking? She'd known this man for scant hours, and she'd nearly gotten naked with him. She hadn't been thinking, period. Frankie swallowed and pushed her fingers into her hair, her mind spinning. She scrambled to her feet, then, feeling naked, jerked up the towel and wrapped it around her waist, sand and all.

Randy pushed himself to his feet and turned around, holding up the pager. "It's the flower shop. Your money must have arrived." His voice sounded a little hoarse, but his expression remained unreadable as he swept her covered figure with his eyes.

She kept her gaze high to resist the impulse to see if he maintained his earlier state of arousal. Her hands felt awkward, so she hugged her arms and strove to look casual. "That's g-good."

His chest expanded as he inhaled deeply, then his mouth formed a grim, straight line. "Considering where this situation was headed—" he gestured vaguely at the towel "—it was also very good timing."

No matter how close he'd come to the truth, heat climbed her neck at his presumption of her willingness to have sex with him. And why not? Hadn't she given him every reason to think she would? Just another in a long line of willing female tourists, no doubt.

Shaken at her near lapse, Frankie squared her shoulders and assumed her most professional face. "Mr. Tate, I think it's better if we say goodbye now. I'll take a taxi to the florist's. Now that I have money, I'll be fine." She stepped toward him, her toes sinking into the silky sand, and stuck out her hand. "Thank you for your, er, hospitality."

His eyebrows rose and he considered the hand she'd extended, not without amusement, she noticed. Frankie immediately regretted her action since her hand wasn't exactly steady. She felt ridiculous, but still she waited. He pursed his mouth, then reached forward and blanketed her fingers with his in a comforting grip. "I'm nothing if not hospitable, *Ms. Jensen*," he said, mocking her formality. "But you'll still be needing a place to stay tonight, and I'd feel better if you'd let me arrange it."

She carefully extracted her hand from his and nodded curtly. "I would appreciate it. Perhaps you could make a call on my behalf?"

"The fellow who owns the place I have in mind will probably be at the bar," Randy said. "After we pick up your money, we'll swing by there." He glanced at his watch. "It's nearly six—I'm expected back soon anyway, and you can talk to Parker about a room. Then," he added lightly, "we can part company."

For the time being, she ignored his comment about parting company because she found the idea so startlingly disappointing. "Parker? You mean the older gentleman I spoke to?"

Randy nodded. "His house is a bed-and-breakfast. I'm sure he can find a place for you to rest your pretty head for a couple of nights."

She tried to ignore his compliment, but failed miserably. "Hopefully just one night," she amended. "If my briefcase turns up by tomorrow, I'll try to get a flight out of here instead of waiting for the ship on Sunday."

He smiled slightly. "Good idea. After all, you wouldn't want to delay your return to the daily grind, and—" his eyes twinkled "—Oscar."

Her face burned. "No, I wouldn't," she said tightly.

"Well, then it's settled," he said matter-of-factly, casually walking backward toward the shore. "Give me a few minutes, and we'll pack up and head back."

Frankie frowned as he increased the distance between them. "A few minutes?"

He squinted into the sun and flashed a sheepish smile as he walked into the shallows. "Excuse me, but I find myself in need of a cold swim." After a quick pivot, he dived into the water with athletic ease.

When she realized he needed to quench his libido, Frankie allowed herself several seconds of smug satisfaction before shaking herself and bending to tidy up the remnants of their picnic. She murmured a word of thanks to the heavens for intervening on her behalf. If that pager hadn't sounded, right now they might be writhing on the towel, their bodies fused in unleashed passion. Frankie swallowed hard, squashing the provocative image. With a frown, she wondered how many conquests the virile Mr. Tate had made beneath this palm tree alone.

Unable to resist a peek in his direction, she scanned the glistening, bobbing waves and watched the perplexing man swim away with powerful strokes. She sighed. He had certainly gone above and beyond the call of duty by stepping in to help her. Granted, he *might* have harbored ulterior motives—like the private picnic—but she had to admit she'd welcomed his attention.

His dark head disappeared beneath the water, evoking a flutter of apprehension in her chest. The wind had kicked up considerably, cultivating the waves until they crashed more forcefully onto the beach. Straightening from her task, Frankie bit her bottom lip and counted the seconds he remained submerged. After ten seconds, she dropped the bag of uneaten crab legs and cupped her hands as she jogged to the water's edge. "Randy!" When he hadn't surfaced in another five seconds, she stepped free of the cumbersome towel and ripped open her shirt, sending buttons flying. "Randy!"

In her haste, Frankie broke the surface of the water with a loud splash, concentrating on the spot she'd last seen him. Out of habit, she opened her eyes under water, only to be reminded instantly that she was swimming in the ocean. Withstanding the stinging saltwater, Frankie swam with strong kicks as long as her lungs would allow, frantically searching the clear depths for her Good Samaritan.

Spotting a dark object several yards in front of her, Frankie surfaced for air, coughed, then propelled herself forward with a jerky overhand crawl. "Randy!" she sputtered. "Can you hear me?"

In the distance, two yacht-size cruisers were passing, blowing air horns. Her heart thudded in her ears. If a man of his size and strength had been pulled down by an undertow, she'd have very little chance of saving him without becoming a victim herself. Diving shallowly, Frankie tensed for any change in the current of the water around her.

At first she thought the shadowy fingers floating below her were kelp or some kind of sea flora, then she realized it was Randy's hair. With a surge of strength, Frankie grabbed a handful and pulled hard while kicking for the surface. To her immense relief, after the initial weight resistance, his body seemed to rise with little effort on her part. Frankie's first thought was that he must be unconscious. But as soon as she broke the surface, she gasped in amazement when he emerged, eyes wide, his head crooked to accommodate her death grip on his hair.

"Gee, Red, if you wanted me back on shore, all you had to do was say so," he said, his voice rich with suppressed laughter.

Frankie released him with a jerk, coming away with more than one strand of honey-colored hair. Anger blazed through her as she gasped for breath. "I thought...you were...in trouble!"

His grin flustered her further. "You swam out to save me?"

"No!" she sputtered. "I mean...yes, dammit!"

His hearty laugh rumbled out, echoing across the water. With his hair slicked back and the sun glinting off his earring, Randy Tate was quite possibly the most outrageously handsome man she'd ever seen. While Frankie burned with embarrassment at coming to his supposed rescue, the man beamed.

She scowled and headed back to shore with as much fervor as she could manage with her rubbery limbs, weak from exertion and relief. She heard Randy following her, his occasional spurts of laughter fueling her exasperation.

He caught up with her in shoulder-deep water. "I do appreciate the gesture," he said, still smiling.

Frankie tried to splash the gloating expression from his face. "What the heck were you doing underwater for so long?"

"I thought you might like this," he said, lifting his hand to reveal a curved shell the size of his palm.

"A conch," she murmured as he placed it in her hand. The hues of the shimmering shell ranged from pale pink to deep rose, with the curved inside nearing purple. "Does it still contain a living animal?"

"Not this one. It's yours if you want it. I'd hate for all your memories of the island to be bad ones."

"It's beautiful," she said, touched. "Thank you, Randy."

He grinned and his eyes lifted at the corners. "You're welcome. And I'm glad we're back on a first-name basis...Frankie."

Ridiculously pleased with his gift and his good humor, she waded out of the water with him, clutching the white suit to her body, recalling the bikini's transparency. He picked up the towel and her shirt where she'd dropped them, but when she reached for the items, he held on to them, making her pause. "Frankie," he said, his voice suddenly serious. "I'm sorry about...earlier."

Surprised, her mind raced for an explanation for his apology. Was it a ruse to catch her off guard, to endear her to him further? She bit the inside of her cheek. He looked so damn sincere...but then, he *was* an actor. Conjuring up a shaky smile, she said, "Let's forget about it, okay?"

"Okay," he agreed with a nod. "Maybe by the time you pick up your money, the police will have found your briefcase."

"And I can be on my way," she said, nodding with him. Except suddenly, stupidly, she hoped the briefcase wouldn't show up until just before the second ship arrived Sunday. She could spend a couple more days on the island relaxing with...alone. Yes, alone on the beach with a book. A nice, platonic nonfiction book. A cookbook.

"On your way back to cold weather," he murmured, retaining his hold on the items between them.

"Back to my job."

"Back to the stress," he said with a pointed look.

"Back to my responsibilities," she corrected gently.

He slowly released the towel and the shirt into her hands. "You're right, of course. Let's get going. I guess the windsurfing lesson will have to wait until another time."

Within a few minutes, they had repacked the cooler and donned their clothing. Since her shirt was missing a few buttons, Frankie tied the ends across her midriff. They remained silent for most of the walk back to the private beach and the spectacular stucco home. Frankie held the gym bag in one hand and the conch shell in her other, rubbing her thumb against the smooth inside wall. The stroking motion seemed to calm her vacillating mood, and she felt a strange attachment to the gift. She occasionally sneaked a peek at the man striding next to her, thinking he would laugh if he knew how much the token had pleased her.

When they stepped within bounds of the nudists, Randy moved closer to her side and touched her waist in a protective gesture that she appreciated, despite the fact that the casual contact set her nerves on end.

He guided her along the outskirts of the sunbathers and Frankie labored to keep from staring. Sheely had turned over on her stomach to give her sleek back and behind equal exposure to her front. "I'd like to pay your friend for the bathing suit," she said. "Will you bring the money back to her on your next visit?"

"I already offered to pay Sheely, but she didn't want the money."

Frankie frowned. "I can't very well give it back to her after wearing it."

"She wants you to keep it."

This habit of accepting charity from strangers left her feeling very...beholden. "Why would she do that?"

He shrugged. "Sheely is a very generous person."

Frankie was glad he didn't expand on the woman's different levels of generosity, but she couldn't resist asking, "Is she an old girlfriend of yours?"

His chuckle rumbled low and mocking. "No. Does it matter?"

"Of course not," she assured him, although she did feel strangely comforted by the disclosure.

The owner of the house loitered near the gate, smoking a short cigar—Frankie strove not to make Freudian comparisons. Trying to keep her eye contact high, Frankie realized with a start that she hadn't craved a cigarette since they'd arrived at the beach.

"Ahhhh, Randy," the balding man crooned. "Surely you're not whisking away this lovely woman so soon."

"I'm afraid we need to get back, Tom."

His friend pulled a face. "You're not fooling anyone, my boy. You simply want to keep her all to yourself."

"How true," Randy said easily, his hand tightening on her waist. With the other hand, he held up the cooler. "Thanks for the crab legs."

Tom winked. "No problem. I figured you two would work up a bit of an appetite."

Frankie narrowed her eyes at Randy, but he simply smiled and shook his head as if to say, "Even if we deny it, no one will believe us." Instead, he said, "I might be back tomorrow afternoon for a little surfing."

The host nodded hospitably, then gestured toward Frankie with his cigar. "Will you be bringing your little tourist treasure?"

Frankie lifted her chin, bristling. The man made her sound like a generic plastic souvenir. She glanced at

Randy and found him studying her with amusement dancing in his eyes. "That's up to Red, I suppose. She seems to be in a hurry to leave our fair island."

Flushing under his mocking gaze, Frankie inclined her head in farewell to his congenial naked millionaire friend, then walked through the gate Randy held open. She stepped onto the shaded path leading to the parking area, feeling self-conscious. Following the path abruptly to the right around a hibiscus bush heavy with fragrant, pink blooms, Frankie lost sight of the men, but she could still hear them talking.

Tom chuckled. "Did you scare her off, Randy?"

Expecting a flippant answer, Frankie smirked. Then Randy's deep voice floated to her, despite his obvious attempt at a lowered tone. "The other way around, my man, the other way around."

7

FRANKIE ONLY half listened as the man at the flower shop counted the bills into her hand. During the entire return trip, the offhand parting comment Randy had made to his friend had darted in and out of her mind much like the way he'd maneuvered the motorcycle in and out of streets and alleys. *She* had scared *him* off? What the heck was that supposed to mean?

After thanking the clerk, she turned to find the man of her musings standing with his foot propped up on the low sill of the display window, his tanned fingers keeping beat with the tune on the radio against his bare knee. Earthy and masculine, Randy Tate looked incongruous standing amidst floor stands of live and silk flowers.

Staring out the window, he appeared bored, and Frankie decided she was making too much of the earlier remark. Considering him now, unobserved and restless, the thought occurred to her that he probably meant she had turned into more trouble than he'd bargained for, what with all the running back and forth. After all, the island was undoubtedly rampant with low-maintenance one-night stands, and he was wasting valuable time with her, a lost cause.

As if he sensed she was thinking about him, he glanced at her and gave her a distant smile. "Ready to go, Red?"

She nodded, then extended a one-hundred-dollar bill in his direction.

He made no move to take the cash. "What's this?"

"For all your trouble," she said simply.

He straightened, frowning. "You don't have to pay me."

Attempting to press the money into his hand, she said, "I owe you a tip anyway."

He pulled his hand away empty and shook his head. "If memory serves, you only owe me a penny."

Frankie hadn't meant to offend him. More impressed with his gallantry than she cared to admit, she tried to lighten the mood. Holding up the bill, she smiled. "So, do you have change for a hundred?"

Thankfully, he laughed. Frankie felt a stab of panic that the rich sound had become so welcome to her ears. "Come on," he said, opening the door and causing a bell to tinkle overhead. "Maybe the bar will."

From the flower shop, they rode to the police station, but Frankie's briefcase still hadn't turned up. Her initial disappointment gave way to bewildering relief, but she chose not to analyze her reaction too closely. On the trip back to Rum King's, Frankie wrung pleasure out of every second of the early-evening breeze cooling her pink skin. The sun in its descent had turned from flaming tangerine to a brilliant coral, with flowing robes of rose and blue clouds gathered around in preparation for a grand exit. Bongos reverberated in the distance, probably a celebration of the impending sunset.

Having acclimated to Randy's rhythm, her body melded with his seamlessly as they swayed around curves, her hair whipping behind her. The skin on his back felt soft and fuzzy with salty residue. The flat planes of his stomach moved beneath her interlocked hands as he shifted on the seat they shared. Frankie clung to his warmth, resisting the overwhelming urge to run her hands freely over the front of his body. The heat, her circumstances, his proximity—all of it combined to make a powerful aphrodisiac. But, she reminded herself, she had always conducted herself with discipline, and she wasn't about to change now.

Still, the thought of what might have happened on the towel beneath the palm trees kept sneaking into her mind, sending arrows of fire to her belly. Would he have been the fiercely gentle lover she'd longed for during the wee hours of countless sleepless nights? Gazing at the ceiling until she'd memorized every crack in the plaster, many times she'd concluded there had to be more to life than the daily grind of corporate drudge. But by the light of day her romantic reflections had seemed silly, and by lunch she'd been reveling in the hectic pace of the day. Her parents had taught her to be strong, independent and resourceful—she didn't need a man to make her feel fulfilled, and certainly not a raggedy vagabond.

As if strengthening her resolve, Frankie tightened her fingers over Randy's midriff, her fingers grazing the indention of his navel, a strangely erotic sensation. Perhaps in response, or maybe not, he rolled his shoulders slightly, pressing back into her breasts. She closed her eyes against the rush of desire that left her neck rubbery, thinking how it was very lucky that she'd escaped the brush with intimacy with this unabashedly appealing man. Otherwise, she might spend the rest of her life looking for a mate with the impossible combination of sex appeal and security. In her opinion, such a man didn't exist because the two drives ran counter to each other. What better example than to compare her hazardous riding companion to her complacent co-worker? Randy evoked a more animal response in her with a single glance than trusty Oscar achieved with the candy and the earnest kiss he'd given her before she left.

Her disturbing thoughts cleared when they stopped at an intersection she recognized. She marveled at the swelling crowds swarming down the sidewalks like so many colorful bees. Randy threaded through the people, at a pace so leisurely he kept his feet down, touching the pavement occasionally to maintain their balance.

After a few turns, they bumped gently into the weedy parking lot they'd left earlier in the day, triggering in her a vague sense of sadness that the ride was over. Randy eased the bike into a grassy spot and killed the engine. He held the motorcycle level while she climbed off, then lowered the kickstand with his foot. Rolling the bike backward, he pulled up on the handlebars to lock the kickstand into place. After removing the clear-lensed glasses he'd traded for his sunglasses in the waning light, he untied their belongings.

"Thanks for the ride," she murmured as she took her straw hat.

"My pleasure," he answered easily, engrossed with loosening the gym bag.

"I always thought motorcycles were dangerous. I didn't know they were so much fun."

"They can be dangerous," he admitted with a quick glance in her direction. The fading light cast most of his face in shadow. "But you're right—there's nothing like having something warm and responsive between your legs."

Frankie froze, wondering if her overblown hormones were prompting her to read more into his comment than he'd intimated. But when she saw the flash of his white teeth, she knew she was indeed being goaded again. "Are you ever serious?" she asked, exasperated.

"Being serious is bad for your health," he asserted. "Between the smoking and your type-A personality, I'll bet your arteries are already clogged."

"My bank account is healthy," she said loftily.

"Oh, well," he said with thinly veiled sarcasm. "At least you'll be able to afford a private hospital room."

"I would be much more stressed if I didn't have the security of a good job," she insisted.

"Define 'good,'" he said as he rummaged in the gym bag.

Frankie frowned. "Hmm?"

"Define a good job." He came up with a T-shirt and then pulled it over his head.

Momentarily distracted by the disappointment she felt when he concealed his smooth, muscled chest, Frankie chewed on the inside of her cheek, then said, "Good—you know, well-paying, stable."

He turned toward the street, stepping between her and a noisy group of college-age kids as they rumbled by in the falling dusk. "You don't ask for much out of your career, Red."

Frankie nearly laughed aloud—a bartender was telling her she didn't ask for much out of her career? She trotted behind him down the short, sparsely lit alley. "Excuse me?"

Randy shrugged. "No offense, but what about spending most of your waking hours doing something you just plain enjoy?"

Ruffled, Frankie pulled away from him as she walked. "I never said I didn't enjoy my job."

"You never said you did." Randy stepped into an opening in the stream of pedestrians on the sidewalk and made room for her.

She followed and raised her voice to be heard over the clatter. "I'm very good at what I do."

He gave her a quick once-over, his eyes sparkling with appreciation. "I'm sure you're good at a lot of things, Red, but just because you're promotable doesn't mean you like what you do."

She flushed under his gaze and the suggestive comment, but considered the wisdom of his words. The man was right, of course, but judging from what she knew of him, he was taking his own advice to the extreme. Deciding the conversation had strayed too close to a topic she didn't want to explore, Frankie scanned their surroundings.

The streets, now awash with light, had taken on a definite carnival appeal. Woe to any driver foolish enough to attempt taking a car down the street, which was swollen with vivid, vibrating bodies. Several establishments broadcast their own music, each louder and happier than the next in order to attract foot traffic. Even Rum King's had assumed a nighttime persona, sporting a huge neon parrot she hadn't noticed in the daylight.

"Did I hit a nerve talking about your job?" he asked near her ear.

She jumped, surprised he hadn't tired of their serious subject. "It's a trade-off," she said as he drew her aside to avoid a wayward partier. "A person can't have fun twenty-four hours a day."

He lifted his eyebrows in obvious disagreement.

"Well," she relented, lifting her hand toward him, "not everyone."

His laugh rolled out as they slowly made their way toward the bar. He placed a warm hand on her waist and she instinctively moved closer. "People like us balance out each other, Red. You're productive enough for both of us, and I'm..." He pursed his mouth as he presumably considered his best traits.

"*Re*productive enough for both of us?" The remark had entered her mind, but she hadn't meant to blurt it out.

But his burst of laughter made it clear she had embarrassed herself far more than she'd embarrassed her companion. Randy squeezed her waist as he steered her through the wide doorway of Rum King's. "We all have our talents." His voice sounded wistful—was he thinking of missed opportunities?

The bar had undergone a transformation in preparation for the night crowd. More tables had been added, and luminaires sat in the center of each table. Strings of white lights sparkled down from the rafters. The waitresses, now wearing short black shorts and tight cropped T-shirts, maneuvered between crowded tables. Reggae music boomed from the speakers. Cigarette smoke hung thick in the air, stirring Frankie's appetite for nicotine and practically obscuring the press of bodies on the patio. The underlying sweetness of citrus and alcohol tickled her nose, but she had the most irritating craving for a beer.

Randy nodded and smiled to a couple of customers who must have been regulars, then led her toward the bar where the blond waitress Kate dispensed drinks with a practiced hand. Tweety squawked like a broken record. "First drink is a quarter, *awk*, first drink is a quarter."

Randy briefly introduced the women. Upon hearing Frankie's name, Tweety dipped his blue head and declared, "Nice ass."

Frankie frowned at the bird and shot an accusing glance at Randy, who simply pressed his lips together and shrugged. Kate flitted her gaze over Frankie, then said, "Hey, Randy, the girls are asking for you out back." She jerked her thumb toward the patio and lifted her eyebrows suggestively. "Remember, it's for a good cause."

Randy squirmed and actually blushed, intriguing Frankie. "What's going on out on the patio?" She craned for a better look.

"Kissing booths," Kate explained.

"Kissing booths?" Frankie asked, then smirked in Randy's direction. "Let me guess—your idea?"

"Of course," chirped the blonde as she splashed rum into a row of glasses on the bar.

Randy reddened. "We have fund-raisers for charity a couple of times a year."

"And since Sunday is Valentine's Day," Kate continued while slicing limes, "Randy thought it would be a good time to raise a few bucks—one smackaroo for one smackaroo." She winked at Randy. "Of course, with some of the talk I overheard, you could probably name your price, boss."

Frankie imagined women standing in line to kiss Randy Tate and experienced a sting of jealousy. He shifted under her gaze, then glossed over the awkward moment by asking Kate several questions related to inventory and the day's receipts. He was making sure everyone else had covered for him in his absence, Frankie noted, probably in case the manager came around asking questions. But when Kate moved down to the other end of the bar, Frankie remembered how the woman had addressed him.

"Do you manage this place?" She gestured vaguely toward the crowd, trying to mask her censure. After all, the man certainly had a right to live his life the way he saw fit.

Randy considered her question as he circled behind the bar to fetch a cold brew. She was fishing, perhaps delving to see if he was really as irresponsible as he seemed. For some bizarre reason, he felt torn between wanting to impress this woman and wanting to maintain the distance they'd established. "Manage? I guess you could say that." She looked duly unimpressed—which was just as well, he decided. "What can I get you to drink, Red?"

She drummed her fingers on the bar, craving a cigarette, he presumed. Her lips moved, but he couldn't hear her over the din, so he cupped a hand behind his ear. Frankie fidgeted, then said loudly, "I'll have a beer."

He started to grin, then realized in the space of a few hours he had introduced the woman to nude beaches and beer—not much to brag about. Feeling like a bona fide bad influence, he pulled two beers from the ice chest, emerged from behind the bar and nodded toward Parker's regular table.

Parker Grimes sat in the same seat, with the same pitcher of frozen margarita in front of him, holding court to a wide-eyed handful of studious-looking patrons. By his animated gestures and facial expressions, Randy knew the silver-haired man was telling one of his famous stories. And by the looks of anticipation on the faces of his audience, he was nearing the end. Suddenly Parker's arms fell down, his shoulders sagged, and the entire table collapsed into gales of laughter. Randy touched Frankie's elbow and forged closer, waiting for a chance to get his friend's attention. The sooner he saw Red squared away with a room for the night, the sooner he could turn his thoughts elsewhere.

When he saw them, Parker's face lit up in greeting and he waved them forward. "Randy! Ms. Jensen! Please come and join us."

Two stools materialized, but Randy chose to remain standing—*for a quick getaway?* his conscience whispered. Frankie climbed onto a seat next to the man who had become a fixture in Rum King's.

Unlike most of the writers who found inspiration living in and around the unique landscape and personalities of Key West, humorist Parker Grimes was widely published, even achieving a good bit of critical acclaim with his second novel. Randy had inherited Parker's magnanimous presence when he'd purchased the bar, and the two had become fast friends. In fact, Parker was the only person with whom he'd shared the details of his prior life.

"I see you made it back safe and sound, Ms. Jensen." Parker looked past Frankie's shoulder and winked at Randy. "She seemed a bit concerned, my boy, that you might ravish her and leave her on the beach."

Randy caught Frankie's guilty gaze and a thousand unspoken words passed between them. For him, Parker's glib comment had the effect of stripping away the crowd and the noise, and sending him back to the stretch of sand he and Frankie had nearly christened. To lighten the moment, Randy conjured up a grin.

"And you assured her, no doubt, Parker, that I had absolutely no intention of leaving her on the beach."

Frankie narrowed her eyes slightly, which he found adorable.

His friend laughed, a rich, mellow sound. "Tell me, Ms. Jensen, did Mr. Tate help you out of your—what did you call it? Bind?"

She turned a shaky smile in Parker's direction. "Um, yes, Mr. Tate was very...accommodating."

Just knowing that Frankie too was thinking about their near romp sent desire pumping through Randy's primed body. He leaned in close, wickedly gratified to see her swallow just before he murmured, "I seem to be collecting adjectives—first, *hospitable* and now, *accommodating*. What next?" Her mouth tightened and Randy remembered the silky feel of her lips beneath his own.

"*Incorrigible* comes to mind," she said sweetly. "Are you going to ask your friend about a place for me to stay or shall I?"

He retreated, reining in his rampaging libido. "Parker, the lady needs a place to stay a night or two—can you put her up?"

The man glanced from Randy to Frankie and back, then bestowed a blustery grin upon them. "I'm sure I can arrange something."

"Great," Randy said, relieved to have one loose end secured. "Listen, Red, if you don't mind hanging out here for a few minutes, I need to check on a couple of things."

"The kissing booth?" she asked with an arched eyebrow.

"No," he said, embarrassed anew, but Frankie wasn't paying attention. She checked her watch, worrying her lower lip with small white teeth. "Do you have to be somewhere?" he asked in a wry tone.

Frankie shook her head. "But I should make a phone call."

"Let me guess—good old Oscar?"

She nodded, blessedly ignorant of his...*jealousy?* Impossible.

"Come on," he said with more impatience than he meant to reveal. The quick flash of hurt on her freckled face as she climbed off the stool filled him with remorse. He sighed. "I'll even give you the quarter," he said, his tone pathetically gentled.

"But I still owe you a penny," she reminded him with a small smile that sent a low throb of panic drumming through Randy's stomach.

Oh, dear God...he liked her.

No, he *wanted* her, he corrected as he led Frankie through a maze of bodies to a door marked Employees Only. Like and want—big difference. Big, big difference.

"Here you are," he said, sweeping an arm into a closet-size room. A naked bulb from the low ceiling cast harsh light over the cluttered contents. "Not much to look at, but a little more quiet." He closed the door behind them and pointed to a battered student's desk in the corner. "Help yourself to the phone. If you don't mind, while I'm here I'll sign a few orders that have to go out in the morning."

Frankie stepped toward the desk, but her gaze was riveted to a picture on the wall, an awkwardly framed newspaper article and photograph of him handing a check to the director of the Dry Tortugas National Park. "You *own* this place," she said, her voice tinged with surprise.

"Guilty as charged," he admitted.

"You said you were the manager."

He laughed. "I *am* the manager—and the janitor, and the bartender if need be." He watched her carefully, although he wasn't sure what kind of reaction he expected.

But she simply turned and set down her bottle by the phone. "I'll leave you some money for this call—I'm already indebted to you enough."

Randy set his beer on a paper-strewn, shoulder-high file cabinet, watching Frankie's red, windswept hair fall over her shoulder when she picked up the handset. Her arms and hands moved gracefully, beautifully. He wasn't quite sure why even her slightest movement spoke to him, made him alternately want to watch her and fold his arms around her.

Giving himself a mental shake, he mined a pen from a pile of debris, turned his back to give her some semblance of privacy, then studied the liquor-order sheets. Muffled laughter and the bass of the music sounded on the other side of the door, but not loud enough to drown out Frankie's voice behind him.

"Hi, Oscar, it's me."

Randy frowned. *Not Ms. Jensen, not Frankie—me. Which means they're on very close terms.*

"Yes, I received the money. I don't know what I would have done without your help."

His rolled his eyes. *Since no one here has lifted a finger.*

"Everything's fine. I'm scheduled to leave on another ship Sunday afternoon, so I'll be home by Monday evening."

Home? Is she talking generalizations, or does she live with the guy?

"The design sheets? I—I—I couldn't locate a fax machine to get them to you today, but— Oscar, I know you need them, but— No, I don't think anyone else has an updated copy, but—Oscar!" She spoke so sharply, he turned to stare. Frankie glanced up guiltily, then gave him a weak smile and turned back to the phone. "If I find a fax machine, I'll send what you need. Otherwise, I'll give you the sheets Monday night."

Monday night? So they are *living together.* A fact which was hard for him to reconcile with the uptight Frankie Jensen he was coming to know. He turned back to his orders.

"How's the testing going on the new compiler?"

Randy listened as she exchanged computer talk with her beloved Oscar—conversation she probably thought would be over Randy's head. Actually, he'd been quite the computer whiz in his day. Then he bit the inside of his cheek. From TV and newspapers, he gathered that computers had changed tremendously in the decade since he'd last touched a keyboard. He'd never even signed on to the Internet. Why did this woman make him suddenly feel as if he was missing something?

The click of her hanging up the phone interrupted his thoughts. He hurriedly scanned and signed the rest of the orders, then pivoted to give her a wide, guileless smile. "How's Oscar?"

In a blink, she erased the concern from her face and casually retrieved her beer. "Fine."

"Missing you, I'll bet."

She shrugged and stood. "He stays busy."

Unable to stop himself, he asked, "And did you tell him how you've been staying busy?"

Frankie leveled her gaze on him. "What's to tell?"

A hot flush singed his neck and he inclined his head

in concession to her candid, if stinging, observation. Then he caught sight of a one-hundred-dollar bill wedged under the phone. He settled his hands on his hips, frowning. "The call didn't cost that much. I thought I made it clear that I'm not going to accept your money."

"Don't get defensive," she said, standing. "If you won't take the money for yourself, take it for your charity fund."

He started to object, then a wicked idea occurred to him and he smiled. "Agreed." He reached her in two lazy strides, and leaned one hand into the wall behind her, leaving mere inches between their bodies. "But doing the math in my head," he whispered, stroking her pink cheek with his thumb. "That comes out to one hundred smackeroos for one hundred smackeroos."

8

BEFORE HE CLAIMED the kiss, Frankie had barely enough time to inhale, let alone voice the feeble protests half formed in her throat. Randy clamped his mouth down on hers with the fierceness of a consummation, although only their lips touched. He bathed her tongue with his, sharing the keen tang of beer and his own pleasing taste. Her body vaulted to life, section by section, as if she were a machine and he the power source.

Desire coiled low in her stomach, then sprang into her torso and electrified her arms and legs, fingers and toes. The low desk bit into the back of her thighs, but she found the numbing pain slightly arousing. She nipped at the end of his tongue and he responded with increased intensity. Their teeth clicked together as they levered for advantage, their heads bobbing as power ebbed and flowed between them. His lips alternately softened and hardened, every few seconds shifting from gentle disclosure to blatant desire, and back. Her need for oxygen ended the kiss, leaving her gulping air. Frankie raised a hand to her tingling mouth, struggling for composure.

Randy's air passages seemed equally compromised, although his golden eyes remained riveted on her. He slipped his arms around her waist and emitted a low whistle of appreciation. "Only ninety-nine more to go."

"Randy," she uttered, turning her head. "We shouldn't."

Unwittingly she'd given him unobstructed access to her neck, which he latched on to, alternating tiny suckling kisses with a hoarse countdown. "Ninety-eight...ninety-seven...ninety-six..."

"Randy," she protested again, even as her hands cradled his dipping head.

"...ninety-five...ninety-four...ninety-three..."

She raised her chin and arched backward as his mouth traveled over the pulse jumping in her neck. "W-we shouldn't let things g-get out of hand..."

"...ninety-four...ninety-five...ninety-six..."

She playfully slapped at his shoulder. "You're counting in the wrong direction."

Frankie felt him grin against her neck. "And you're supposed to be too distracted to notice."

She pushed him away in exasperation and crossed her arms in a literal effort to hold herself together. "Perhaps I should add *conceited* to your list."

Lifting his shoulders in a too-innocent shrug, he said, "Since the kissing booths were my idea, I figure it's my responsibility to make sure you get your money's worth."

The hunger in his eyes sent alarms screaming through her body, because she suspected he saw the same desire reflected in her baby blues. Panicked, Frankie spun to face the wall, fighting for control. Too late, she realized she faced a picture-size mirror, and Randy Tate was not someone she should have turned her back on.

A good six inches taller, he stood behind her and

caught her gaze in the reflection. With his mussed tawny hair and his sparkling gilded eyes, he reminded her of a lion circling a female he might either ravish or eat alive—or both—depending on his whim.

He reached around and hooked his bronze fingers in the mass of red hair that had fallen forward to brush her collarbone. Frankie held her breath as he drew the tresses back over her shoulder, exposing the sensitive zone behind her ear. With a sinking heart, she realized her neck tingled in anticipation of his unbelievably talented mouth. But rather than planting a kiss, he lowered his head, making the light glint off his earring, and stroked her neck with his chin, his evening beard rasping along her skin. "So?" he muttered.

She closed her eyes and released the pent-up breath, rolling her head to the other side as goose bumps raced along her shoulders. "So...what?" she gasped.

He continued the stroking motion, nuzzling her hairline. "So, do you think you're getting your money's worth?"

In answer, she eased back into him, wrapping her hands around his hips, pulling his hardened sex into the curve of her buttocks. He groaned and smoothed his hands inside her gaping shirt, massaging her breasts through the thin fabric of the white bikini top, budding her nipples with his thumbs. His breathing became erratic in her ear as his tongue lapped at her earlobe. "Frankie, I can't keep my hands off you."

She moaned her acquiescence and opened her eyes just as he slid the two triangles of the bathing-suit top aside, exposing her paper-pale breasts. Fascinated by the sight of his brown fingers against her skin in the mirror, Frankie rubbed back against his arousal, eliciting another groan. He deftly untied her knotted shirt, then slid his hands over her stomach and into the loose waistband of her disheveled shorts.

Liquid fire flamed through her body when he cupped his hands over the flimsy bikini bottom that stood between her nest and his apt fingers. With eyes glazed with desire, he met her gaze while pressing their bodies together with increasingly firm movements that promised a level of passion and expertise she had not yet experienced.

She'd have to be an idiot to not know how much he wanted her. And she wanted him, too, with a fierceness that absolutely terrified her. Wanted him right here, right now, in a cramped closet of an office, with unsuspecting people on the other side of the wall.

But when he slipped a finger beneath the inadequate scrap of fabric at the juncture of her thighs, the intimacy of the gesture shook her to her senses. Frankie stiffened. She was behaving like a coed on spring break, literally falling into the hands of the smooth-talking bartender. She dropped her arms and tugged his hand from the front of her shorts.

He seemed surprised, but to his credit, he didn't resist. He took a step back and dragged his hand over his face. "Frankie—"

"Randy," she cut in, frantically righting her clothes, gauging his reaction in the mirror, "I apologize for my behavior." She paused to catch her breath, then bit her lip hard, hoping the pain would help to clear her head, help to banish the passion that threatened to render her powerless to think. She glanced down to ensure body parts and clothing were back in place before she turned to face him.

At the expression of anger on his face, she nearly faltered. But she lifted her chin and forged ahead. "I do appreciate all you've done for me, but weekend-vacation flings are not my style. This—" she gestured in circles, searching for the right word "—this, this, this...*attraction* is a pleasant diversion from my dreadful predicament, but I've—" She stopped and laughed, sounding hysterical even to her own ears. After a moment, she put a shaking hand to her temple and squeezed her eyes shut. Frankie swallowed, then said almost to herself, "I've got to face the fact that if I don't find that briefcase, I might as well not even go back to Cincinnati."

"And what would be so terrible about that?"

She glanced up and nearly laughed aloud at his simplistic solution. "I was being facetious—I *have* to go back."

He pursed his lips and pulled a dubious face. "Why?"

Frankie blinked. Why, he asked? Randy Tate lived life by the seat of his raggedy cutoffs—how could he comprehend the responsibility she held or the magnitude of her blunder? How she not only had compromised *her* job by hoarding the plans for the project, but also the reputation of the entire team if the system were delayed due to her negligence? The full force of her dilemma hit her anew and nausea welled in her stomach. She shook her head in disbelief. Why was this happening to her? "I've got to get out of here." She pivoted toward the door, but Randy caught her by the wrist.

"Let go of me," she bit out. "I know you're angry, but—"

"Frankie," he said firmly, loosening his grip, but maintaining his hold. His eyes grew serious. "I'm not angry at you, I'm angry at myself for pushing you—I'm sorry. And I know you're worried about finding your briefcase, but leaving like this won't help anything."

Was he sincere, or simply giving a convincing performance? She had to admit he had risen above and beyond the call of duty at every step to help her. Was it possible she had underestimated the man when she assumed he had ulterior motives? His gaze bore into her—not the suggestive, flirty gaze of a ladykiller, but the somber, affectionate gaze of a man who...*understood*? Impossible.

"Thank you for helping me find a place to stay," she said, extracting her wrist from his gentle hold. "I need to buy a few personal items and some clothes." She attempted an optimistic smile. "And who knows? Maybe tomorrow my bag will turn up."

"And you can go back early?" His eyes mocked her.

"Yes," she said simply. "Why on earth would I stay?" *And increase the odds of going to bed with the likes of you?*

"Why indeed?"

"Exactly," she murmured.

"Exactly," he repeated.

The energy of their earlier passion seemed to hang in the air around them, thickening the atmosphere. Remembering her forwardness, Frankie flushed and pushed her hand through her tangled hair. "After I get directions to the B&B from Mr. Grimes, I'll pick up the things I need. Then I'll probably turn in early—it's been a very trying day."

Trying. Randy silently agreed. He'd spent the entire day *trying*. Trying to resist becoming involved in this woman's situation, then trying to squash the compelling physical attraction he felt for her, then trying to ignore the feelings of failure and inadequacy she resurrected with her concern for her job.

He sighed. Key West boasted more bars per capita than any other place in the world—so why did she have to wander into *his* peaceful little hole in the wall? Oh sure, she could turn and march out into the street and disappear, but dammit, she'd already set wheels into motion that wouldn't be so easily slowed again. During the ride back from the beach, his thoughts had run amok, darting between the incredible pleasure of having Frankie's body jammed up next to his and long-forgotten curiosities like how the new tax laws might affect capital gains.

She put her hand on the doorknob, and Randy realized that despite the havoc she had wreaked in his life in the space of a few short hours, he wasn't willing to let go just yet. "I'll go with you."

Frankie turned back, a frown knitting her eyebrows. "I don't think that's a good idea."

She hadn't said no—a good sign. "What's *not* a good idea is you walking around the streets by yourself at night. You can buy the things you need, we'll grab a quick bite to eat, then I'll drop you off at the B&B."

She squinted, bit her bottom lip and considered his words for several seconds, during which he strove to hide his pathetic hopefulness. "Then we say goodbye?" she asked, obviously wary.

"Then we say goodbye," he agreed with a nod.

"No more..." She gestured vaguely between them.

"No more," he vowed recklessly, raising his hand.

"Okay," she relented, turning the doorknob.

"Okay," he repeated, ridiculously pleased.

"You're starting to sound like your parrot," she said over her shoulder as she opened the door.

Randy's gaze dropped to her rounded rear and Tweety's newest phrase came to mind, but he wisely held his tongue.

FRANKIE WALKED her fingers through a rack of blouses, conscious of Randy's eyes on her from a few feet away. Under her lashes, she studied him leaning against a rack, holding a small bag of travel-size toiletries she'd purchased at a drugstore. For the umpteenth time since they'd left the bar, she wondered if she was compounding earlier mistakes by not taking leave of his company when she had the chance. At the same time, she had to admit she felt better knowing he would see her to bed, er, to the bed-and-breakfast inn.

They were two of only a handful of customers in the clothing store. Music, laughter and the buzz of voices filtered in through the front door, which had been propped open with a chair. The youngish salesclerk stood gazing longingly at the happy people milling by, their faces lit beneath the glare of neon lights. Distracted, but trying to hurry, Frankie pulled out a plain beige cotton shirt and folded it over the pair of pleated long navy shorts on her arm—simple and sensible.

"How about this?"

Randy's voice startled her. She glanced over to see him fingering a short water-green silk skirt.

"It's a nice color and it feels good," he urged.

Mildly surprised, she walked toward him, still carrying her own choices. "It's pretty," she agreed, noting the wraparound style. "But not very practical."

He frowned. "Why not?"

"Well, I typically wear matched suits to work."

He pursed his lips. "Strict dress code?"

Frankie shook her head. "Personal preference."

"At least try it on."

She rubbed the fabric between her fingers, its texture so soft it felt almost oily. "It is a nice color, isn't it?" she mused, then spotted a pale yellow silk blouse hanging on the next rack that would make a striking combination. Feeling indulgent, she conceded his good taste and added both garments to her arm.

The dressing rooms offered questionable privacy since they faced the foot-traffic area and the doors were curtains that hung from neck to knee. The inside was even less impressive, with no mirror and one itty-bitty hook on which to hang both her old and new clothes. Muttering under her breath, Frankie slipped off her loafers and disrobed self-consciously, leaving on the bikini bottoms, which had become increasingly elusive and uncomfortable.

"How does it look?"

Frankie jumped, then glanced up to see Randy standing at arm's length from the so-called door. She held the beige shirt over her breasts, even though he couldn't see them—and even though he'd *already* seen them. "I'm not dressed yet."

He gave her a lopsided grin. "Then it must look pretty good."

She flushed to the roots of her hair and ignored him, pulling on the shirt and shorts.

"There's a mirror out here," he said, pointing to his left.

She shoved aside the curtain and emerged, aware of his perusal. Stepping in front of the mirror, she checked the modest length of the shorts and the shoulder seams of the simple shirt. She glanced in the mirror at Randy and saw him crinkle his nose.

"What?" she asked, frowning.

He straightened and shook his head. "Nothing."

She turned to check the rear fit. A little loose, but adequate in a pinch.

"Hmm."

Frankie looked back to the source of the grunt. "What's wrong?"

He shook his head again. "Nothing."

She started back to the changing booth.

"It's just that..."

She sighed. *"What?"*

"Well..." He tilted his head to one side, scanning her figure. "That outfit's kind of plain, don't you think?"

She looked down at the neat, unadorned garments. "So?"

"So try on the other one."

Flustered at his familiarity, she nodded to his shabby cutoffs and threadbare T-shirt. "For some reason, I assumed clothes didn't mean much to you."

He shrugged good-naturedly. "If I'd known you'd be dropping in the bar today, I'd have worn my good T-shirt."

She closed the curtain with a snap and kept her gaze averted while removing the clothing as quickly as her quaking hands would allow. There was something undoubtedly erotic about undressing with Randy in plain sight...she might as well be performing a striptease.

With burning cheeks, she shimmied the yellow silk tank over her head. The thin fabric settled over her breasts with a whisper, the slight friction instantly pearling the tips. She wrapped the skirt around her hips, and even before she secured the ties at the side, she knew the garment was perfect—a perfect fit to mold her hips, the perfect color for her pale skin and the perfect length to show off her long legs...but where on earth would she wear the outfit when she returned home?

"So?" he asked, still loitering nearby.

Frankie swallowed and pushed back the curtain, foolishly gratified when Randy straightened and his eyes grew large. "Wow, Red."

Embarrassed, she gave him a wry smile and stepped in front of the mirror. The garments were indeed flattering, she decided as she turned sideways. Still dubious, she glanced down at her white feet. "But I'll need shoes."

At last the preoccupied salesclerk turned, surveyed Frankie's outfit and smiled. "We have a few pairs of sandals in the back."

Randy looked to Frankie with eyebrows raised.

She sighed and nodded to the girl. "Eight and a half."

With ballooning confidence, Frankie chose a few more items—white gauze drawstring pants, a floral skort, a soft pink T-shirt dress, a one-piece teal swimsuit, two casual tops and a thin white cardigan for the cool evenings on the return cruise. The clerk returned with a selection of shoes, and Frankie chose a pair of strappy green sandals to go with the silk skirt, and a pair of low-heeled white mules to go with everything else.

"Why don't you wear the skirt to dinner?" he suggested, grinning. "I'm dressed like a bum, but no one will be looking at me anyway."

Pleased beyond understanding, Frankie nodded and ducked back into the changing room to dress in the outfit. She was looking forward to a nice, conversational meal, fully dressed, with a table wedged safely between them.

"Will there be anything else, ma'am?" the girl asked when Frankie carried the purchases to the cash register.

"Yes." She leaned forward and whispered, "Underwear."

Standing a few feet away, Randy coughed and she shot him a warning glance.

"Right this way, ma'am," the clerk said, heading toward a counter in the back of the store.

In case he had notions of "helping" again, she pointed a finger in his direction. "Don't move from that spot."

He held up his hands in a gesture of innocence, which she didn't believe. Thankfully, Frankie was able to select a few undergarments without him looking over her shoulder, but she had to admit, she chose styles that were more brief and lacy than her normal fare.

"All done?" he asked pleasantly, while craning for a peek as the salesclerk tucked the filmy garments into bags.

"Yes," she said primly, and he chuckled.

Not amused, she removed a black canvas bag and nylon wallet from a rack, in resignation to the fact that she might never see her briefcase and wallet again. Her expression must have betrayed her thoughts because when she looked at him again, he gave her a comforting wink. "It'll turn up," he said quietly. And once again, she believed him.

"I suppose I'll have to buy a suitcase tomorrow," she said with a laugh, to change the subject.

The bounty took a good portion of the cash Oscar had wired her, but she didn't worry because she'd be able to pick up replacement traveler's checks in the morning. She did experience a pang of guilt when she thought about her would-be boyfriend who was genuinely worried about her while she spent the evening in the company of an undeniably attractive man...a man who had become entirely too easy to kiss in the— she checked her watch—good Lord, seven hours she'd known him. *Seven hours.* Frankie shook her head and glanced sideways at her companion as they gathered up bags.

"What have I done now?" he asked with a smirk.

"Nothing," she said quickly, stepping through the open door onto the sidewalk.

"Good, because I'm trying to be on my best behavior." The thinly veiled remark indicating he'd like to finish what they'd started—twice—sent a thrill to her stomach, but she decided she was hungry and ready for another beer.

She stopped and looked down at their burdens. "How are we going to get all these packages to the inn on the back of your motorcycle?"

"No problem," Randy said, then walked to the end of the curb and lifted his hand to hail a cabbie sitting on the corner. Immediately, the lights flashed and the driver pulled forward. After taking the bags from her arms, Randy loaded all the packages into the back seat, walked around to the driver side and leaned down.

"Hey, Tippy," he said to the tiny man.

Tippy grinned and put out his hand for Randy to palm. "What's happening, my man?"

After a glance to ensure Frankie hadn't followed him, Randy returned the smooth handshake, leaving a fifty behind.

Tippy's eyes bugged. "Where to?"

"Take these packages to Parker's and have them delivered to the room he reserved for a Miss Frankie Jensen."

"Done."

"One more thing, Tippy—I've got a business proposition for you."

The man instantly turned serious. "I'm listening."

"I'm looking for a woman's briefcase that was scarfed earlier today." He squinted, trying to recall the descriptions she'd given the police officer. "Black and soft-sided, like a purse. The guy who took it was young, white, with short hair, wearing jeans and a green T-shirt. If you find the punk and he hasn't dumped the bag, I want it."

Tippy nodded and considered his words. "How bad do you want it?"

"Five hundred for the briefcase, contents intact."

The man shook his head. "Any money and jewelry are long gone, man."

Randy dismissed the comment. "I'm interested in some papers and CD's that were in the bag, but I'll throw in a hundred-dollar bonus for the wallet, minus the cards and cash. Got it?"

"Yeah. Where can I find you?"

"Leave me a message at the bar."

The little man sneaked a peek at Frankie standing on the curb under the streetlight and whistled low. "Six hundred dollars, huh? I hope she's worth it."

"She is," Randy said without thinking, then pushed away from the cab with a stone of anxiety in his stomach.

9

HE STOOD long after the cab had pulled away, staring at the woman standing on the sidewalk who had so thoroughly captured his...attention. Her long curls swirled around her shoulders in the light breeze, and the new clothes showed off her fabulous figure. Unbeknownst to her, she was turning the head of every man who passed. And she was his date for the evening, a thought that made his stomach clench with possessive masculine pride.

The fact that she was stranded and had practically no other choice was inconsequential, he decided.

She smiled. "Are you going to stand in the middle of the street all night or are you going to feed me?"

"Feed you," he relented. With a strange tightening in his chest, he rejoined her, then turned in the direction of his favorite restaurant, Jordy's Shell House. On the way, his southern manners resurfaced, rusty from disuse. In the decade since he'd arrived, his encounters with women had been short-lived and superficial. He couldn't remember ever taking a woman to dinner with the express determination to *not* bed her afterward.

Sex with Frankie would be incredible, he knew, and therein lay the paradox. Randy had the unsettling feeling that if she'd already affected his mind-set in such a short time, making love to her might have him doing something really crazy...like asking her to stay here with him instead of going back home to her boyfriend and her *Fortune 500* job.

"You're awfully quiet," she observed.

Randy started from his musings, suddenly realizing that they only had a few more hours together, and he wanted to make the most of it. He had no doubt that Tippy would smoke out the thug eventually, but if the police hadn't yet recovered the briefcase, chances were slim the kid hadn't sunk the bag or burned it. Either way, she'd be leaving on another cruise ship Sunday at the very latest. "Just enjoying the scenery," he said, thinking she'd grown more lovely with each passing minute. "Are you cold?"

"Cool," she admitted, then unfolded the white cardigan.

He took the sweater from her and placed it around her shoulders, resisting the urge to leave his arm there. Everywhere he looked, couples held hands, danced, kissed—and more. Gearing up for Valentine's Day, he supposed. Funny, other than the opportunity to raise money for charity at the bar, Valentine's had always been just another day to him. Now he wondered if he would remember it as the day Frankie Jensen sailed out of his life.

"So tell me about this big project you're working on," he said to keep his mind from wandering into dangerous areas.

She laughed. "It's very boring, actually."

"Try me."

Frankie shrugged, then said, "It's a computer system to track inventory of road-paving materials. The company I work for bids on state and federal road jobs, and up until now, inventory control has been haphazard."

He frowned. "Doesn't sound like much of a way to run a business, much less a huge business."

"You're right, but the raw materials used in our line of work—like rock, sand, asphalt, concrete—are difficult to track. The material might be mixed at a plant and trucked over, or mixed on the job site. And since most of the materials are stored in piles that sit out in the elements, there's a lot of waste—" She stopped and laughed. "See, I told you it was boring."

"Not at all," he corrected her. "But I admit to being a little surprised to hear that your specialty is asphalt inventory systems."

"My specialty is systems analysis and design," she said. "It just so happens that Ohio Roadmakers made me the best offer out of college." She pressed her lips together. "Looks like I'll be job hunting soon."

"It can't be that bad," he insisted. "Maybe you're overreacting."

Frankie shook her head. "No. If that documentation doesn't show up, it could take us weeks to piece together the information the vendor needs to get the new compiler working. The new system has to be in place before construction season, which is just around the corner. If we miss this deadline, we'll have to wait until November or December when activity at the job sites slows down again, and we'll have sacrificed an entire season's worth of productivity gains—" She stopped again and sighed. "I'm sorry, this isn't your problem."

"That's all right, it sounds interesting," he confessed, aware of the stir in unused areas of his brain. Ohio Roadmakers sounded familiar—did it trade on the New York or the American stock exchange? He should at least renew his subscription to the *Wall Street*

Journal, he decided. "I'm glad to listen if it helps to talk about it."

Frankie shook her head. "I think I'd rather try to enjoy the rest of the night, um, evening."

"Here we are," he said, stopping in front of a tiny rounded awning, suddenly wondering if Frankie would be disappointed to find Jordy's absent of white tablecloths and upscale patrons. His doubts were erased, however, when they stepped inside and she brought her hands together.

"How charming," she murmured, her eyes bright and darting.

"Part museum, part pub," Randy said. "As seedy as it sounds, piracy was one of the industries on which Key West was founded."

She nodded. "I think I read that in the cruise literature."

He gestured to the documents and artifacts mounted on walls and within small cases. "Jordy's great-great-grandfather was supposedly one of the most infamous swashbucklers. He keeps the old man's glass eye in a case beside the bar cash register."

Her eyes widened like a child's. "He doesn't!"

"What did you call it? Ambience?" he teased.

Busy even for a Friday night, the little place overflowed with customers. They joined the long line behind the authentic ship wheel that served as a makeshift hostess station, but when their turn to be seated arrived, Jordy's daughter beamed, exchanged small talk with Frankie, then led them directly to a choice table. Randy nodded to Antony, an ancient islander strolling the catwalk above them, playing a soothing piccolo. The man nodded and winked, never missing a note.

"I see you're a regular," Frankie noted as he held out her seat.

"Good food and great people," he said easily. "I usually eat here at least once a week."

"With a date?"

He glanced up in surprise as he sat down across from her. "Sometimes," he admitted. "But more often not." A waiter arrived immediately with two wine-glasses and a bottle of Randy's favorite merlot. "Do you like red wine?" Randy asked Frankie.

She nodded absently, still engaged by the decor.

"Thanks, Chapel, I'll open the wine," he said, taking the bottle and the corkscrew from the young man.

"This is simply marvelous," she said, fingering the lighthouse that served as their centerpiece.

"I think Jordy's wife collects lighthouses." He chuckled over her shining enthusiasm. "You must love restaurants."

"I do—my parents own a family restaurant in Cincy, and I grew up waiting tables and helping in the kitchen."

"Ah," he said as he popped the cork on the bottle. Filling her glass, he said, "And you didn't want to follow family tradition?"

She picked up the tiny chalkboard on which the day's menu had been handwritten. "Actually, I *did* want to."

He splashed the berry-colored wine into his own glass, surprised at this side of Frankie. "So why didn't you?"

She shrugged her lovely shoulders and sipped the wine, nodding with approval. "My parents convinced me there are easier ways to make a living."

"Like designing asphalt inventory systems?"

A smile danced on her lips, wet with wine. She had definitely gotten some sun today, and it became more noticeable as the evening wore on. Her cheeks fairly glowed and Randy decided she was simply the most compelling woman he'd ever met—beautiful to distraction and diligent to a fault. "I have a good job."

"So you've said before. But do you like it?"

"I like the insurance and the steady income."

"Stability means a lot to you," he stated, probing. He hated to belabor the point, but he wanted to prove to himself on a deeper level that a romantic entanglement with Frankie Jensen was a lost cause, that she wanted the very things in life he'd sworn never to be a slave to again.

"I suppose," she said.

The waiter returned with entrée recommendations. Randy ordered conch fritters for an appetizer and grouper for dinner. Frankie ordered yellowfin tuna. Then Randy encouraged her to bring her glass of wine and join him on a quick tour. For the next twenty minutes, they strolled around the restaurant and Randy pointed out the more interesting items in Jordy's collection, including the notorious glass eye.

On the way back to the table, Frankie asked, "Randy, have you ever thought about turning your bar into a restaurant?"

He pursed his lips as they reclaimed their seats. "Not really. I'd probably make a lot more money, but the upgrades to be able to serve food would be considerable, plus a new decor, a larger staff...more responsibility."

She conceded with a smile. "How did you make the jump from being an actor to being a bar owner?"

Randy blinked, recalling her earlier assumption, but

saw no reason to correct her. Time had healed some of the wounds of his failed career and bankrupted customers—he didn't wish to open the wounds again now with someone who would be leaving the day after tomorrow, or sooner if her missing bag turned up. He refilled their glasses to buy a few seconds, then decided to stay on the periphery of the truth.

"When my career ended in Atlanta, I decided I needed a change of venue. I came here for a few days and struck up a friendship with Parker and a man named King who had owned Rum King's for over twenty years. I'd been here, oh, about a month when the bar owner decided to retire. It was Parker's idea that I buy the bar. I inherited good employees, and the place practically runs itself. I own a small place nearby, and find time to surf almost every day. I'm happy."

"Sounds like your life is perfect," she agreed, sipping from her glass. "Have you ever been married?"

"No." He couldn't take his eyes off the way her fingers wrapped around the stem of the glass. "Never had the inclination." His gaze darted to her unadorned fingers, then back. "You?"

She shook her head and when he opened his mouth to ask if she and Oscar had planned that far ahead, the conch fritters arrived, saving him from asking and having to hear her answer. Because if she'd said yes, finishing dinner while thinking about Frankie with some faceless man would have been...well, *trying*. And if she'd said no, he might have been tempted to convince her to spend the night with him, which he'd as good as promised her he wouldn't do. Not to mention his weighty suspicion that bedding her would spell disaster for life as he knew it.

Squirming, he watched as Frankie sampled one of

the spicy fritters that resembled hush puppies. Her eyebrows shot up in an impressive salute. "These are really good."

Still rattled over his own revelation, he drank deeply before eating one of the conch morsels. If he had any sense at all, he'd manufacture some emergency at the bar and leave her cab fare to Parker's.

"Do you miss acting?" she asked, oblivious to his struggle.

"No," he said, reasoning it wasn't a lie—he couldn't miss something he'd never done.

She seemed surprised. "You don't miss *anything* about your previous career?"

With jarring clarity, Randy remembered the zing of elation when a stock he recommended or a portfolio he assembled had performed well. He'd felt so invincible that he'd had no trouble convincing clients to put their life savings in his hands. Indeed, he'd grown the funds considerably for most of his customers. But it was the few dozen who'd lost nearly everything who still haunted him. He often wondered what had happened to Mr. and Mrs. Oldham, who'd been looking forward to retirement. And Mr. Chandler, who'd intended to set up a trust fund for his grandson. And Mrs. Quillion, who'd been terrified of ending up in a nursing home in the event she lasted longer than her money.

"Ah, here's our food," he said, immensely grateful for the interruption as their waiter placed the steaming plates before them. The aromas were as tempting as always, and the presentation flawless, but Randy's hunger for food had fled in the wake of an overriding preoccupation with the woman across from him. Still, he squeezed fresh lemon juice over the grouper and forked a flaky bite into his mouth, hoping to jump-start his appetite.

Frankie closed her eyes in appreciation and pronounced the tuna wonderful just as Jordy stopped by on his nightly rounds from table to table. Randy made the introductions and stood to shake the old man's hand in greeting. Frankie raved about the tavern, her eyes shining. The man was instantly enchanted, Randy noted with relief—at least he wasn't the only one to fall under her spell. In fact, the longer Jordy loitered, the more outrageously the gray-haired man flirted. When the stabs of jealousy over their banter threatened to banish even his shrunken appetite, Randy gently cut in.

"Jordy, if you like, I'll pick up your liquor order after we finish eating."

The older man flushed guiltily and bid them an enjoyable evening before moving on.

Despite Frankie's declaration about the food, he noticed she was so busy watching the waiters, hostesses and musicians, she scarcely ate, although he filled her wineglass a third time. She asked dozens of questions about the patronage, local seafood sources and liquor laws. He didn't feel slighted by the fact that she seemed more taken with the restaurant itself than with her dinner companion. Indeed, he was thankful that she alone had the presence of mind to resist fostering their accidental attraction with lingering looks and coy small talk.

But her elusive attention gave him free license to study her...the fluidity with which she moved her head and hands, her sharp, absorbing gaze, the way her lips tightened and pursed sporadically as if her mind was whirling and she was about to blurt out her thoughts. Randy sipped his wine, looking for some answer in the slight buzz of the alcohol to explain why this woman so captivated him.

She was beautiful, no doubt, but so were any number of women he met on a daily basis. Sexy and passionate? Sure, but so was Sheely and he'd never been enticed to sleep with her. Intelligent and inquisitive? Yes, but not all the women in his bed had been empty-headed, either.

"Do I have something on my chin?" she asked, holding up her napkin.

"No," he replied with a laugh. "I didn't mean to stare."

"You were a million miles away, I think."

"No, I rarely let my thoughts and plans wander past the boundaries of the island," he lied, although he wanted it to be true.

"It must be nice to feel so at peace with your... decisions," she said, her voice wine-wistful.

Her words raised a disturbing question in his mind: Was he truly making proactive decisions about his life, or had he simply bowed to serendipity by staying in Key West? To evade commenting, he turned the misguided observations around. "Earlier today when you claimed to be happy, you weren't being truthful?"

She slowly pushed aside her plate and leaned forward on her elbows, her arms crossed at her slim wrists. "I was being as truthful as I knew to be," she said, her too-bright eyes testifying to the effects of the wine. "But when I see people like you and Jordy living exactly the life you want to—and living it in paradise...well, you have to admit that writing code for a computer in Ohio pales a bit in comparison."

"It's a good job," he said, mimicking her words.

"Yes," she agreed. "But when you consider that you spend the better part of your waking hours at your job—and more time with your co-workers than your own family—you should really love who you do, er, I mean *what* you do."

Randy wet his lips, ignoring her slip. "Of course, some would argue that what I do doesn't exactly contribute to the quality fabric of society."

She shrugged in an exaggerated fashion. "That's for you to decide."

He frowned. *Decide...decisions.*

"I'd give anything for a cigarette," she said, leaning closer. Her eyes drooped and her lips pouted.

Randy swallowed. "Anything?"

She smiled lazily and nodded. "And anything twice for two."

He stood up suddenly, sending his chair crashing to the floor and gathering the attention of couples seated around them. "I—I'll get Jordy's order and see if I can find you a smoke," he said, righting the chair and snatching his napkin from the floor. After smoothing the cloth next to his abandoned plate, Randy gave her a smile he hoped was stronger than his resolve to resist her, then strode in the direction of the kitchen.

Jordy stood in the steamy, bustling kitchen wearing a stained apron and sampling a pinkish soup that Randy recognized as lobster bisque.

"Randy, are you leaving so soon?" The man wagged his silver eyebrows. "Not that I blame you—your Ms. Jensen is quite a dish."

He frowned. "She's not *mine*, Jordy. I came to get your liquor order."

"So testy," the man said, tsk-tsking. "She seems like a very special young woman."

Randy clenched his jaw under the man's watchful gaze. "Just a pretty tourist, Jordy, who had her purse stolen and missed her cruise ship."

"And I suppose you're simply helping her out in a jam?"

"That's right."

Jordy's laugh was gratuitous. "Well, if that isn't a case of the fox taking care of the henhouse, I don't know what is."

Randy sighed and rubbed his hand over his face. "You're a riot, Jordy. Where's your liquor order?"

The old man chuckled as he pulled a folded sheet of paper from his apron pocket. "If I didn't know better, my boy, I'd say Cupid has clipped you with his arrow."

Rankled, Randy protested hotly, "Yeah, well, don't worry—" He stopped, then sighed as he looked into the wrinkled face of a true friend, and clapped Jordy on the back. "Don't worry, old man, it's just a flesh wound." He took the order form and started to retreat, more anxious than ever to deposit Frankie safely at the B&B. Then he snapped his fingers. "I almost forgot— do you know where I can get a couple of cigarettes?"

"I didn't realize you smoked."

Randy gave him a wry smile. "It's for the hen."

"Ah. Check at the bar. Good night, lad, and good luck."

Taking the long way back to the table, Randy fought to get a grip on himself. No woman could wield so much power in his life unless he allowed it. Just because Frankie Jensen had unwittingly pushed old buttons didn't mean he had to assign her a special place in his life. She was an acquaintance, that's all—and a passing acquaintance at that.

But when he neared the table, he acknowledged the quickening of his pulse at the mere sight of her and ground his teeth. Her smile widened to a grin, melting his heart when he produced the unopened pack of menthol cigarettes—a harbinger of things to come, he feared.

"No Key lime pie for dessert?" he asked, holding back the pack.

"This will be my dessert," she said, plucking the package out of his hand. "And another glass of wine."

Randy eyed her dubiously as he sat down. "How about a half glass?"

She leaned forward, looking hurt. "I thought you wanted me to relax."

Red was nursing a good buzz—beautifully. Her chiseled features were soft around the edges and her eyes luminous. Desire beat a rhythm through his loins, torturing him. He sighed. "I do, but I don't want you to fall off the bike, either."

She shrugged, hurriedly tapping out a cigarette. "Okay." She lit the smoke with a hand that shook slightly.

He frowned as he poured her a half glass, pushing his own glass aside in preparation for driving home. "You're hooked on those things."

She inhaled deeply, drawing in her cheeks until her eyes bugged, then turned her head to exhale. "No, I'm not."

Scoffing, he asked, "Are you the same woman who just promised 'anything twice' for a couple of lousy cigarettes?"

A smile moved languidly across her pink, freckled features. The cigarette dangled from her long fingers, the tip sending up a curling wisp of smoke. "Surely you didn't take me literally."

Her words had indeed telegraphed pictures to his mind of various types of repayment. "Of course not," he said, glancing at his watch. Ten-fifteen. He could drop off Frankie, then head back to the bar for closing. Perhaps the kissing booths would still be open and he could find a substitute for—

"Am I keeping you from something you'd rather be doing?" she asked, taking another drink of the heady wine.

"No," he assured her quickly. "I'd just lost track of time, that's all."

She smiled again. "Does that mean you're having fun?"

"No." He winced, and held up one hand. "I mean, yes, I'm enjoying, um...dinner."

"But dinner is over," she pressed, gesturing to the near-empty table. Their plates had been cleared in his absence. "Are you still having fun?"

"Yes," he said politely, deciding not to elaborate. He signaled the waiter for the check and reached up to run a finger around his shirt collar, only to remember he was wearing a T-shirt. The unconscious gesture astounded him because it was a habit he'd dropped ten years ago when he'd adopted the dress code of the island. So why did he suddenly feel as if he had an eighty-dollar shirt collar pulled tight around his neck with a sixty-dollar tie?

"No Key lime pie for dessert?" she asked, sounding amused.

"Uh, no," he said, drumming his fingers on the table. He glanced up at Antony who strolled the catwalk playing "My Funny Valentine" on his silver piccolo.

Randy lifted his hand, and Antony gave him a thumbs-up, gesturing toward Frankie. Flustered, Randy shot him a tight smile and nodded curtly.

The waiter came by and handed him a note. "Where's the check?" Randy asked.

"Mr. Jordy asked me to give you this, sir. Good night." The young man nodded to Frankie. "Ma'am."

Perplexed, Randy opened the note. *Accept dinner with my compliments. Happy Valentine's Day to you and your Ms. Jensen. This is a special night, I think.*

"What does it say?" she asked, draining her wineglass.

"Dinner's on the house," he said, refolding the note. Rankled, he pulled out his wallet and withdrew a hefty tip just as she snuffed out the cigarette in a small tin ashtray. "Are you ready to go?" he asked, trying not to betray his desire to be rid of her as soon as possible.

She smiled and nodded, then pushed herself to her feet using her lower arms. Randy recognized the symptom of someone who might not be feeling so well in the morning and was by her side in a flash. "Easy," he said when she swayed and raised a hand to her temple. "I think you had a little too much wine, Red."

"No, red wine," she corrected, then cracked up at her own terrible joke. "Get it?"

"I got it," Randy said sourly. "Everyone's a comedian tonight. Come on, Red, the ride home will be cool enough to help sober you up."

"I hope Parker has a big hot-water heater," she said. "Because I can't wait to take a long, hot shower."

Cold for me, he thought as he took her arm and led her toward the entrance. At least she was a happy drunk, he noted as they left and she said goodbye to everyone. Out on the sidewalk, she shivered and he helped her into her sweater—not an easy task where armholes were concerned. Once tucked inside, she leaned into him and he slid his arm around her shoulders to make sure she didn't break her pretty neck in her new high-heeled sandals.

"Mmm," she murmured, settling next to him. The temperature had cooled considerably, but Randy wasn't cold—probably because his blood pressure and other vital signs had kicked into overdrive. The street celebrations were in full swing, and would be for another few hours. He steered her in and out of heavy pedestrian traffic. Wobbly at first, she had revived somewhat by the time he led her carefully down the short alley toward the parking lot where he'd parked the bike. He considered putting her into a cab, but since the drive to the B&B was such a short distance, he decided she'd be okay. He nearly changed his mind, though, when he realized the skirt she wore might make for a compromising ride. Not that he hadn't already seen most of her assets, he noted dryly.

Straddling the bike, Randy turned on the headlight and backed the motorcycle out of its spot, then motioned for Frankie to climb on. She did, albeit awkwardly, with her new bag on her shoulder and no complaints about her hiked-up skirt. If he had concerns about her ability to hold on, they were banished immediately when she wrapped her arms around him securely and tucked her chin next to his ear.

Randy felt a rush of affection for the woman folded around him, and realized with a start that he might very well be saying goodbye to her within a few minutes. After all, he really had no good excuse to see her in the morning. And if the police had recovered her bag, she might simply hightail it to the airport for a standby flight, or grab a taxi to Miami, where her chances of catching an outbound flight would be better.

Once they left the crowds behind, Randy slowed the bike to a crawl, stunned at the thought he would miss seeing her tomorrow, and the next day, and the next day.

Even at the slower pace, they reached Parker's B&B in short order. He wheeled around to the side of the familiar house and braked to a stop. When she pulled her arms away from his waist, Randy felt cold and...alone. He twisted to help her climb off, relieved to see that despite her windblown appearance, she seemed a bit more alert than when they'd left the restaurant.

"I guess this is almost goodbye," she said with a strange timbre in her voice. He couldn't read her eyes in the darkness.

"Almost," he agreed in a tone more cheerful than he felt. "Did Parker say which room he'd put you in?" he asked, trying to determine the closest entrance.

She nodded, then frowned slightly, reached into the black canvas bag and withdrew a small slip of folded paper. "It says I should ask for the extra bed in the guest house."

Randy felt his smile drop. "It doesn't."

"Sure it does," she said, relinquishing the note.

He glanced at the scrap of paper, then shook his head and muttered a curse to himself. That son of a gun!

"What's wrong?"

He winced and pinched the bridge of his nose, his mind spinning. "I don't know how to tell you this, Red, but *I* live in the guest house."

10

APPREHENSION TENSED Frankie's muscles, then she frowned, having already forgotten what Randy had said, but knowing it had rattled her. She squinted, trying to remember. "Say that again."

"*I live in the guest house.*"

Touching her forehead as if to force the information to remain close by, she murmured, "That's nice." Randy stared at her for so long she wondered if she'd said something wrong. "I'm really tired," she added in a feeble attempt to end the evening. She'd hoped the wine would dull her senses enough to forget... something, and to resist...someone. She bit her lip and suspiciously studied the man standing before her. Was it Randy she was trying to avoid? He didn't look very scary. In fact, he looked—Frankie tilted her head and giggled—nervous.

"Are you okay with this?" he asked.

She detected a note of concern and inhaled the clean fresh air, trying to clear the fog from the corners of her brain. "Shouldn't I be?"

He clasped her by the arms. "Look at me, Red."

You're so handsome, she thought, realizing with a start that she'd said the words aloud.

He sighed, then turned her to the right—no, left—and steered her toward a tiny cottage built on stilts and not much larger than a child's playhouse, a comparison which made her giggle again. After a few steps, she decided to kick off her shoes, and walked the rest of the way barefoot, carrying her sandals. Randy didn't say a word, just tightened up his face like she was being a big pain in the patootie.

"Do you think I'm a big pain in the patootie?" she asked, gazing up at him.

"If a patootie is one of two things," he said dryly, helping her up stone steps, "then yes."

Hurt ripped through her. "I'm sorry."

He made a face while he unlocked the front door. "I shouldn't have said that."

"I don't blame you for being angry."

"I'm not angry," he said, swinging open the door and reaching around the frame to flip on a light. "Come on in and have a seat while I make a phone call."

Frankie stepped inside, nearly tripping over the bags and boxes of clothing she'd purchased earlier, which had somehow materialized. Barely noting her surroundings, she made a beeline for an overstuffed gray sofa. She sank into the cushions and started to lie down when she remembered she'd walked barefoot through wet grass. Wriggling her greenish toes on the pale wooden floor, she heard him talking behind her.

"Hello, Nina? It's Randy—Parker wouldn't happen to be around, would he?" He sighed. "That's what I was afraid of. Listen, do you have any available beds tonight, any at all?"

Frankie pushed herself to her feet. "Randy," she whispered loudly. "Where's the bathroom?"

He pointed, then turned his attention back to the phone. "It's a friend of mine and I don't think she'd be comfortable staying here."

Walking through a doorway, Frankie felt for a light switch. Illumination spilled over his bedroom, and a rattan ceiling fan began to whir softly. Here the wooden floor gave way to a taupe-colored sisal rug. Frankie stood at the threshold, hesitant to cross into his domain. Randy had made his bed in a hurry, yanking the navy-and-white-striped comforter up to the headboard, the pillows still situated awkwardly beneath. Resisting the urge to stretch out for a catnap, she strolled through the basically neat room to a door she assumed was the bathroom.

At the sight of the glass-walled shower, Frankie began stripping off her clothes, rationalizing she would be finished by the time Randy found her a place to sleep. She turned on the spray of water and adjusted the temperature, then stepped inside, delighted with the pulsing action of good water pressure against her sun-tinged skin.

Too late she remembered she'd left her toiletries in the black canvas bag in the other room. Borrowing a palmful of Randy's shampoo, she quickly soaped her hair and rinsed, then touched up her legs with a disposable razor and a puff of shaving cream. Lathering with his bar of soap seemed almost too intimate, however, since the planes of Randy's body had contoured the waxy shape. Wicked images flashed through her head as she smoothed the suds over her skin, but the shower had sobered her enough to know that train of thought led to dangerous territory.

She rinsed and turned off the water, and claimed a clean, fluffy white towel from the stack on the back of the commode. Frankie picked up the borrowed bikini and shook her head, then held the fabric under running water in the ancient porcelain sink. After hanging the suit from the showerhead, she felt loath to put on the silk skirt and blouse again without clean under-wear. Deciding that wearing the towel by itself was too provocative, she poked through the garments hanging on the back of the door—a black cotton robe, a pair of pajama pants and a T-shirt, all undoubtedly Randy's.

Settling on the soft robe as the most concealing and unsexy garment in which to retrieve her underwear from the living room, Frankie walked out, sorting snip-pets of their earlier conversation in her clearing head. Apparently Parker had put one over on them, saying he had a place for her to stay when all along he'd planned for her to sleep at Randy's. She frowned. Was Randy perhaps in on the deception? And how often did he offer overnight lodging to lonely tourists?

When she emerged, he stood across the room, pacing the floor in front of the kitchen counter. From the look in his eyes when he saw her, she realized the thin silk garments might indeed have been the better choice, as opposed to being wrapped head to calves in his sleep-wear. She stopped just outside the doorway, deter-mined to keep the situation light. "So?" she asked brightly, double-knotting the ties at her waist.

He smoothed a hand back over his hair and leaned against the counter. "So, the nearest available room is in Islamorada. I'm sorry—Parker's never done any-thing like this before."

She pressed her lips together, sensing the ball was in her court. Pointing to the couch, she asked, "Is that the lumpy sofa you offered me earlier today?" The episode at the police station seemed to have unfolded aeons ago.

One side of his mouth climbed in a wry smile. "Yeah."

Despite the safety zone of distance between them, Frankie felt a pull emanating from him, tugging at her middle as surely as if they were connected by a steel cable. Trying to neutralize the sexually charged atmosphere, she attempted a laugh. "Well, either I'm very tired, or you were exaggerating, because it didn't feel lumpy to me."

"You're being a good sport about this."

She laughed again. "Me? Once again I'm indebted to your hospitality."

"I was afraid you'd think that Parker and I set this up."

Frankie angled her chin at him. "And did you?"

"No." He held up his hands. "Absolutely not."

He looked so mortified, she believed him. Which meant, she realized, that he wasn't too crazy about her spending the night in close proximity. "I hate to intrude," she remarked softly.

"Don't be silly," he said, straightening. "I'll take the couch and you can have my, um, bed."

She hugged herself tight and shook her head. "I insist on taking the sofa, and thank you...again."

He inhaled deeply and shifted from foot to foot, seemingly at a loss as to what to do with his hands. "You're feeling better?"

She glanced down, then gave him a sheepish smile. "Yes. I showered and helped myself to your robe."

He wet his lips slowly. "I noticed."

After moving self-consciously to her packages, she leaned over. "I'm going to change right away." She straightened.

"What?"

Burning with embarrassment, she asked, "I don't suppose I could borrow a T-shirt to sleep in?"

He pushed away from the counter and walked toward the bedroom. "*That* I can help you with."

She followed him and stood in the doorway while he rummaged in a dresser drawer. He removed a new white T-shirt with a colorful parrot logo that read Rum King's—Where the First Drink Is a Quarter.

"I like it," she said with a wide smile.

"Keep it," he said, handing her the shirt. "I know the boss, I can get another one."

Her gaze locked with his for several seconds, her senses thrumming at the nearness of him and his bed. Frankie cleared her throat and swept her arm toward the living area. "You have a very nice place."

"Thanks." He tugged on the hem of his shirt, then pulled it over his head, baring his chest. "The balcony off the kitchen has a decent view."

Frankie stood, mesmerized by her own view. "Wh-what are you doing?"

"Taking a shower," he said, nodding toward the bathroom. The muscles in his forearms and chest bunched as he balled up the shirt and banked it into a huge straw basket containing other clothes. "I thought I'd swing back by the bar for closing and let you get some rest." When he unbuttoned his cutoffs to reveal a slice of the neon orange swim trunks, she took a step backward and bumped into the door frame. His shorts hit the ground and he stepped out of them, then tossed them into the basket. The ridge of his erection strained at the thin material.

Her feet refused to move.

He hooked his thumbs in the waistband of the swim trunks and sighed. "Look, Red, we said no hanky-panky, and as much as I'd like to lay you down on my bed, I won't, because I told you I wouldn't. But I'm only human, so if you don't mind..."

Frankie turned and fled to the living area, her heart pounding. Her body tingled all over and her head swam with erotic images as she heard the faint click of the shower door closing. Then she stopped and looked over her shoulder. They were unfettered, consenting adults. He wanted her, she wanted him—what was keeping them apart? She took a step in the direction of the bedroom.

The fact that they'd only known each other for a day? She'd shared more with him in a few hours than she'd shared with her boyfriend wannabe, Oscar, or anyone else for that matter. She walked to the bedroom doorway and shivered at the sound of the shower coming from the bathroom door standing ajar.

Randy was a fabulous-looking man with mysterious insight and a sense of appreciation for the simpler life. Perhaps their chance meeting on Valentine's Day weekend wasn't by chance at all—maybe she was predestined to cross paths with Randy Tate so she could learn to follow her instincts.

Frankie stepped to the dressing mirror in his bedroom and peered at her reflection. Still wet from the shower, her hair lay skimmed back from her face and down her back. The sun had coaxed even more freckles to bloom across her nose and cheeks, but there wasn't much she could do about it now. With one glance in the direction of the bathroom, she inhaled and straightened her shoulders, then loosened the robe ties, allowing the thin garment to hang open a few inches.

In the next room, the shower fell silent, sending her heart pumping into overdrive, but she lifted her chin in determination. Maybe her courage came from the lingering effects of the wine, but she suspected she would look back on this moment as a pivotal point in her life...when she learned to take a chance.

She turned as the bathroom door opened and Randy emerged nude, toweling his hair dry. She had a few seconds to absorb the sheer beauty of his damp, muscled body before he realized she was in the room. Broad, brown shoulders transitioned into a smooth chest, with mahogany nipples accenting firm, slanted pecs. His ribs, waist and stomach were compact planes of separated muscle and sinew. The wall of abdominal strength gave way to slim hips. His manhood hung in a tangle of dark hair, flanked by pale skin, indicating his participation at the nude beach was not as extensive as she'd assumed. Sun-lightened hair covered the length of his powerful thighs and calves. Her throat constricted and she worried if she'd bitten off more than she could chew. No matter, she decided—what she lacked in experience, she would make up for in enthusiasm. If he still wanted her, that is.

He stopped and blinked, then his gaze flew to the opening in the black robe, which revealed one of the few areas of her body he had not already seen. Immediately his erection began climbing and his towel slipped from his hands. His expression was part wonder, part confusion. His molten eyes were alive with desire, but he made no move toward her.

Emboldened by his unabashed nakedness and obvious passion for her, Frankie took a deep breath and pulled open the lapels of the robe. With a flick of her wrists, she let the soft garment slide off her shoulders and into a pool at her feet. Immediately her nipples peaked and she felt moisture between her thighs.

His erection sprang up, enormous and straining, as

he surveyed her body, but otherwise he remained completely still. At last Frankie could no longer tolerate the silence. "Randy, say something."

His chest heaved as he filled his lungs, then he slowly exhaled. "Come to me, Frankie."

She did. With long, slow strides, she walked toward him, her breasts high and taut, her fingers twitching in anticipation of touching every part of his body. They came together in a leisurely embrace during which her gaze remained locked with his. He dipped his head and urged her mouth open with his tongue, then smoothed his hands down to cup her rear and lift her against him. Somewhere in her muddled mind, she registered that he had shaved, and she relished the smoothness even as she missed the sandpaper texture. Their moans mingled and vibrated inside their kiss over the sizzling shock of their bodies touching intimately for the first time.

A thousand fires started in different places in her body, whooshing together in one consuming flame. His hands were gentle and firm, massaging her flesh in a way that promised he wouldn't release her until they were both fully sated. Caught between his pleasing hands and his branding shaft, Frankie had never felt so drunk with need and want. Standing on the balls of her feet, she clung to him, running her hands down the hard muscles in his back, squeezing his buttocks as he pulsed against her.

He tore his mouth from hers long enough to scoop her into his arms and carry her to the bed, his mouth nuzzling her forehead. "Frankie," he murmured as he lay down next to her. "Are you absolutely sure about this?" His breathing had become ragged and his expression serious.

Only one thing could change her mind. "Do you have protection?" she whispered.

"Of course."

She closed her eyes in blatant relief. "Then, yes, I'm sure."

Randy sighed and cupped her breast, guiding her rosy nipple into his mouth. Waves of warm pleasure washed over her and she arched upward, tangling her hands in his thick, wet hair, urging him to draw on her breast harder, deeper, longer. He flicked his tongue over the hardened peak before transferring his attention to the other side.

Aching to touch him, she lifted her leg and stroked his arousal with the sensitive inside of her knee. He halted his ministrations long enough to moan and undulate, moistening her skin. Nipping at her rib cage, Randy licked a path down to her navel, then grasped her hips and splayed his hands over her waist. He grazed his thumbs over the area around her mound and blew gently into her curls, torturing her.

She gathered fistfuls of the comforter to leverage her body higher, closer to any contact that would grant her relief from the intense pressure building in her belly. "Randy," she urged. "Please...please."

With the gentleness of a longtime lover, he combed the moist curls with his fingers, grazing the pearl of her desire until she shivered. When he slid one, then two fingers inside her, she gasped and tore at the covers, arching into his strong hand. He explored her tenderly at first, then plunged farther and harder, readying her for later, she knew. She followed his rhythm, thrusting to meet his strokes while he whispered erotic words over her stomach. The tension in her body swelled with each expressive move of his hand, and when he lowered his thumb to the tiny knob in her folds, she cried out. Her body hummed with burgeoning release. Just when she thought her muscles would fail, a flood of relief crashed over her. She called his name, and bore down on the resistance he offered as she descended from her rocking orgasm.

With great restraint, Randy waited until she had quieted, until the convulsions around his wet fingers had ceased. Then he withdrew his hand carefully and kissed his way from her navel to her ear. Frankie recovered and ran her fingers up and down his spine, her short nails biting into his flesh with enough pressure to heighten his senses. In fact, her every touch made him harder and more eager to make love to her. She opened her knees and he sighed against her cheek at the overwhelming invitation. Maintaining his hold around her waist, Randy stretched and retrieved a condom from a drawer in the nightstand, drawing away only long enough to roll it on.

Her eyes were soft and luminous when he lowered himself against her. "You are so beautiful," he murmured, caressing her cheek. He probed at the threshold to his fulfillment and she opened herself to him. With one long, slow stroke, he entered her, the sensation of her body closing around him so exquisite, he set his jaw to maintain control. Masculine pride welled when Frankie's lashes fluttered and her mouth opened in a silent gasp. He paused a few seconds, absorbing the tight cushion of her femaleness, then pulled back and experienced the thrill of joining her body again, this time eliciting a joyous little sound from her. Randy kissed her chin, her cheek, her ear—anywhere but her mouth because he wanted her lips free to voice the pleasure she experienced.

As for himself, every thrust brought a higher plane of satisfaction and every withdrawal a keener sense of anticipation. He clasped her hands and entwined their fingers, holding her arms above her head, excited by the way she held his gaze throughout. Her eyes were so brilliantly blue, the color could only be natural. Wide and expressive, they echoed every nuance of enjoyment she uttered.

Randy felt his body boiling close to release and strove to extend the lovemaking by slowing down. But when Frankie's murmurings became more frantic and she tightened around him in another climax, he lost control and shuddered, falling into her again and again. He sagged against her, feeling more vulnerable in those few seconds than he dared admit. In fact, even before he regained his composure, Randy was already wondering how he'd say goodbye to this wonderfully complex woman who made him feel alive again. And how far he'd have to flee and how many bars he'd have to buy to put yet another life-altering event behind him.

FRANKIE BLINKED into the light blazing above, then shielded her face and glanced at the clock on the nightstand. Two thirty-five in the morning. Randy lay asleep beside her on top of the comforter, and despite the slight chill in the air, she felt warm because his body still touched hers in so many places.

A flush enveloped her as she remembered their lovemaking session, the intensity of which must have completed her exhaustion of the disturbing day, since she didn't remember leaving the bed afterward. But one quick look at the man next to her told her he had at least disposed of the condom before falling asleep.

Seeking a drink of water, she disentangled herself from Randy's grasp and left his bed. Immediately, her muscles complained and her nipples budded from the coolness. She scooped up the T-shirt he'd given her on the way to the bathroom and pulled it over her head. Inside the tiny room, she cupped her hand and drank from the tap water. She avoided the mirror as she extinguished the bathroom light because she didn't want to invite self-analysis at the moment.

But as she stared at Randy, lying asleep on his side, his arms out to accommodate her when she returned, she acknowledged that, considering the circumstances, spending a few seconds taking stock seemed appropriate.

Two thirty-five in the morning on an island she shouldn't be on, in a bed she shouldn't be in, with a man she shouldn't be with…and she'd never felt more content.

How utterly depressing.

11

FRANKIE AWOKE in the early-morning light to the sound of the shower going in the next room. She sat up and pushed her hands through her hair as images of their lovemaking bombarded her. Leaning on her knees, she sighed. Now what? Act casual, as if one-night stands weren't a novelty for her? Pack up her shopping bags and be gone by the time he emerged? Join him in the shower? She brightened at the last option, then stopped and shook herself. What was she thinking?

She climbed from the bed and straightened the covers, carefully stretching sore muscles as she reached, her mind whirling. Her search for the black canvas bag that held the scavenged pack of cigarettes ended at the living-room sofa, where she stopped to appreciate the efficient layout of his home in the pinkish glow of the morning sun.

The living area consisted of the gray couch and two worn navy leather chairs grouped around a sleek entertainment center that featured a television, stereo system and an extensive selection of CD's. The pale walls were empty, save for a couple of black-and-white landscape photographs attractively matted and framed in silver hues. Assuming the furniture and decor were his idea, she approved of his minimalist style—functional furniture with clean lines in cool shades of white, gray and blue.

The far end of the long room housed a white kitchenette with a breakfast bar, but the focal point of the room, surely the star feature of the house, was the panoramic view of—she squinted to get her bearings from the sun—the Atlantic Ocean. Impulsively, she opened the partially drawn vertical blinds to reveal a virtual wall of screened, sliding glass doors. Frankie sighed at the glorious display of natural beauty and idly entertained the thought of waking up in paradise every day with a man like Randy Tate. An absurd notion, she knew, aware that the black cloud hanging over her career at the moment would make any alternative, no matter how preposterous, seem viable.

With unlit cigarette in hand, she was hesitant at first to look past the surfaces of the white kitchen counters for a light. Then she scoffed. Randy had shared his body with her—surely he wouldn't begrudge her a match. Gingerly, she opened a couple of drawers, finding surprisingly neat contents of utensils and emergency supplies: batteries, candles, flashlight, and yes, matches. She opened one of the sliding glass doors, partially closed the screen behind her and stepped outside with Randy's oversize T-shirt flapping around her knees.

Protected by a scalloped awning, the six-foot-wide balcony ran the width of the cottage. Tropical trees and vines effectively screened out neighbors on either side, although she caught a glimpse of the B&B to the right. The roofs of many buildings were visible between Randy's place and the faraway shore, but the elevation and landscape lent the perception of a private view.

The sturdy iron balcony could easily accommodate a

table and chairs. Instead, a single director's chair with a faded blue seat cover sat in the farthest corner at an angle, suggesting that he often perused the horizon alone. She could picture him sitting in the chair holding a beer, with his feet propped up on the railing. Since he probably could have his pick of women if he were looking for a companion, the fact that he seemed to revel in his hedonistic bachelorhood confirmed her suspicion that Randy Tate was not the kind of man who valued commitment and responsibility. She wondered how many women had made the mistake of falling for him only to discover that sobering fact.

Even at this distance, the roar of the ocean thundered in her ears as she leaned on the metal railing. She smelled and tasted salt in the breeze that ruffled the ends of her hair and made it difficult to light the cigarette. At last, though, the tip caught and she took a minty drag, exhaling a thin stream of smoke into the air as she considered her newest predicament.

She was becoming emotionally invested in a man she hadn't even met this time yesterday. Frankie ground her teeth in frustration. She knew that her chaotic condition could be attributed to her current state of vulnerability, but since when did the heart listen to reason? The systems engineer in her could retrace her actions and reactions since the moment her bag was stolen and predict this morning's outcome just as surely as if she herself were programmed, but all the motivation and excuses and rationalizations didn't make the fallout any easier to deal with.

"Coffee?"

She'd been so engrossed in her self-examination, she hadn't heard Randy emerge. Wearing only black swim trunks, he held two mugs of coffee, one toward her.

His hair was slicked back and he smelled like soap and talc. His expression was neither sultry nor overly friendly, simply polite. Would he gloss over their intimacy with glibness? Had their lovemaking meant so little to him?

"It's not hazelnut, and I was out of cinnamon," he added with a hint of a smile. "But I added sugar and a little cream."

Her pulse kicked up, sending adrenaline pumping after the nicotine she had ingested. Why not add caffeine to the mix? "Thank you," she said, reaching for the cup. "I'm surprised you remembered."

He shrugged. "Bartenders remember what people drink." His gaze slid over her once. "I can whip up an omelette if you're hungry."

"No, thanks. I rarely eat breakfast." How odd to think that he knew what sounds she made during lovemaking, but not that she typically skipped the first meal of the day. She sipped her coffee, then smiled awkwardly, her gaze landing on his arm. "Where did you get the tattoo?"

Randy glanced down and flexed his arm as if he rarely noticed the swirling design. He smiled wryly. "A local artist ran up a tab he couldn't pay and offered to trade." He shrugged. "It seemed like a good idea at the time."

"You don't like it?"

"I don't dislike it," he hedged, turning to face the scenery in blatant dismissal of the subject.

So much for conversation. She puffed on her cigarette, careful to exhale in the opposite direction. Neither of them spoke, and Frankie was beginning to think she might have imagined their previous intimacy.

Lifting his mug to his mouth, he said, "Looks like the day's going to be a beaut."

"Yes, beautiful," she agreed.

After several seconds of silence, he cleared his throat. "Not a cloud in the sky."

"Uh-huh, cloudless," she confirmed, nodding.

More quietness ensued, then he said, "And maybe enough of a breeze this afternoon to catch a sail."

"Maybe."

The silence stretched taut between them. They turned to face each other and spoke at the same time.

"Frankie—"

"Randy—"

"—about last night—"

"—you don't have to—"

"—we were simply—"

"—say anything—"

"—caught up in the moment—"

"—things got out of hand—"

"—at least it's out of our systems—"

"—it was just one of those things—"

"—and won't happen again."

"—and won't happen again." She stared at him, part of her relieved, part of her disappointed. To cover, she turned back to the railing and took a deep drink of coffee. Out of the corner of her eye, she saw that the horizon had reclaimed his attention also.

A fishing boat bobbed into view on its way back from an early-morning jaunt. In the trees flanking the balcony, two birds sang to each other, warbling tirelessly it seemed to Frankie—they obviously hadn't had sex yet.

"What are your plans today?" he asked after another significant pause.

And just like that, Frankie realized, they had officially dismissed the mind-blowing love they'd made as an incidental occurrence—like a flat tire or a dental appointment. Apparently the experience hadn't been such a revelation for him. She tapped her cigarette ash over the edge and took a short drag. "Back to the police station, I suppose. And then I have to pick up replacement traveler's checks."

He nodded, still looking toward the horizon.

"And check in with—I mean, at home," she stammered, not wanting to even think about Oscar right now. But her original ship would be docking in Miami today, so she should at least call her parents and let them know she was okay before her cousin Emily relayed some kind of embellished horror story after touching down in Cincinnati.

"You can use my phone to call...whomever you need to," he offered, his tone abrupt.

She nodded. "Do you mind if I shower first?" After knowing each other intimately, they had regressed to tight politeness.

"Not at all. In fact, I'll phone the police station while you're getting ready."

"Thank you."

"You're welcome."

RANDY HUNG UP the phone and exhaled in a mixture of frustration and relief. Frankie's bag hadn't yet surfaced at the police station and Tippy hadn't left any messages at the bar. One minute he was resigned to be rid of her as soon as possible, and the next he was stupidly happy her departure would be delayed a few more hours.

Last night after they'd made love and she'd fallen

asleep, he'd lain awake with the overhead light on to stare at her, to try to get his fill of her. He'd memorized every contour and freckle on her face—how her left eyebrow arched slightly higher than the right one, how her eyelashes were dark at the base and gold at the tip, and how her nose twitched in her sleep. She had gravitated toward him, and he couldn't resist the opportunity to hold her close without her knowing and, consequently, perhaps reading more into his actions than was warranted. After all, this uncommon attraction was simply a novelty, undoubtedly heightened by the knowledge that their time together was limited.

Since the shower still ran in the bathroom, Randy gauged it fairly safe to return to the bedroom and finish dressing. Telling himself he was not upgrading his dress code on Frankie's account, he withdrew a new red T-shirt from the bottom of his drawer and donned the only pair of denim shorts he owned that were not raveled cutoffs.

He tamed his hair with a palmful of gel, recalling a time when he visited a barber every two weeks to keep his hair from touching his collar. And the earring and tattoo? Sometimes he wondered if he'd defaced his body upon coming to the Keys to seal his resolve to never return again to staid corporate life. He frowned ruefully. Of course, now tattoos were all the rage and earrings no longer the sign of a rebel—go figure.

The water shut off, cutting into his thoughts. Unwilling to test his willpower to resist her if she came out wearing a towel and smelling like the sun, he scooted into the living room. To keep from thinking about Frankie being naked only a few steps away, he sank into one of the leather armchairs and flipped on the television. The set stayed tuned almost exclusively to the cable sports station. He watched ten minutes of a middleweight boxing match before growing restless. His eyes kept darting to the mirror hanging on the wall adjacent to the bedroom door, a silly reaction since the reflection revealed nothing, and he'd already seen, touched and tasted her bare body in most places.

Randy glanced back to the TV. Slowly, he began to flip through the stations, mindful of the network identifier in the bottom right corner of the screen. When a twenty-four-hour news station appeared, he hesitated and moved on, then switched back. Two ribbons of stock symbols and corresponding prices moved across the bottom of the screen, sharing space with a market-summary update—the numbers startlingly high—and a breaking news event in a tiny screen in the top corner. When a live broadcast from the floor of the New York Stock Exchange came on, he turned up the volume and leaned forward, his pulse bumping slightly higher.

"Sorry to keep you waiting," Frankie said, breezing into the living room and flashing him a smile. "Did you get through to the police station?"

He cut off the television abruptly and stood. She wore what looked like a floral wraparound skirt, but when she moved, the flap revealed shorts underneath. A bright pink shirt suited her complexion, and she'd twisted her hair into a loose knot, contained with some kind of comb-claw thing. She wore no makeup that he could tell, and her skin positively glowed. She looked happily beautiful, giving no indication whatsoever that their night together had given her pause to reevaluate *her* life—after all, her life had purpose, meaning.

"Your bag hasn't turned up yet," he said, hating the sudden frown that overtook her face. She'd been hoping to leave today, he knew. "But the day's not over," he added.

She nodded absently, folding emptied shopping bags. "Would you mind if I made a phone call?"

"Not at all," he replied, gesturing toward the phone. He moved toward the kitchen under the pretense of straightening up, in order to give her privacy. Indeed, with her back turned to him, he could barely hear her words and hummed to himself to try to drown out her voice altogether.

"...fine...I'm positive...police station..."

She was obviously trying to reassure Oscar that she had survived the night. Randy swallowed a sour taste in his mouth, telling himself how ridiculous it was to be jealous. After all, if the guy really cared about her, he was probably going crazy.

"...ship tomorrow...bed-and-breakfast..."

He smirked. No doubt she would leave off the part about having a quickie fling with a bartender.

"...Tuesday...I love you..."

His hand stopped midmotion. So she was more involved with this man than she'd previously let on. Love? Randy shook his head. He'd known a few women in his life for whom he'd felt affection, but while establishing his career, he hadn't had time for a relationship. And while crashing to the ground after the S&L failure, he hadn't wanted to expose yet another innocent person to the melee. Since arriving in Key West, he hadn't wanted the complications or responsibility of a permanent companion.

"Thanks," she said from across the room where she'd replaced the handset. "Are you going into work this morning?"

He nodded and gave her a wry smile. "I guess I'd

better, since I didn't make it back for closing last night."

Her cheeks reddened and she fidgeted before asking, "If I haven't worn out my welcome, can I bum a ride to the bar?"

"Sure."

She slipped her feet into the low-heeled white sandals she'd purchased last night—not the best shoes for riding, he noted—and slung her canvas bag over her shoulder. "I'll walk to the bank from there," she said primly, jamming on her sunglasses.

Amused at her sudden streak of independence, he nodded. "And then what?"

"Find a place to stay tonight."

He straightened, more than a little unsettled at the thought of her spending the night elsewhere. Feeling as if she were slipping through his fingers, he walked toward her slowly and smiled with as much nonchalance as he could summon. "That's not necessary, Frankie."

"I think it might be."

"No," he assured her. "I will definitely take the couch."

She bit her bottom lip. "I feel like I'm taking advantage of your generosity."

"Don't," he said simply. "I wouldn't offer if I didn't want you—" Randy cleared his throat to cover the slip "—want you to be safe."

She hesitated and he wished he could see her eyes. "Thanks, but I'll see what I can find," Frankie said softly. She held up a single, bulging shopping bag, indicating she was taking all her worldly possessions with her in case she found another place to stay.

Relenting with a swallow, he said, "Wait a minute."

He strode to the bedroom and knelt beside the bed, then lifted the edge of the comforter and felt around in the darkness. When his fingers seized upon the handle of a suitcase, he withdrew the tan leather bag, now gray from a decade's worth of dust bunnies. Randy restored the small case to its original condition with a T-shirt long overdue for the rag bag, all the while thinking of the day he'd packed the suitcase in the vacant bedroom in his huge Atlanta home. Inside he'd put a couple pairs of jeans, a few casual shirts, underwear and an Atlanta Braves cap. Everything else— Hugo Boss suits included—was sent to Goodwill. He smoothed a hand over the rich leather bag, an award for some sales record or another, then carried the piece of luggage into the living room and handed it to her.

"What's this?"

"You can't go around looking like a bag lady," he said with a wry smile. "Put your things in here."

She removed her sunglasses, her eyes wide. "I can't take your suitcase."

"Sure you can—I have no use for it."

Frankie scoffed. "Everyone needs a suitcase."

"Not if they're never planning to leave," he reasoned.

Her eyebrows crinkled slightly and she seemed at a loss for an argument. "You should never say never," she said finally, caressing the fine leather handle.

He considered her words, then to voice his own resolve that he was exactly where he wanted to be, he said, "Never." The word came out sounding more brusque than he'd intended, so he added, "You can send it back to me when you get home and let me know how the job situation worked out."

Frankie fingered the small leather bag, hesitant to

become further entwined in Randy Tate's life, but absurdly willing to maintain a thread of a connection to him after she returned to Cincinnati. "All right," she agreed, kneeling to transfer the clothing from the shopping bag. When she lifted the new bathing suit, Randy's hand snaked out to touch hers.

"If you're still up for that windsurfing lesson," he said, "leave out your suit."

Again, she hesitated.

"Come on, enjoy your last day," he urged with a heart-stopping grin. "Take home a good memory."

That was the problem, she noted dryly—she would be taking home too many good and disturbing memories already. "Okay," she said with a sigh. "But go easy on me. The way my luck is running, I'll probably break both legs."

His eyes danced. "Maybe your boss will take pity on you if you're in traction."

She'd chickened out on calling Oscar a few minutes ago, dialing her parents instead to give them peace of mind, and to give herself momentary relief from the disastrous work situation that awaited her. "Perhaps I should aim for a broken neck," she said miserably.

But when Randy's good-natured laugh made her chest expand with unexpected longing, she realized she'd be lucky to escape Key West without a broken heart.

12

FRANKIE SURFACED and gulped air into her straining lungs. "I was only kidding about the broken-leg thing!"

Randy's laugh reached her. She blinked him into view, chagrined to find him magnificently clad in his black wet suit, straddling the surfboard and paddling toward her, the sail sagging—again.

"I'll never get the hang of it," she complained, shivering despite the borrowed wet suit she wore. The water temperature had dropped considerably after they'd swum past the sun-warmed shallows. Having landed in the chilly depths headfirst at least a dozen times, she felt a bit waterlogged. By comparison, Randy's hair was still dry above his ears.

"You're doing great," he said, reaching down for her hand. Then he grinned. "You sailors aren't used to being in the water, eh?"

Frankie summoned a sweet smile, reaching up to take his hand. "No!" She levered her body and yanked hard, gratified at the look of surprise on his face as he lost his balance and toppled into the water, leaving the surfboard rocking. He came up gasping. Frankie laughed and kicked toward the safety of the board to avoid retaliation, squealing when she felt his hand close around her ankle.

He easily pulled her backward and clasped her to his

chest, wrapping his arms around her from behind. A sensual thrill raced through her as he laughed like an evil villain who had captured his unfortunate victim.

"Ah, my careless mermaid," he murmured behind her ear. "Don't you know there are sharks in these waters?"

Frankie rolled her neck and squeezed his arms interlocked over her chest. He tread water for both of them, and while she knew she wouldn't drown, she felt far from safe in this man's embrace. A chill raced over her skin.

"Hungry sharks," he said, nipping at the back of her neck. "Just waiting...to eat you up." He growled against her wet, cold skin, laving the sensitive curve with a warm tongue before clamping down in a playful bite.

Desire struck her low and hard as she squirmed. "Help," she whispered lazily, her voice hoarse. "Save me...someone."

He chuckled against her neck, gently sinking his teeth deeper into her flesh. The pleasing pain awakened every nerve ending, hardening her nipples to the point of chafing. She pulled his arms against her, guiding his hands to cover her breasts. He groaned and obligingly massaged her through the rubbery material. The tip of his tongue danced across the patch of skin he'd captured, sending shudders over her body that engulfed her so completely, her teeth chattered uncontrollably.

Randy lifted his head and rolled onto his back, dragging her with him. "Let's get you back to shore." He kicked hard, propelling them toward the wayward surfboard.

"I'm f-f-fine," she protested, but went along willingly.

They caught up with the surfboard, which had fallen onto its side, leaving the slack sail to float on top of the bobbing waves. He released her long enough to right the board, then held it steady with one hand and helped hoist her astride with the other. Trembling both from the cold and his touch, Frankie balanced herself and smiled down at him. He winked and patted her leg, the simple gesture making her heart flutter. Then he positioned himself near the back of the board and kicked, acting as the motor and rudder, to propel them back to the shallows. Frankie used her hands and legs to speed their progress, and soon they were in warmer, shoulder-deep water.

She slid off the surfboard and helped Randy walk it ashore near where their towels lay under the same bowed palm trees as yesterday. Far to their right in front of the nude beach, a few guests bobbed in the waves, batting a huge inflated ball back and forth. To their left, a lone—and clothed—couple walked hand in hand away from them, apparently seeing and heeding the signs posted for the private beach. On the horizon, a couple of windsurfers and Jet Skis were visible. Based on their traffic patterns, a two-story cruiser chugging slowly behind the smaller watercraft appeared to be serving as a home base.

Exhausted, Frankie tipped her face up to the sun, welcoming the warmth, then pronounced, "I am one lousy windsurfer."

"Not true. The water's too cold," he offered. "Otherwise, you'd get the hang of it in no time."

She surveyed the silhouette of his fabulous body in the second-skin black wet suit, trying not to stare as he stripped it off with the ease of practice, the rubbery fabric making little sucking noises of resistance. Underneath, his black swim trunks had molded to his body, outlining his maleness. Frankie wheeled, fumbling with the back zipper of her own suit. "The water is pretty cold," she agreed, noting her encased nipples were still rock-hard.

He walked up behind her, brushed away her hands and unzipped her wet suit. His hands lingered on her waist, and she moistened her lips, tense with anticipation. "You know, Frankie," he said, his voice low and casual. "If you could be here when the water warms up, I promise you would love it."

Her breath caught in her chest. *It?* Key West? Surfboarding? Or being with Randy? Was he tempting her to stay, or simply teasing her? "Wh-when will the water warm up?"

The sun heated her back where he separated the suit and pulled the stretchy fabric from her shoulders. "In a couple of months it'll feel like bathwater."

She pressed her lips together and reached up to help tug the rubbery suit away from her cold skin. "In a couple of months I'll be knee-deep into the rollout of my project."

"I thought you were going to be fired."

She peeled the wet suit down her arms. "Thanks for reminding me."

Pulling from behind, he helped her slide the suit down her hips. "So?"

Tingling from his touch, she leaned over and tugged off the cumbersome garment one leg at a time. "So what?"

He took the heavy suit from her and squatted to spread it out in the sun next to his. His silence further stirred her curiosity, but she held her tongue. Slowly he stood, pursing his mouth, then captured her hand and led her back to their shady spot. She stared at their entwined fingers, bronze and pink, marveling over the simple pleasure of holding hands with someone you...were physically attracted to.

They settled onto their respective towels, with Randy maintaining a loose hold on her hand. When he turned over her palm and traced the outline with a pumice-textured finger, she languidly thought he'd decided not to answer. Then he raised his eyebrows and shrugged casually. "So...why not stay with me...for a while?"

Stunned, Frankie studied him, gauging his seriousness—and her own reaction. *For a while*...no strings, no commitment. She had to admit the notion sounded more appealing than returning to a hornet's nest at work.

He tilted his head. "Does that little crooked-eyebrow thing mean you're thinking about it?"

"It's crazy," she said, shaking her head.

"Preposterous," he agreed, leaning forward to nuzzle her hairline.

"Ridiculous," she murmured, lifting her mouth for a kiss.

"Absurd," he whispered as he covered her mouth with his.

Frankie sank against his body and lifted her hands to caress his hard chest, to thumb his dark nipples. He smoothed his hands down the indention of her spine and over the rounds of her hips, easing his fingers inside the thin fabric of her bathing suit to knead her skin. Knowing all too well what pleasures his hands could unlock, she shuddered with desire.

He lifted his head, his eyes dancing. "Is that a yes?"

She tried to analyze the situation as objectively as possible under the extraordinary influences of an incredibly sexy man and a tropical breeze. She acknowledged the temptation of chucking it all. She could call Oscar and her boss, apologize for what happened, tender her resignation and stay in paradise with Randy...for a while.

Still, as appealing as the idea sounded, she knew herself well enough to know that she couldn't simply walk away from her responsibilities. And she'd probably be bored silly within days. After all—she swallowed—there was more to life than romping on the beach and windsurfing. Besides, could she afford to become more attached to someone whose life-style was so contrary to her own?

She shook her head and opened her mouth to tell Randy his suggestion was out of the question, but he placed a finger on her lips, silencing her words. "Just think about it, Red," he urged in a too-sexy rumble. Then he smiled, his even teeth startlingly white against his dark skin, and leaned forward to brush his lips against hers. "Meanwhile, here's some food for thought." And he kissed her with such depth and sweetness that all thoughts of...whatever else she'd been thinking...were banished.

He eased her back on the towel, then lifted his head and gazed at her. A few wisps of tawny hair danced around his eyes. "Frankie, I want to see you tremble in my arms again."

Her body screamed yes, but her head told her to retreat. She murmured, "Randy, two wrongs don't make a right."

He gave her an unabashed grin. "How about three wrongs?"

In spite of her reservations, she giggled. He was an impossible charmer.

"Four?" he pressed, kissing her neck. "I'm not young, but still relatively healthy." He kissed her thoroughly, gathering her beneath him, caressing her waist and the back of her thighs. She sighed into his mouth, cheerfully resigned to his lovemaking and willing to postpone reality for the time being. He moved his mouth to her shoulder, nudging down the strap of her bathing suit. Frankie absorbed her surroundings through half-closed eyes while she held his head next to her body.

Palm fronds swayed above them, the leaf edges curling like fingers. The sun trickled through, splashing her face with brilliant sunlight, then retreating. The sand dune next to them partially blocked the early-afternoon breeze, but occasionally a cool gust enveloped them.

Giving in to the erotic perfection of the moment, Frankie closed her eyes and groaned when he untangled the straps from her arms and pushed the swimsuit to her waist. Her breasts immediately tightened, her nipples bracing for his onslaught. He stopped long enough to brand each breast with an attentive, suckling kiss, then moved lower, peeling down her bathing suit to make way for his hungry mouth.

She moved her hips in small circles to the music he unleashed in her body, but paused when he slid the suit past her hips, exposing her swollen mound. "Randy," she whispered in protest.

"We're alone, Frankie," he assured her, moving his lips across her stomach. "Give in to the fantasy.

Doesn't it feel good to have the wind and sun on your body?"

She sighed in agreement, willing away the inhibitions that tightened her muscles and opening her knees enough for him to shimmy the suit down her legs. Randy laid her bathing suit aside, then stood and stared down at her. Suddenly self-conscious, Frankie started to sit up, but he raised his hand. "Please don't move."

Flushing with pleasure and the titillating sensation of indulging in a sexual daydream, Frankie lay back on the towel and closed her eyes. At that moment she understood the allure for the nudists. There was definitely something wickedly wonderful about baring your body outside the privacy of your home.

"Frankie, you have to be the most beautiful woman I've ever seen," Randy said, his voice gravelly. A rustling sound caused her to open her eyes. Randy had shed his trunks and stood above her, the water and sun to his back, his arousal jutting full and proud.

She reveled in his compliment, and stared openly at his nakedness. "That's probably what you tell all the stranded tourists."

"No," he breathed as he knelt between her legs. "Not by a long shot." He hooked his arms under her knees and pulled her gently toward his mouth. Inhaling sharply, she froze, mesmerized by the sight of his head dipping between her thighs. "Relax," he whispered against her triangle of red curls. "Let me do all the work."

Her muscles dissolved on their own accord, unable to withstand the proximity of his mouth to her sex. She felt his breath first, hot and diffused against the sensitive folds, then his tongue, strong and probing, delivering promises. Frankie gasped and convulsed beneath him, and the world fell away around them as his lips closed firmly upon the stiff little nub imbedded in her nest.

"Randy," she whimpered, clutching at his shoulders, digging in her nails.

He moaned in response, the vibration of his deep voice against her skin sending warm ripples through her stomach, triggering an intense swell of longing that foreshadowed an unprecedented climax. Frankie began to undulate, to meet the thrusts of his tongue as he made savory love to her. As desire ballooned in her loins, she urged him to greater fervor with murmured assurances of what was to come, and very shortly. He hastened her rhythm, coaxing the burning orgasm to the surface with patient, steady pressure.

When she clenched her knees against his shoulders in preparation for her deliverance, he squeezed her thighs with strong hands, and sent her soaring over the edge with an animal growl against the swollen bead. Frankie cried out his name and bucked under his kneading mouth, relishing the long, languid flood of release between each contraction. She descended with slow, satisfying spasms which he matched with unerring perception. At last she quieted, shrinking from his mouth when even the gentlest pressure was torture for her engorged flesh. She sighed in bliss, reveling in the perfection of one of the most basic of human acts.

But she didn't have long to ponder how Randy had managed to elevate the essential mechanics of sex to a satisfying emotional experience. He crawled higher, his face a mask of smug maleness. She had the fleeting thought that he might pound his chest, but instead he planted a quick kiss on her mouth, then reached for his gym bag. He unzipped two pockets before withdrawing a condom, which he lay next to her shoulder. "You," he said as he dropped another kiss on her lips, "have very strong legs."

She laughed, heady with her own scent and musky taste lingering on his mouth. Reaching down to stroke his erection, she murmured, "Did I hurt you?"

Randy caught his breath and bit back a healthy curse. "You're killing me." If he didn't get a grip, he would explode within Frankie Jensen's small white hands and end their pleasure much too soon. Her enthusiastic response to his sensual tongue-lashing and her vocal climax had stoked his fires to heights he hadn't experienced since his teenage years, when sex had been new and so incredibly exciting. For an instant, he wished he and Frankie could have known each other then, could have explored the blush of erotic discovery together. Then he bit his tongue. With his youthful ready-at-a-moment's-notice libido, he couldn't have handled her back then—hell's bells, she was almost too taxing *now* for him. He closed his hand over hers, stilling her nimble fingers. "Ease up a minute, love. You make my body forget how decrepit it is."

She laughed, a confident, sexy laugh of a woman in control. In answer, she sat up and climbed over his body until she knelt between his knees. Randy swallowed and ground his teeth for restraint as her long, curly hair swept over his stomach. The carpet of red tresses blocked his view, but her intentions were clear enough, and indeed, clinched when her mouth closed over the tip of his arousal.

His eyes rolled back in his head and he exhaled quickly, trying to concentrate on their surroundings to distance himself somewhat from the enormous pleasure coursing through his body. But her tongue commanded his attention, circling, lapping, drawing moisture from his primed manhood. She drew him inside her mouth and he groaned at the exquisite torture, burying his hands in her hair. "Slowly," he pleaded. "Frankie, please go slowly."

To her credit, she withdrew with infinite slowness and descended again with even more deliberate care. But the incredible textures in her mouth and the steady pressure set his life fluid boiling, and after only a few strokes he had to still her once again. He swept aside the fall of hair for one glance of her devouring him, and the sight alone was almost too much for him to bear.

"I need your body, Frankie," he said hoarsely. "Make love to me."

She lifted her head and felt on the towel for the condom. As if sensing his urgency, she tore open the package and rolled the thin casement over him, another exercise in control, he discovered. Then she straddled him, her blue eyes heavy-lidded, pausing to give him a few seconds to compose himself, he presumed. And when her silken glove closed around him, he was grateful for the hesitation...so grateful.

"*Aaahhhhhhhhh,*" he breathed, settling his hands on her slim waist as she accepted his length with a gasp. She threw her head back, then rocked forward and leaned on his chest for support. Randy groaned and covered her breasts with his hands, tweaking her hardened nipples until they glowed. She tightened around his shaft, and moved up and down in a slow, agonizing rhythm that soon told him there was no turning back. He plunged into her with the increasing intensity of a lost but driven man. Frankie's moans echoed his, and when he realized in a blinding flash that she was going to climax again, he arched into her with a massive thrust and shuddered, grinding their hips together. Her soft cries came on the heels of his powerful release, and they swayed, interlocked, until their bodies cooled and their pulses calmed.

Randy sighed heavily and pulled Frankie down to lie against his chest. He closed his eyes and stroked her hair, his heart swelling with an unfamiliar, scary emotion. He had become amazingly attached to this woman in such a short time—he wished they had a few more days to explore their amazing chemistry. Would she forsake her boyfriend and job in Cincinnati and agree to stay with him...for a while?

"Yes," Frankie whispered against his shoulder.

His hand stilled upon her hair and his eyes flew open. Had he spoken aloud? "Yes, what?" he asked, his heart thudding.

"Yes, I'll stay with you," she said, then added, "for a while."

His heart vaulted with mixed sentiments—surprise, happiness, fear, anxiety.

She lifted her head from his chest and smiled. "It sounds like you're going to have a heart attack. Have you already changed your mind?"

He hadn't realized how much he would have missed her until he looked into her velvety blue eyes. "No," he said with a slow grin and pulled her close for a welcoming kiss. "Guess this means I'll have to buy a cappuccino machine."

13

STILL REELING from her spontaneous announcement to stay in Key West, Frankie's mind whirled like the wheels beneath her during the motorcycle ride back to the bar. What would her parents say? She'd never done anything so crazy in her entire life. But telling her folks she'd quit her job to live with a beach-bum bar owner in Key West sounded better than admitting she'd been fired for her own stupidity and relegated to look for another job, with no references. Either way, she'd lose her job, but this way, she'd have Randy, she reasoned. And while he wasn't the long-term, settling-down kind of man she might have hoped for, he was kind and passionate and free-spirited and...easy to love.

She wasn't a fool—she knew Randy's interest in her was more of a physical nature than spiritual. Naturally she herself recognized the powerful sexual chemistry between them. But she also harbored true affection for the man, and something else...gratitude. Because during the short time she'd spent in Randy Tate's company, he had unwittingly shown her she was living her life as if at the end she could trade it in for another one. Of course she couldn't expect Randy to reciprocate those strong feelings, because he couldn't appreciate her revelation.

She could help him run the bar until she decided what to do next. She had a healthy savings account for several months' living expenses, and thanks to her company's stock rising and splitting twice in the last decade, she'd accumulated a couple hundred thousand in her retirement account if she needed to tap into those funds. Frankie knew her open-ended plan was preposterous. For the first time, she was working without a net, and the experience felt...liberating. At the same time, doubts niggled the back of her mind, raising concerns that she might already be in over her heart where Randy was concerned. Would more time spent in his bed cure the condition or kindle it?

As if he suspected she might be having second thoughts, Randy reached back and gave her thigh a comforting pat, then winked at her in the side mirror. They'd spent the rest of the afternoon making love and napping beneath the palm trees, talking about sailing and surfing and more about their families. But they'd scrupulously evaded the topic of Frankie agreeing to stay, as if they both realized her resolve was shaky and best left alone for now. Frankie smiled into his neck and hugged him closer as they drove down the now-familiar street toward the bar parking lot.

As she climbed off the bike, Frankie decided she'd definitely have to invest in a few casual clothes—namely, tennis shoes—if the bike was to be their primary means of transportation. *Their*...even the simple pronoun carried intimate implications that kicked up her pulse. She decided to look into buying a moped, which would be more her speed. Then Frankie stopped. How empty her life had to have been that she could so easily acclimate herself to a new environment. When Randy dropped a kiss on her temple, her throat constricted. Very empty indeed.

His expression turned to teasing as he unhooked the

suitcase he'd given her this morning when she'd insisted upon finding another place to stay the night. They'd been carrying it around all day and now would be taking the piece of luggage back home with them.

"A woman's prerogative," she said simply, offering to take the bag.

But he only shook his head and, smiling like a man who knew when to be quiet, led the way to the bar. Frankie smoothed a hand over her hair and down the rumpled skort and pink T-shirt, which had spent most of the day folded into little squares inside her canvas bag. "How do I look?"

He grinned. "Like you've been tumbled."

"Thanks," she said with a dry laugh.

"No, thank *you*."

Scoffing, she preceded him into the bar, amazed that her fateful trek into this unassuming little place only yesterday had so changed her life. At six o'clock, the Saturday-night crowd was beginning to pick up, although a few empty tables remained. The interior felt cool and inviting, the fans overhead busily circulating air. Bob Marley's distinctive reggae boomed from the rafters, and the pale sand on the floor glistened in the low lighting. The Valentine's kissing booths sat unoccupied on the patio, but Frankie suspected they would be busy before the night ended and the beer stopped flowing.

Kate once again staffed the bar, her eyes lighting up when she saw Randy, then dimming when she spotted Frankie. A pang of jealousy struck Frankie. Were the two of them involved, or had they been at some point? With a sinking heart, she realized the longer she stayed in Key West, the better her chances of running into an old lover of Randy's. How soon would she, too, be relegated to the "ex" pile?

"Are you leaving?" Kate asked cheerfully when Randy set the suitcase on a bar stool.

"Uh, no," Frankie replied with an awkward glance in Randy's direction.

He smiled, seemingly ignorant of the competitive undercurrent. "Frankie's staying in Key West for a while, Kate. I'm going to leave this suitcase in the office." Glancing toward the covered cage above them, he grimaced. "Tweety sleeping off a hangover?"

Kate nodded. "Some bozo slipped a shot glass of tequila into his cage. The poor little guy couldn't even hang on to his perch."

Randy shook his head. "Remind me to get a lock, will you. I doubt if my health insurance will cover rehab for a bird. How's business?"

"Business is good, as always," the woman replied with little enthusiasm. "A lot of people have been asking for you."

Randy raised his eyebrows. "Tippy?"

Another lover? Frankie wondered, watching from beneath her lashes. Kate shook her head, and Frankie couldn't read Randy's reaction. But his sudden change in demeanor indicated he wasn't interested in what anyone else might have wanted. He removed two bottled waters from the cooler behind the bar and handed one to Frankie. The peal of a ringing telephone sounded behind the office door. "I'll get that," Randy said, grabbing the suitcase and pivoting toward the noise. He flashed an apologetic grin at Frankie. "Back to work."

"Good to have you back," Kate called after him, then settled a sullen gaze on Frankie.

She twisted the cap off the bottle of water and took a shallow drink, hoping Kate might move on down the bar. She didn't. "Have you worked for Randy long?" Frankie finally asked, adopting a friendly tone.

The waitress smiled tightly. "Long enough to see lots of his girlfriends come and go."

Frankie's smile dropped.

"See you around," Kate said over her shoulder as she moved toward a customer. "For a little while, that is."

Embarrassment flooded Frankie, warming her cheeks as she averted her eyes. Was she making such a fool of herself by willingly adding a notch to Randy Tate's bedpost?

"Pay her no mind, Ms. Jensen."

Frankie turned as Parker Grimes settled himself onto the stool next to her. He'd apparently overheard their exchange.

"Schoolgirl crush," he said, nodding toward Kate. "She's actually a very nice young lady, but her infatuation with Mr. Tate has sharpened her tongue."

"Were they...involved?" Frankie asked, squirming.

Parker laughed. "Certainly not. Randy has better sense than to dally with an employee. In fact, he has a rule about never dating local women."

She frowned. "What's wrong with local women?"

He shrugged congenially. "They are *here*, my dear."

Realization dawned. "You mean Randy only dates tourists?"

"You could say that."

"I did say that."

His smile spread wide. "So you did."

Worry chewed at her stomach. "He only dates tourists because they're temporary, right?"

He shrugged again. "You may draw your own conclusions. But know this—Randy is a good fellow who would never intentionally hurt a soul. And," he added with a look toward the office door, "I overheard him say you would be staying for a while?"

"For a while," she parroted, the words sounding more vague every time they ran through her head.

"So," he said with a toothy grin, "I gather your sleeping arrangements were satisfactory."

"You tricked us," she accused.

"So I did," he admitted with a smug expression. "But truthfully, Ms. Jensen, I knew you were in capable and trustworthy hands. And may I say, the two of you make a delightful couple."

"Thank you," she said, struck by her new status as part of a "couple."

Randy suddenly appeared behind Parker, and her heart lifted appallingly at the mere sight of him. "Don't even try to steal her away, old man," he said, giving Frankie a wink.

"Just keeping you on your toes, my boy."

Randy shot him a warning look, then said, "Frankie, I need to run a quick errand. Would you mind hanging out here for a while?"

She blinked, then chastised herself. She hadn't expected to spend every minute with him, had she? "Of course I don't mind," she said quickly, thinking she might take the opportunity to make a couple of very difficult long-distance phone calls.

"Great." He held up the suitcase. "I'll run this by the house while I'm at it, and I'll be back soon. Make yourself at home." After dropping a chaste kiss on her temple, he disappeared. Frankie stared after him thoughtfully. Had it been her imagination, or was he avoiding direct eye contact?

"My dear, would you care to join me at my table?" Parker asked.

Frankie nodded, intrigued by the distinguished writer Randy had mentioned often and with such obvious affection. She accompanied him to what must have been his regular roost. He offered her a drink from the half-filled pitcher in front of him, but she declined, noting the strong aroma of tequila.

"Randy told me you encouraged him to buy this place," she said, glancing around, her mind spinning with the possibilities—live entertainment, an appetizer menu.

"Considering the size of my weekly tab," he muttered, "I should have bought the place myself."

She laughed and gestured to the blank legal pad. Reading glasses rested next to a dull, gnawed pencil. "Do you spend your days here writing?"

"Some days writing, some days thinking of writing."

"What inspires you?"

He frowned as he perused the ceiling, giving the question theatrical regard. "A snatch of overheard conversation, a line in a song—" he glanced at her pointedly "—a look between lovers."

She felt herself blush.

"You're a nice change for Randy," he declared, pouncing on the subject of their fledgling relationship with little provocation and with the gusto of a father. "Someone to jump-start his mind again."

"I'm afraid I have no idea what you're talking about," Frankie said, wondering if he was slightly drunk.

"The boy has a brilliant talent," Parker said as he refilled his glass from the pitcher. "And what does he do with his gift? Serve drinks to people who typically have more money than good sense."

Frankie smiled at Parker's praise—the man obviously adored Randy. "Randy was modest when he told me about his career in Atlanta."

The older man nodded. "He's very circumspect about the entire affair. I wouldn't have known myself, save for an acquaintance of mine there who raved about the boy's uncanny ability to pick technical stocks. Randy made the gentleman quite a tidy sum before he sadly gave up the game and left town."

"Was the man an actor?"

Parker frowned. "No, he was in commercial real estate."

Confused, Frankie opened her mouth to ask a few questions, then realized she might learn more if she played along. Anxiety curled low in her stomach at the thought that she was snooping into Randy's background, but she reminded herself she had a right to know about the man who had captured her heart, darn him. Actor, schmactor. "Yes, the circumstances under which Randy left Atlanta would make a good plot for a book, wouldn't you agree?"

"...THREE HUNDRED, four hundred, five hundred."

"Sorry about the wallet," Tippy said, folding the bills into his shirt pocket. "But the kid couldn't remember where he ditched it."

Randy frowned ruefully at the man sitting in the dark cab. "How much of this money are you giving to the punk?"

Tippy's teeth flashed in the dark. "Just enough to pay the fine for the shoplifting charge."

"Shoplifting?"

"Uh-huh. Tomorrow morning the police will receive an anonymous tip that the kid has a radio that was stolen last week from the audio shop."

Randy smiled. "You're a good man, Tippy."

The cabdriver reached into his pocket and withdrew a one-hundred-dollar bill, then shoved it back into Randy's hand. "All's well that ends well," he said, and pulled away from the curb.

"All's well that ends well," Randy repeated to himself as he stared down at the dirty black briefcase Tippy had given him. Having given the contents only a perfunctory glance earlier, he leaned against the seat of his motorcycle and angled the bag under the glow of the streetlight. The leather was of superb quality, but he'd expected no less from a woman who appreciated good penny loafers. His favorite briefcase had been a burgundy leather and canvas expandable bag—great for the oversize printouts he'd taken home every night to read until he fell asleep.

He lifted the side flap and withdrew a portfolio bearing the name Ohio Roadmakers and a hard-hat logo. Inside were the precious compact discs and endless charts and notes that Frankie had been agonizing over...until this afternoon. This afternoon at the beach she had rounded a mental corner, gaining perspective on the matter thanks to a little time and diversion. And she'd decided to turn her back on the corporate world and stay with him...for a while.

Her resolve to quit reinforced his belief that big companies gobbled up juicy people and chewed on them until the flavor was gone, then discarded them like a piece of old gum. Yessir, he'd been lucky to escape ten years ago with his sanity intact. And here he was, enjoying life more than he'd ever thought possible.

Randy frowned, running his finger around the edge of a CD which, according to the label, could hold more information than the entire desktop computer in his old office had held on the hard drive. A sigh escaped him. Okay, so he hadn't realized how intellectually stale he'd become, but just knowing that Frankie would be there in the morning renewed his zest for island life. They'd talk about...not computers, since he didn't know much about them anymore. And not the stock market, since he hadn't kept up with the numbers. And not foreign policy, since he no longer watched world news—and damn little domestic news, for that matter. He hadn't even voted in the last two presidential elections.

Then he brightened—sports! They could always discuss sports. Sailing and windsurfing and...sailing.

He scanned the pages of notes, not that he understood much of the vocabulary, but because he found her handwriting so intriguing. She was a jotter—someone who had diagrams and phrases scribbled on every square inch of the margins. *He*, on the other hand, had been a one-idea-to-one-sheet-of-paper kind of businessman, with neat, organized stacks of papers on his desk.

Randy set aside memories of his fast-paced days and replaced the portfolio inside the briefcase, thinking how jubilant Frankie would be when he handed her the briefcase. She could overnight the documentation and resign without thinking she'd undermined the project.

Then he stopped. With the briefcase in hand, what if

she decided to return to Cincinnati? What if the only reason she was staying with him was that she didn't want to face the firing she was convinced awaited her if she returned without the portfolio?

Randy chewed his lip furiously. Was it really necessary that Frankie know he had the briefcase? Now that she'd decided to give up her job and stay with him, what would it matter if he simply chucked the bag into the ocean?

What mattered, he realized, was that an entire team of people were relying on the information in the portfolio, and he didn't want to be responsible for disrupting untold dozens of lives, just like before. Then again, he could simply drop the portfolio anonymously into the mail to Ohio Roadmakers with a note about finding the folder in Key West, blah, blah, blah.

Yes, he decided suddenly. He would send the portfolio back to the company in a week or so, and if Frankie discovered someday that the materials had been returned, she'd be so entrenched in Conch life, in *his* life, the job in Cincinnati wouldn't matter.

Easier thought than done, he realized later when he reunited with Frankie at the bar. She kept looking at him with those big, blue eyes as if he had betrayed her somehow, even though he knew it was his own guilt eating at him. They had a few beers and he sat with her at Parker's table, listening to the old man's stories and laughing as if he hadn't already heard the yarns dozens of times. Often he sneaked glimpses of Frankie's profile, loving the way the tip of her nose lifted when she laughed, his heart squeezing when she turned her wide smile in his direction.

The rowdy atmosphere prevented them from conversing much, but even so, she seemed withdrawn. She didn't shrink from his touch, though, and on the late ride back to his place, she clung so tightly, she seemed part of his own body. Despite his hurry to get Frankie home and in his bed, Randy drove slowly, allowing the wind and the vibration of the bike to take over, acutely aware of both sets of curves—the ones beneath his wheels and the ones pressing into his back.

From the bike to the bedroom, they barely spoke. She seemed as anxious as he to make love. Ignoring the pangs of guilt, Randy deposited the gym bag that held her briefcase in his closet, then tugged her to the bathroom. While the shower ran warm, he undressed her carefully, christening every revealed patch of skin with lingering kisses. But her hands and mouth carried more urgency, and by the time they were both naked and standing under the water, Randy had gladly adopted her edgy pace.

They lathered each other's bodies with fresh-smelling soap, then Frankie scrubbed his back with a stiff brush, the act strangely more intimate than their nakedness, the friction more erotic than if she'd touched his private zones. By the time they rinsed, Randy wasn't sure they'd make it to the bed. Indeed, he'd barely grabbed a condom from the nightstand when Frankie pulled him down on top of her on the hard, nubby texture of the sisal rug. They kissed and wrestled until she again straddled him in what was fast becoming his favorite position.

Her body accepted his in one thrilling downstroke, then she rocked with him inside her in a quick, controlled rhythm. Between the biting surface of the carpet at his back, and the soft, giving contours of the woman on top of him, every nerve screamed, every response stimulated. When her moans escalated, he stroked her with his thumb until she came in great, heaving spasms, then he readied himself for a powerful climax. Lifting his body into hers with a final massive thrust, he clutched her waist and held her against him as he shuddered his release again and again, murmuring, "Frankie...oh, yes...Frankie, Frankie."

Her body fell limp and she might have fallen asleep on the scratchy rug had he let her. Instead, he scooped her up and laid her in his bed, then climbed in next to her and tucked the sheet around them. While his body recovered, his thoughts whirled at a dizzying pace. He'd always enjoyed sex, but this, this...emotional afterglow made for an exceptionally memorable experience. He sighed and debated the wisdom of never leaving this room again, of simply keeping Frankie as close to him as possible for as long as possible. When the thought of her briefcase stashed in his closet loomed large, he squeezed her close, then forced himself to close his eyes and sleep.

FRANKIE TRIED TO SLEEP. Her body ached, and after the mental gymnastics of the past several hours, so did her mind. She couldn't stay in Key West. She wanted to, but she was already too emotionally attached to Randy Tate. After her illuminating chat with Parker, she realized how little she really knew about the man to whom she'd so willingly handed her body...and her heart.

She'd mistaken physical chemistry and comfortable compatibility for affection, and while she might have his attention for a few days or weeks, she knew she'd never have his heart—he kept himself too well guarded. She'd wager that if he let her get close enough to share the tribulations of his past, he'd push her away shortly thereafter.

Frankie held her breath and listened to Randy's even breathing, then slid out of bed as silently as possible. Pausing long enough to grab his robe and her cigarettes, she made her way to the balcony and eased open one of the sliding glass doors, closing the screen behind her. The night setting was so incredibly beautiful, she had to smile. The nearly full moon spread its glow across the bumpy surface of the water, silhouetting trees and buildings so perfectly, the only thing missing was a hand-in-hand couple. She would always remember this weekend as one of enlightenment and romance.

She closed her eyes, almost wishing she was the kind of woman who *could* become so wrapped up in a weekend fling that she'd throw away everything. But she couldn't sacrifice it all for anything less than love. Besides, she'd left loose ends in Cincinnati, and she owed it to herself to tidy them up before getting on with her life.

Feeling around on the shadowy balcony, she claimed Randy's director's chair and tapped out a cigarette. The sound of the match striking sounded loud in the confines of the quiet little corner of the world. She drew on the cigarette, thinking she needed to quit, then laid her head back and exhaled.

"Those things'll kill you," Randy said behind her.

Frankie's heart jumped and she lifted her head. "That's what I've heard," she said softly without turning around. She even craved the sound of his voice.

"Insomnia?"

"You could say that."

"Mind if I join you?"

She laughed. "It's your balcony."

The screen door opened and closed. "I have something to tell you."

Feeling falsely brave, she said, "Let me guess—you were never an actor?"

After a few seconds of silence, he said, "You're right, I was never an actor. I was an investment broker. The company I worked for went bankrupt and took several of my customers down with it."

She paused. "Did you do anything illegal?"

"Not knowingly."

"Then what's with all the secrecy?"

She couldn't see him, but heard footfalls as he stepped up next to the chair, and the slight whisper of his arm against metal as he leaned forward on the railing. "It was a long time ago, and I was a different person. In fact, when I first met you, I saw a lot of my old self in you—driven, goal-oriented, a real workaholic."

A horrible thought occurred to her. "And you thought you'd save me from myself?"

"I guess so," he confessed.

A stone of embarrassment fell to the bottom of her stomach. She'd fallen for him and he'd viewed her as a project, a fixer-upper. "Gee, thanks."

"You didn't seem happy."

"I'd just been mugged," she reminded him.

"You know what I mean."

She put the cigarette to her mouth for a quick puff. "So maybe I'm not ecstatic about my job. Who is, besides the Ben & Jerry's ice-cream taster? I'm a good analyst, I make a decent living and I work with great people."

"Like Oscar?"

"Like Oscar," she agreed, wondering how her friend would react when he heard about the lost documentation. Poor thing—he must be going out of his mind waiting for that fax she'd promised him. "He's a real gem to put up with me."

"You're leaving on that ship today, aren't you?"

She tried to read something into his voice—longing, regret, *something*—but he had said the words as casually as if he'd asked her what she wanted to drink. "Yes. You might be happy here, Randy, but if I stayed, I'd just be running away from my problems."

"What will you do if you're fired?"

Frankie shrugged, then realized he probably couldn't see her. "I don't know—start interviewing, I guess. Something will come up." After another drag on the cigarette, she asked, "You had something to tell me?"

"Yes," he said softly. "I have something for you."

Knowing he didn't care for her the same way she cared for him freed her tongue. "What is it, and don't tell me you're naked."

He chuckled. "I am... But I was referring to something else, and considering the fact that you're going back to your job, it seems all the more appropriate."

"What?" she asked, startled when he laid a heavy item in her lap. "What—my briefcase!" She stuffed the cigarette in her mouth to free her hands. "Oh my God—where did you find it?" she mumbled. Feeling for the side flap, she slipped her hand inside and breathed a sigh of relief when her fingers touched the familiar smooth portfolio.

"A friend of mine found it."

"What friend?" she asked, instantly suspicious.

"A cabbie with his ear to the ground."

"When did your friend find it?"

"This evening," he said. "That was my errand—to meet him."

"Why didn't you take me with you?"

"I didn't want to get your hopes up."

"Then why did you wait so long to give it to me?"

"I, um, well...didn't want you to feel like you *have* to go back to your job."

"I don't," she snapped, furious.

"But you *are*."

"I mean, I *didn't* feel like I had to go back to my job," she blustered. "I wanted—*want*—to go back."

"Oh," he said simply. "In that case...good—I mean, I guess this nixes plans for the cappuccino machine."

So he was glad she had changed her mind about staying. Frankie pushed herself to her feet, clasping the briefcase as if her love, er, life depended on it. "I guess I'd better get some sleep." She didn't move, knowing he stood nearby, and naked. And she certainly couldn't spend the rest of the night in his bed.

They spoke at the same time.

"I'll take the couch," she offered.

"I'll take the couch," he declared.

Before he could suggest that they both take the couch, Frankie said, "Okay. See you in the morning." Then she brushed past him, glad for the cover of darkness to hide her welling tears.

14

WITH HER STOMACH tied in knots, Frankie joined the line of passengers waiting to board the cruise ship that sounded its horn every two minutes. Randy had driven her to the dock and insisted on waiting with her while the lines formed. "I can't thank you enough," she said, flashing him her brightest smile. "For everything—the windsurfing lesson, a place to stay—" She blushed. "And especially for getting my briefcase back. I don't know what I would have done—"

"Slow down, Red," he said with a tight smile and a wink. "I would've done the same for any—" He broke off and cleared his throat. "That is, um—"

"I know you would have," Frankie rushed to assure him even while her heart hung heavy in her chest. How much clearer could he make it that their couple of days together meant so little to him? "I'll send your suitcase back soon."

"No hurry," he said, shrugging his shoulders.

He'd worn a fairly new T-shirt for the occasion, and looked amazingly handsome. Frankie realized she didn't even have a picture of him and wondered how long she would keep his face in her memory. Hoping he would forget the way she looked when they first met, she wore the white gauze pants and a new turquoise tank top for her send-off, but Randy hadn't seemed to notice. "It's hot," she announced unnecessarily, stuffing her battered hat on her head.

"This is Key West," he answered easily, glancing over his shoulder, obviously anxious to be rid of her and on his way.

Saddened and embarrassed, she deferred to silence as the line snaked around, then realized with dread that a ship photographer stood on the ready to snap pictures of passengers as they embarked. And not just any picture, but in front of a huge red heart frame. With a jolt of surprise, she realized today was Valentine's Day. Great—once again everyone on the cruise would be paired up.

"Is Oscar picking you up at the airport?" Randy asked.

"Probably." Thankfully, this morning she'd been able to fax Oscar copies of the design sheets he needed. "He'll want to bring me up to speed on a few systems modifications that were made in my absence."

"No doubt," he said, nodding.

The closer she got to the photographer, the more she tried to convince Randy to leave. "You wouldn't want to get caught in all that, um, foot traffic on the way out."

"Frankie, I'd like to stick it out the last five feet," he remarked wryly.

And so she fidgeted, wondering if he might kiss her before she stepped on board, or shake her hand, or maybe even pop her one for being such a pain. "I can't thank you enough," she babbled.

"You said that already," he murmured with a smile. "And you're welcome."

"A picture of the couple for Valentine's Day?" the

photographer asked in a thick Spanish accent. He grinned and gestured toward the huge heart.

Frankie shook her head, but Randy said, "Sure, Pops," and steered her toward the prop.

"Randy—"

"You don't have to buy it," he said, laughing. "But I have to admit I was hoping for a goodbye kiss, and at least this way we'll be semi-alone."

She inhaled deeply, hating to admit she was hoping for the same. "Okay, but make it quick. I wouldn't want to miss this ship, too."

"If I remember correctly," he said as he pulled her close, "*quick* wasn't on my adjective list." Since her hands were full, she could only lift her lips. His mouth covered hers in a sweet, lingering, completely possessive and uncomfortably familiar kiss. His tongue thrashed against hers, dredging up desire she'd suppressed the remainder of the night without him next to her. She savored the sensory details, committing to memory the scent of his fresh soap and minty shaving cream, the feel of his hands kneading her back and waist, the rumble of his slight groan as her tongue said farewell to his. *Goodbye... Bon voyage... Don't forget to write.*

"Is enough kiss!" the man exclaimed, finally gaining their attention. They parted to the tune of hearty laughter from other passengers.

Frankie wet her lips and looked toward the stairs leading to the entranceway. "I guess this is goodbye then."

"I guess so," he said with a slow wink. "It's been a pleasure, Red."

Since no words came to mind, she simply nodded and started backing toward the stairs.

"Let me know how that project of yours turns out," he called.

Frankie nodded again and, feeling suspiciously close to tears, wheeled and hurried toward the stairs. She knew he'd be gone by the time she boarded, but once on deck, she walked to the railing and looked over anyway. Her heart fell lower and lower in her chest as she scanned the crowd. Finally she had to admit she would never see him again. The ship's horn blasted so long and loud, she covered her ears. Within minutes, the stairs were pulled away from the ship and the huge vessel began to tremble, then move. The crowd on the dock started to dance and sing in a collective send-off, put into motion by the beat of a snare drum.

She searched the crowd frantically, hoping to catch one more glimpse of him.

"Hey, Red, over here!" she heard above the din.

When she caught sight of him directly below her on the dock, waving both arms, she grinned wide, and waved back, crowding close to the railing. For a few frantic seconds, she wished she had stayed, wished he had cared for her as much as she cared for him, wished their life-styles weren't a world apart.

On impulse, she dug deep in the corner of her resurrected briefcase and seized a penny. As luck would have it, the coin was newly minted, shining so brightly it almost looked counterfeit. Stretching out over the railing, she called, "Here's the penny I owe you for the coffee!"

She dropped the coin, and watched it spiral through the air, glinting in the sun. Several feet below he caught the penny, juggled it, then held it up in triumph. Cupping his hands like a megaphone, he yelled, "What, no tip?"

She laughed. "Yeah—buy a motorcycle helmet!"

He made a face, but kept waving until he blended in with the crowd that grew ever smaller as the cruise ship pulled away. She stood by the railing waving when all the other passengers had dispersed. At last, Key West disappeared from the horizon and Frankie stared at the gigantic body of water around her, feeling very alone. Being in love for the first time had a way of ennobling a person, of stripping away nonsensical baggage until only those things most important remained. She was a happier person for having met Randy Tate. Really, she was.

She enjoyed the return journey to Miami, even though she spent most of the time gazing out over the frothy wake behind the ship. Sunday afternoon she spent on the uppermost deck, safely swathed in towels and sunscreen, thinking hard about the philosophical wake-up call she'd been delivered. And Randy was never more than a heartbeat from her thoughts.

Sunday evening she found the lovely pinkish conch shell he had given her, and thereafter kept it tucked in a pocket. She tossed her half-smoked pack of cigarettes overboard Sunday night, and Monday morning, began recording her trip in a journal. By the time the ship docked Monday afternoon, she'd reconstructed most of her hours in Key West, down to what she wore and phrases of the islanders, to sketches of the fanciful buildings. And throughout the partially illustrated, pieced-together snippets were Randy's face and laughter and bar and motorcycle and tattoo and parrot and countless other memories.

With only the small suitcase, she was one of the first passengers to disembark in Miami. She caught a cab straight to the airport and turned in her unused ticket to Cincinnati toward another flight—a roundabout trip back to Cincinnati that included a two-night stay in Atlanta. Then she fished out a business card Parker had given her and headed toward a pay phone.

RANDY ACHED for Frankie—her face, her body and her laugh plagued him at all hours of the day. He'd drilled a hole in the penny she'd thrown him and wore it on a leather thong around his neck. He became moody, sniping at the waitresses and even yelling at Tweety like an idiot.

One night Parker clamped a hand on his shoulder. "Just because you were foolish enough to let her go, don't take it out on the rest of us, son."

Randy had scoffed and denied anything was wrong. And if something *were* wrong, he added loudly, it had nothing to do with Frankie Jensen.

"Do us all a favor," Parker had said. "Call the lady."

So late one night when he was sitting out on the balcony, he'd called directory assistance, only to find her number was unlisted. Then he'd called Ohio Roadmakers and had listened to her voice message like a coward—twice—before hanging up without a word. She was getting on with her life. It wasn't her fault that he didn't have much of a life to get on with. One thing was certain...the woman had left him with enough fantasies to keep his sheets wet into the foreseeable future.

A few restless days later, he bought and read the first copy of the *Wall Street Journal* he had consumed since arriving in Key West. Suddenly the televisions in the bar were tuned to all news, all day. The only way he could keep thoughts of her at bay for any length of time was to engross himself in financial journals and tax codes.

In mid-March, Randy received a suitcase-size package from Cincinnati. His heart pounded like a child's as he opened the box, knowing full well it contained only his piece of luggage, but hoping it would include a long, rambling letter from Red letting him know how the project was progressing, or how the weather was miserable, or how much she missed him. Instead, she'd packed a slightly smaller, but heavy box in the suitcase, which he lifted with a wry laugh.

She'd sent him a black motorcycle helmet, the old-fashioned half-helmet style with a chin strap—very hip and good for warm-weather riding. There was no letter and no return address, just a simple yellow memo square that read: *I gave up smoking, so you have to start wearing a helmet. Frankie.*

He sat on the balcony wearing the helmet and staring at the note all evening, the wheels turning in his head. He'd simply not gotten his fill of her, that was all. Maybe if he at least saw Frankie again, outside of the island atmosphere, and realized that the novelty of their attraction had worn off, he could get her out of his system. Baseball season was right around the corner— he could take a long weekend to go to Riverfront Stadium and stop by to see her. To see how she and good ole Oscar were doing. To see if her eyes were still as blue as the water around the Keys.

Before he could change his mind, he picked up the phone and called her voice mail at work. Her voice came on the line, slightly lower-pitched and well-modulated for business. "Hi, this is Frankie Jensen with Ohio Roadmakers. Please leave a detailed message and I will return your call as soon as possible."

When the beep sounded, his mouth went completely dry. "Uh, hey, Frankie. This is Randy...Randy Tate. Today is Friday, March the nineteenth, and you've probably already left for the day. Um, I got your package today. Thanks for the helmet—I really love...it. The helmet, that is. And congrats on giving up the cigarettes. Uh, listen—" He cut off as a piercing tone interrupted, then a mechanical voice said, "Thank you," and disconnected the call.

He swore a blue streak and stabbed in the number again.

"Hi, this is Frankie Jensen with Ohio Roadmakers. Please leave a detailed message and I will return your call as soon as possible."

"Hey, Frankie, it's Randy again...I was cut off before. Listen, I was thinking about heading to Riverfront for a Reds game sometime soon, you know, make a long weekend out of it. I was wondering if you would be available to go out with me, maybe get a bite to eat...or something...afterward. If you would—" The tone and voice cut him off again and disconnected the call.

"Dammit!" he thundered, then hit the redial button.

"Hi, this is Frankie Jensen with Ohio Roadmakers. Please leave a detailed message and I will return your call as soon as possible."

"Frankie, this is Randy—again. If you'd like to take in a game, call me and I'll fly up. Three zero five, five five five, one two one three. Bye." He hung up, then regretted his hasty goodbye. He should have told her he was looking forward to seeing her, talking to her, lying down with her...

Oh, well, he decided, locking his hands behind his new helmet and propping up his feet. Now the ball was in her court. If she wanted to see him again, she'd call.

"I CAN'T BELIEVE you're really leaving, Frankie." Oscar shook his head sadly and cupped both hands around his beer.

"Yeah," Susan chimed in. "How long has it been— nine years?"

Frankie glanced at the date on her watch. "Let's see...March nineteenth. In another six weeks I would've celebrated my ten-year anniversary." She smiled happily and shrugged. "Except I won't!"

"A toast," Oscar said, lifting his glass. "To fearless Frankie, may she be the most successful restaurateur in the entire city of Atlanta!"

"Hear, hear!" chorused the group.

Frankie looked around the table at the more than two dozen co-workers, her eyes glistening. "Thank you, everyone," she said, blinking rapidly.

"Speech, speech!" someone yelled, and others joined in.

She shook her head and drank from a frosty beer glass, relenting when the chant deafened her. "Okay, okay." She cleared her throat, then said, "Thanks to all of you who made every day a great challenge. I'm so glad to be going out on the tail end of a successful project."

"That's the understatement of the year," Susan piped in, and everyone laughed.

Frankie nodded. "You're right, Susan, we did good. And I'm going to miss all of you so much." Her gaze rested on Oscar. She gave him a wink and a friendly pat on the hand. He'd taken her leaving almost as hard as her parents, but she'd convinced him they had no romantic future together, regardless of whether she stayed. He'd been hurt at first, but after a few weeks, Oscar had finally come around, filling Frankie with relief that they were parting friends. Following another round of drinks, and a few war stories, people started checking their watches and pushing back their chairs to go home to their families. One by one they came by to shake Frankie's hand and say goodbye.

"So if your restaurant falls through, will you be coming back?" Charley asked.

Oscar scoffed. "It won't fall through, you dolt. Frankie said a restaurant would have to be pretty bad to fail in Atlanta, didn't you, Frankie?"

She nodded, her cheeks warming when she remembered Randy's words. "Someone told me that once—I certainly hope it's true." What would he say if he could see her now? Thinking of the Valentine's bon voyage picture stuck in her vanity drawer at home brought an affectionate smile to her face. Randy had been on her mind all day, probably because he should receive her package soon. She wondered what he would think of the helmet, and if it would fit.

"What's so funny?" Oscar asked, looking morose.

"I'm just happy, that's all," she answered quietly.

"I'd like to know what happened to you in Key West," he muttered. "Did you have a near-death experience or something?"

"No," she said, laughing. "Sometimes getting away just gives you a little...perspective. Thanks for putting together this little going-away gig."

"Glad to do it," he said, nodding at the last people to leave. "Can I give you a lift home, Frankie?" He looked hopeful.

"No, thanks," she answered gently. "I didn't have time to load a couple of boxes of desk junk into my car before dropping by here, so I need to swing back by the office."

"I saw the boxes and carried them down," he said with a defeated shrug. "It'll only take me a couple of minutes to transfer them from my trunk to yours."

She gave him a fond smile. "Thanks, now I won't have to go back to that empty office." Frankie hesitated, wondering if she should record another voice message to say she'd left the company. Then she changed her mind. Everyone who knew her knew she was leaving...everyone who cared, that is.

As THE WEEKS PASSED into May, Randy's hurt that Frankie hadn't returned his call dulled, then flamed to anger. She'd been stranded, broke, dirty and scared when he first met her, and he'd gone so far as to extend his home to her. The least she could do was acknowledge his phone call and spare five minutes to see him if he came to *her* city.

Friday nights were the worst, and this particular Friday night he found himself sitting in the bar office, tinkering with his new desktop computer and holding the phone, considering leaving her another message. He drank a mouthful of beer, then hesitated. Maybe he should wait until Monday during the day and try to catch her in her office. Then he sighed and rubbed his hand down his face. What did he care? He'd left Frankie a message—three of them, he recalled wryly—and she hadn't bothered to call back with so much as a howdy-doo for the man whom she "couldn't thank enough" for all he'd done for her.

A rap on the door broke into his thoughts. "Yeah?"

Parker stuck his head inside. "A minute of your time, Randy?"

"Sure, come on in."

The older man closed the door, removed his reading

glasses and poked the tip of the earpiece into his mouth. ''Randy, I realize only a few days have passed, but I'm anxious to know if you've given any thought to my offer.''

Randy sat up and crossed his arms. ''Well, sure I have, Parker. It's too much money not to give the idea some thought. But for the life of me, I can't imagine why you'd want this place.''

Parker's mouth turned down in a thoughtful frown. ''It's not so complicated, my boy. I have the money, I'm here more often than not anyway, and, well, quite frankly, my agent thinks a tavern of my own would be good for publicity.''

Randy's eyebrows rose and his companion had the grace to blush. ''Thinking of changing the name, are you?''

Parker shrugged as a sheepish smile lifted one corner of his mouth. ''Perhaps.''

Randy chuckled, shaking his head. ''There's just one problem, old man.''

''And that is?''

''What the heck would I do?''

Parker scoffed, dismissing Randy's concern. ''You've had your little rest, now it's high time you got on with your life. Get back into investments where you belong.''

Randy frowned wryly. ''Parker, I know there's a lot of money in Key West, but this isn't exactly the financial pulse of the South.''

''You're a free man, you can go anywhere—Miami, Orlando...Atlanta.''

Randy tensed for the sick feeling that descended every time he thought about Atlanta, but it didn't come. Instead, flashes of the things he loved about the city entered his mind: the skyline, the hectic pace, the mild climate; blazing azaleas, pine trees and the Braves.

He mulled over the idea for a while, then glanced up and shrugged. "Maybe I'll...give it another try...someday."

"You can go into business for yourself this time."

Randy pursed his mouth, nodding slowly. "Develop my own portfolios and treat clients *my* way." Warming to the idea, he squeezed his fingers to his temples, shaking his head. "Dammit, Parker, just *think* of all the money I've missed out on making for other people over these last ten years."

The old man smiled. "There will always be more money to be made, my boy." He clucked. "But I can see in your eyes that you are making a wise decision in this new direction. You already seem more...energetic. I sensed you were looking to make a change ever since the girl left."

Randy didn't have to ask who "the girl" was. In fact, for once he felt too good to argue, so he simply nodded. Loving Frankie—he stopped, then pressed on— loving Frankie had been a catalyst for his mind and body, reminding him he was alive, with a searching intellect. "I'll need to take some refresher courses, renew my license, find an office..."

"You can maintain your little home here—I'll rent it out for you if you like. And with the money from the tavern, you should be able to secure a nice office space, say in Midtown?"

Randy pointed his index finger toward Parker. "Midtown—now you're talking."

"A chum of mine is refurbishing a charming old building to house apartments, professional offices, eateries, and the like. We can jet up next weekend and take a look around."

"Sounds great," Randy agreed, his adrenaline churning. He trusted Parker's taste implicitly.

"So, do we have a deal on the bar?" Parker extended his hand.

Randy looked around the tiny, shabby office for a few seconds, contemplating all the soul-searching and drinking he'd performed within the confines of its walls over the last ten years or so. Then he glanced to his friend and stood, accepting his hand with a firm shake. "Deal."

15

FRANKIE FELT CLOSER to Randy in Atlanta, and not just in terms of physical miles. Since her café served only breakfast and lunch, occasionally she explored the city in the evenings on foot. At times, she experienced a tightness in her chest or a tingling over her skin and she would imagine she and Randy had walked over the same ground. The notion was silly, she knew, but since moving to the city, she'd become more susceptible to daydreaming and flights of fancy. The experiences of the past few months had freed her mind and spirit—she was determined to make a go of the café, and in time, when her heart had rebounded, she'd find a man who would help her forget about Randy Tate.

Thanks to Parker's friend, she had found a decent apartment on the outskirts of Midtown, a leisurely walk from her brand-new eatery. She'd decided to take decorating chances in the one-bedroom flat she wouldn't have considered in her conservative condo in Cincinnati. A couple of gallons of paint and a hundred yards of brilliantly colored fabric later, she had transformed the ho-hum quarters into a wonderfully eclectic living space, appropriately hip for the artsy area of town. Frankie immersed herself in her new life-style, dividing her time between working at the café, planting a herb garden on her apartment terrace, dining with neighbors, avoiding her parents...and missing Randy.

She had planned to be so busy with the café that she'd scarcely have time to think about him, but for some reason he preyed on her mind with increasing intensity. The nights were the worst. From her pillow, she had a clear view of the *D* in the huge neon All-Night Diner sign on the other side of the wide street. The bright illumination reminded her of the lights of Key West, and a flood of other memories invariably followed. A spring heat wave forced Frankie to sleep with the windows open to cool her un-air-conditioned rooms. She lay on her new, crisp sheets and imagined Randy's big, tanned body next to her, their legs tangled, their desires sated. Indeed, instead of his memory growing dim, he seemed to have mined his way deeper into her heart.

RANDY SAT on the windowsill of his open bedroom window in his boxers, perspiring. Late spring, and the Atlanta air already hung hot and heavy. The heat wave was a freak of nature, he knew, ill timed to aggravate his restlessness, reminding him of two steamy nights in Key West with one Frankie Jensen in his bed.

He turned his face toward Cincinnati, wondering what she was doing and who she was doing it with. Unfortunately, the neon sign across the street for the all-night diner blocked his view. Randy sighed, hoping the adrenaline of building his new business would sustain him through the inevitable lows of missing Frankie.

He stood and massaged his neck, then eased into bed and pulled an extra pillow close to his chest.

THE MEMORY-INDUCED insomnia was taking its toll, Frankie acknowledged with a yawn the next morning as she unlocked the door to the café. Of course, naming the place the Shiny Penny was probably not the best way to get Randy Tate off her mind. But since he'd inspired her to strike out on her own, she wanted to pay him homage in some way, even if she was the only person who knew.

Small and scrupulously neat, tables and booths inside the café featured hundreds of pennies sealed under thick sheets of clear acrylic. The breakfast menu boasted fresh doughnuts, croissants, bagels, coffee and cappuccino. For lunch, the eatery offered gourmet salads, sandwiches, soups and desserts. Frankie prided herself on using the freshest ingredients and rotating the items for new selections every day. Customers were served in a cafeteria-style line run by herself and a promising young woman named Jan she'd found through a local university's culinary program.

Within a few weeks, the lunch crowd had grown to profitable proportions, but the morning trade left a bit to be desired. Since she'd been lucky enough to land a choice spot in an older building that was being refurbished, her initial morning customers were construction workers who drank their weight each day in coffee. But once the workers dwindled, the gourmet java houses down the street were difficult to compete with.

"You need a gimmick," Jan announced.

And so, she borrowed one. Remembering the claim from Rum King's sign, she posted a huge sign in the window—7:00 to 9:00 a.m., First Cup of Coffee for a Penny.

The plan worked. Before long, the yuppies who were rapidly filling the offices in the building discovered the café, came in early to buy a cup of coffee for a penny and typically ended up buying a couple of doughnuts or a bagel.

Frankie and her accountant marveled over the numbers. By the end of May she added another worker to handle take-out orders and had been approached for several catering jobs. She welcomed the extra workload—the money was good and it would help take her mind off other less attainable goals.

"Mr. Red Tie is definitely flirting with you," Jan whispered one day at the end of the morning rush.

Frankie used tongs to transfer slices of fresh banana bread to the deli case. "I'm not interested," she murmured, then stopped and stared as a knot of people bustled by the window in the pouring rain.

Jan craned her neck. "See someone you know?"

"No," Frankie said softly, shaking her head. She really was losing her mind if she was seeing Randy Tate in the faces of businessmen on the street in Atlanta.

"Why don't you take five?" Jan suggested. "It's starting to slow down and I can handle the orders."

Frankie nodded gratefully and headed to her tiny office, where she sank into her desk chair and sighed, listening to the rain on the tiny window. Except for sending the motorcycle helmet, she had refrained from contacting Randy, afraid he would be his charming, flirtatious self and her heart would be falsely cheered. But today she felt overwhelmingly compelled to reach out to him. She checked her watch—almost nine o'clock. Since no one would be in the bar at this hour, she could leave him a breezy message. Somewhat buoyed, she picked up the phone and dialed directory assistance for Key West and asked for the number for Rum King's.

"I'm sorry ma'am. I don't show a listing for Rum King's."

"It's a bar," Frankie added. "On Herald Street."

"I'm sorry, ma'am, no listing."

Frowning, she suspected a mistake in the directory, then asked, "How about Tate? Randy Tate?"

"I have a Randolph Tate the third."

Frankie smiled in surprise. "Yes, connect me please."

The phone rang three times, during which her heart thudded out of control. What would she say? *Just loving you to distraction and thought I'd give you a call?* But when a woman answered the phone—a young, firm-sounding woman—she froze, her heart jammed in her throat.

"Hello?" the woman repeated. "Is anyone there?"

Frankie replaced the handset gently in its cradle. So much for fantasies of Randy pining for her.

RANDY STOPPED inside the entrance to the building that housed the office he'd leased last week and shook his umbrella over a huge floor mat. He pushed his fingers through his hair to disperse a few wayward drops. He'd shorn his hair the day he received his broker's license, and swapped a tiny gold stud for the hoop earring when he met with the lessor of the office space he'd chosen. He'd traded his cutoffs and old T-shirts for jeans and new T-shirts—minus the beer logos—and acquired a few sport coats for legitimacy.

Having entered the building through a different door to escape the weather, he glanced around to get his bearings. Straight ahead was a dry cleaner's, a branch-bank office and a mini drugstore. To the right, elevators servicing the ten-story building and a long hallway that led to the west side of the building—the area where his office was located on the eighth floor. To the left, a newsstand and a small café.

He smiled at the name of the eatery and lifted a hand to rub the small sphere under his T-shirt. Try as he might these last few months, he hadn't been able to get Frankie out of his mind. Granted, wearing the crude necklace he'd fashioned from her tossed penny hadn't helped matters, but the piece of makeshift jewelry gave him comfort and inspiration, so he wore it.

When he spotted the sign in the window about the first cup of coffee for a penny, his chest squeezed at the coincidence and he moved toward the café. Then he shook his head and pivoted toward the elevators. He was looking for reminders of Frankie, he told himself as he glanced over his shoulder. He could remember her coming into the bar and pitifully gathering her coins for the cup of coffee as clearly as if he were seeing her now. Randy squinted and his heart contracted again as he caught a flash of red hair though the window.

He stopped several yards away and stared into the café, incredulity flooding him as his mind assimilated the possibility that Frankie was not only here in Atlanta, but she worked in a café in the same building where his office was located. Still unconvinced, he stepped closer, dodging bodies rushing to their own destinations, his throat constricting. He collided twice with harried businessmen.

It was her. His mouth went completely dry. She smiled at someone he couldn't see and handed them a disposable cup and a small brown bag, her lips moving. She was beautiful, her hair caught up on her head, and pale as ever, especially against the white apron she wore. His mind whirled at the amazing turn of events. How was it possible they could be in the same place at the same time? Then his shoulders sagged and he laughed at his own gullibility.

Parker. Parker had talked him into selling the bar. Parker had put the idea of moving to Atlanta into his head. Parker had introduced him to the man who owned this building. He'd bet his bottom line that Parker had somehow been in touch with Frankie and convinced her to relocate to the same darn building. That sly dog. He knew Randy was hopelessly in love with her, even if Randy himself wouldn't admit it.

Walking slowly toward the Shiny Penny, his blood pounded in his ears. Was the name of the café an indication she'd thought of him, that she'd put some emotional stock in their brief affair? What would he say? *The weather's lousy today...? How about those Braves...? You changed my life in one weekend and I can't live without you...?*

She stood with her back turned, chopping lettuce on a cutting board an arm's length behind the counter. At this distance he saw that a hair net held her piled tresses in place, and she wore thin plastic gloves. The apron draped over her slight curves, cinched loosely around her slender waist. His fingers curled, itching to touch her. His throat closed and his muscles refused to respond.

An attractive dark-haired woman asked, ''May I help you?''

He kept his gaze on Frankie's slender back, then said, ''Coffee, please. Hazelnut, with sugar, cream and a little cinnamon.''

Frankie's hands stilled when she heard the voice, heard the words. Her heart vaulted. It was impossible, of course—Randy couldn't be here. Almost afraid to burst the bubble of her fantasy, she turned around slowly. The man before the counter stared at her, a slow grin spreading across his face. He bore little resemblance to the raggedy beach bum she'd last seen in Key West, having shorter hair, a gold stud earring, and handsomely clad in a sport coat and jeans. But she'd never forget Randy's unmistakable golden eyes. Her voice nearly failed her. "Randy?"

"Hi, Red." He moved closer to the counter, his face wreathed in smiles. "Small world."

"What are you doing here?" she asked, still unable to believe he stood before her.

"Buying coffee," he answered smoothly.

Her heart fluttered cautiously, warning against reading too much into the fact that he was here. Just because he'd worn a path in her heart didn't mean he felt the same about her. Looking for something to do with her hands, she retrieved a cup and filled it with dark, rich brew. Despite his order, she knew he preferred his coffee black. "Here you go," she said, sliding it across the counter with a hesitant smile. "Sorry—no Kahlúa."

They stared at each other in silence for several seconds. Frankie didn't know what to think, but she knew she had to say something. "How did you know where to find me?"

"I didn't," he said. "Until I walked in here, I had no idea you were living in Atlanta. I moved here two weeks ago. My office is on the eighth floor of this building."

Her heart fell, but she managed to smile. "So this is just a coincidence?"

"When Parker Grimes is involved, there's no such thing as coincidence."

Parker had somehow set them up. So Randy hadn't hunted her down...he'd probably never given her a second thought once her ship disappeared. She felt like an idiot, pining for a man who obviously didn't feel the same way about her.

"Frankie, when did you move?"

"Mid-March," she said brightly, the date indelibly etched on her mind. "The nineteenth."

A smile—of relief?—lit up Randy's face, confusing her. Then just as quickly, it disappeared. "Did your boyfriend come with you?"

"Boyfriend?"

"Osgood?"

She angled her head. "You mean Oscar? Of course not. We were never involved."

He nodded, fidgeting. He dropped his gaze and his expression became unreadable. She hated the stiff formality that resonated between them. The casual ease, the chemistry of Key West, was apparently as fleeting as her unplanned visit to the island. Was Randy now thinking of a way to politely evade her since it seemed likely they would cross each other's paths?

With a sinking heart, she glanced toward a line forming at the counter. "I should get back to my customers," she murmured. "It was nice to see you again. Perhaps next time you can tell me about your business."

Randy nodded. "Uh, sure. That would be great." He stepped away from the counter, then snapped his fingers and turned back with an apologetic smile. "I almost forgot to pay for the coffee."

Frankie wished they hadn't run into each other again—at least her memories would have remained unblemished. Faking nonchalance, she dismissed his comment with a glib wave. "D-don't be silly. It's on the house."

"Oh, no," he said, shaking his head. "I insist."

Feeling dangerously close to tears, she relented with a nod, wanting to end the scene as quickly as possible. Conjuring up a smile, she punched a key on the cash register. "Okay. That'll be one penny."

She watched as he ran a finger around his neck, then pulled a leather cord over his head. When he lay the necklace on the counter, she spotted the penny...the shiny penny she'd thrown to him from the ship... He'd kept it close to his heart. Her lungs expanded as she lifted her gaze to him in wonder.

"I love you, Frankie." He reached across the counter and pulled her to him for a hungry kiss. She met his mouth with a glad cry, forgetting her customers, forgetting everything but his words and the wonderful pressure of his lips upon hers. Her heart threatened to burst. At last they parted and she murmured, "I love you, too."

He sighed. "Why didn't you tell me?"

"Why didn't you tell *me*?"

"I called, but when you didn't call back—"

"You called?" she gasped. "When?"

"The same day you moved here," he said, shaking his head. "Can you believe the rotten luck? I left you a voice message at the office begging you to let me come see you."

She grinned and looped her arms around his neck, drinking in his new appearance. "Begging?"

He blushed. "Well, sort of. I bought a cappuccino machine."

Laughter bubbled in her throat. "So did I—call, I mean."

His eyes bugged. "When?"

"About an hour ago. A woman answered your phone."

"Renters," he explained, touching his forehead to hers. "Did you call to beg me to let you come see me?"

Her heart sang. "Well, sort of."

His smile widened. "Think we should give Parker a call and thank him?"

She nodded. "Afterward."

His eyebrows climbed, then he groaned and tugged on her arms. "Let's go to my office. *Now.*"

Frankie emerged from behind the deli case, fumbling with her apron strings and informing Jan she'd be taking a long lunch. But she paused to lift the make-shift necklace from the counter and held it up to the light. Who would have known that setting sail on that silly Club Cupid wedding cruise would have landed her a Valentine for all time. Randy squeezed her hand and her heart swelled with love for the man who had redirected her life course.

As the coin spun, glinting, she caught his loving gaze and winked. "Who says a penny doesn't go very far?"

Dear Reader,

You can't imagine how thrilled I was at the opportunity to hit the shelves with one of my real-life heroines, ultratalented Stephanie Bond. The icing on the cake was being asked to write a story that would be released with *Club Cupid,* a sexy tale set in a tropical paradise. You see, I just happened to have been knee-deep in penning SINGLE IN SOUTH BEACH, a sultry miniseries set in a tropical haven nearby. And I had characters popping up everywhere, begging for stories of their own.

So *Valentine Vixen* was born! I hope you enjoy this story of sensual challenge and steamy stakes. Driven and determined Lucky Adams made his first appearance in Blaze #108, *Girl's Guide to Hunting & Kissing,* and I simpy *had* to help him find the right woman. Francesca Donzinetti might not be America's choice for this oh-so-eligible bachelor in the world of reality romance, but she's definitely snagged Lucky's eye!

If you enjoy this peek into my SINGLE IN SOUTH BEACH miniseries, I hope you'll join me for new stories coming in May, June and July 2004. I love to hear from readers, so please visit me at www.JoanneRock.com to learn more about my future releases or to let me know what you think about *Valentine Vixen!*

Happy reading,

Joanne Rock

VALENTINE VIXEN

Joanne Rock

For my Valentine—
Thank you, Dean, for all the inspiration.

OF ALL THE EXOTIC resort hotels on South Beach, why did Lucky Adams have to walk into mine?

Francesca Donzinetti darted behind the concierge's desk at the posh singles' playground Club Paradise and prayed the gorgeous man who just strode through the main doors into the lobby wouldn't see her. Highly unlikely considering it was 6:00 a.m. and she'd only just returned from an all-night Vintage Vinyl party down the street.

Sure, the South Beach locals had understood that meant vintage *music*, but New Jersey girl Francesca had taken the theme to heart. Now here she stood, cowering behind a news rack stuffed full of brochures for regional attractions while dressed in a black-and-white-checkered miniskirt and white vinyl go-go boots.

Yeah, she blended.

Holding her breath as the sleek stud of reality TV show fame approached the check-in desk, Fran pretended great interest in a pamphlet describing the thrill of alligator watching in the Everglades.

Of course, she shouldn't be surprised that Lucky, featured bachelor in the latest installment of "Eligible Male," would show up at Club Paradise. It only made sense he would stay at the hotel hosting the elaborate post-production wrap party for the show on Valentine's Day. Fran just hadn't expected him to complete taping the necessary interviews and assorted hoopla on the private island off Florida's coast for a few more days.

Wishing her checkerboard miniskirt wouldn't keep creeping up her thighs, Fran grumbled to herself over the fact that she'd finished *her* part of the marathon broadcast five days ago. As an unwilling participant in the stupid show, she shouldn't have minded being the first woman to be voted off by viewers who called in via toll-free hotline. But considering she'd initially experienced a few hot flashes over bachelor number one, she wasn't looking forward to coming face-to-face with him now with the questionable status of grade-A reject stamped across her forehead.

Especially while wearing vintage vinyl at six o'clock in the morning.

Positioning the alligator pamphlet up high to cover most of her face, Fran turned oh-so-casually to scope the whereabouts of the man she desperately wanted to avoid. Peering right and left, she spied him already engaged in registering and oblivious to her presence. No sign of his happily-ever-after bachelorette on his arm.

Because Fran had continued to watch the show after being voted off that week, she happened to know that America had chosen uppity Marley Sinclair as Lucky's dream date. Bully for Marley and her blue-eyed, whitebread upbringing. If America couldn't see the merit of a Jersey girl who put herself through college by starting her own pizza shop, then she didn't want their hoity-toity eligible male anyway.

So there.

She made sure the coast was clear, pilfered a few more flyers and inched away from the concierge's desk. Inch by miniskirt-restricting inch.

No wonder vinyl ranked as a vintage fabric. It possessed all the give of industrial-strength steel.

She made it almost two feet across the coral-colored tiles of the Mediterranean-inspired lobby when the concierge returned to his station. A sleek, endlessly tall black man with horn-rimmed glasses and a neatly trimmed mustache, he flashed Fran an indulgent smile.

"The Vintage Vinyl party is a good time, isn't it?" The distinguished gentleman adjusted his glasses, although Fran had the feeling he was squinting for a better view of her checkerboard.

Keeping one eye on Lucky Adams's broad shoulders at the registration desk, Fran nodded agreement over the top of her alligator brochure. "Very fun." She whispered just in case Lucky might be able to identify her voice from eight feet away. "Although next time your staff sees a woman walking out of here dressed like this, you might suggest they step in to save her some embarrassment."

Scooting across the floor with inchworm speed, Fran cursed her cousin Giselle for roping her into the stupid stint on "Eligible Male" in the first place.

While she had appreciated the bonus tropical vacation that came with it, she definitely hadn't signed on for nationally broadcast humiliation or embarrassing run-ins with highbrow bachelors.

Nearing the middle of the lobby, she decided it was almost safe enough to turn tail and dash for the elevator bank. She kept her gaze on Lucky for another moment just to be sure he didn't see her as he turned to retrieve something from the pocket of his luggage.

Struck anew by the impressive lines of his profile, she paused behind him, her tired legs swaying just a little in her platform go-go boots. Despite his classic navy suit and slick power tie, his features possessed a rugged masculinity that would look equally comfortable in jeans and leather.

Or so her overactive feminine imagination liked to think.

Caught up in admiring his chocolate-brown eyes and the way his neatly cropped dark locks insisted on curling against the line of his haircut, she didn't notice the busload of tourists pouring in the front door until they were filling up the lobby and blocking her path to escape.

Seeing Lucky finishing up his transaction at the registration counter, Fran shuffled faster, hoping to blend with the batch of new tourists. Until she realized the travelers packing the lobby were all wearing warm-up suits with the name of a college lacrosse team stitched across the shoulders.

And, frustratingly, they were all men.

Still, they were very big guys. If she could only ease into their fold, she would be hidden from Lucky's view by the never ending mob of blue-letter jackets. With quiet stealth she glided into their midst just as Lucky hiked his bag onto his shoulder.

She was almost within spitting distance of the elevator bank and delicious freedom when the wolf whistles began.

LUCKY ADAMS drummed his fingers on the smooth granite counter of the registration desk while waiting for the clerk to print his receipt and decided he had never felt so ill-named in all his life. After a week of mortifying embarrassment served up to the American public for nightly entertainment, he knew without a doubt he wasn't one bit lucky.

He'd never live down his stint as America's latest eligible male. Moreover, after building a strong career as a campaign manager for the movers and shakers of southern Florida, he'd finally realized he couldn't continue to climb his way to the top. Not when a profession built on asking for favors came back to bite him in the ass the way it had this time.

Sure he'd expected to have to occasionally reciprocate to people for helping him out with campaigns or lobby efforts. But not in his wildest dreams had he ever envisioned having to repay a video engineer who'd made some great television spots for one his clients this way. He'd suffered through nearly two weeks as the freaking eligible male now that the video engineer was an executive producer on the show.

No matter that Washington was calling Lucky with great regularity. As of now, he was out of the campaign business for good. He didn't need a job that would keep him indebted all the time, damn it. He might thrive on politics, but he sure as hell didn't need the cash. Definitely time for some serious rethinking.

Snatching the receipt from the desk clerk's hands, he turned on his heel to find his room when a cacophony of wolf whistles caught his attention. Near the elevator bank, a sea of male heads turned, all eyes locked on a slow-moving object at the center of the crowd.

A slow-moving object with incredible legs and an impossibly sexy miniskirt. Pleasantly distracted from his somber thoughts, Lucky paused to watch the show, grateful that he was no longer the center of attention the way he had been during the whole week of taping.

Of course the spectacle in Club Paradise's posh Mediterranean lobby was made all the more enticing by the fact that the woman's legs bore delicious resemblance to Francesca Donzinetti's.

Francesca.

Another reason his week had sucked. The down-to-earth Jersey girl with more practicality in her little finger than the television industry possessed in its entire fold had been voted off the reality show as a prospective date for Lucky on the very first episode. Instead, TV voters wanted to see him get together with a deceptively sweet-looking political barracuda who probably ate guys like him for breakfast.

Shifting the weight of his garment bag on his shoulder, Lucky plowed into the thicket of ogling lacrosse players, determined to get to his room and to put an end to this hellacious week. He needed to bury his head under a few dozen pillows until he figured out what to do with his career. Or at least until he figured out how to escape man-eating Marley Sinclair.

Picking up his pace as the elevator doors slid open a few yards away, Lucky nearly collided with the miniskirted object of every man's attention. Dressed head to toe in a shiny vinyl outfit that had either originated in the sixties or in some space-age society, the woman hidden behind a pamphlet advertising Everglade adventure edged her way onto the elevator the same time he did. Only when she had tucked herself into the furthest corner of the elevator cabin did she drop the brochure.

To reveal a face he'd dreamed about all week.

"Francesca?" Her name sounded soft and exotic on his lips, totally at odds with whatever souped-up costume she was wearing. Her skirt looked like a game board with big black-and-white checks all over it.

Lucky could definitely think of a few games he'd like to play with this woman.

"Crap." Francesca's throaty New Jersey accent added a powerful punch to an already-loaded word. Belatedly she attempted to lift at least one corner of her mouth in a halfhearted smile. "I mean—Hi."

Well how was that for a greeting?

"Going up?" His hand hovered over the elevator buttons since he was determined to be polite despite the less than enthusiastic response from the sexy brunette. With long, dark hair spilling over her shoulders, complete with sun-streaked pieces framing her heart-shaped face, Francesca possessed an earthy sensuality that every man in the Club Paradise lobby had recognized.

"I'm on four." She carefully refolded the travel brochure she'd been holding, her movements clipped. Tense.

"Me, too." He punched the number and indulged himself in a good long look at her while the elevator swooped them upward. "I almost didn't recognize you in the vinyl outfit. You look a lot different than you did earlier this week."

"You mean I don't look like the travel-weary frump with no clue I was going to be on national television the way I did when we first met? No surprise there since I rarely get in front of a camera while still under the influence of motion sickness medicine."

Lucky blinked, absorbed her rapid-fire words while she talked with her hands. His brain seemed to run a few moments behind her mouth.

Amused, he stifled a grin. "Are you suggesting you were drugged when we first met?"

"I'm suggesting I was drugged when I met all of

America." Her voice rose with the words, her expressive hands making a sweeping gesture. Then, as if realizing how much emotion she put behind the sentiment, she waved it away. "Not that it matters."

"I have the feeling I met Francesca Donzinetti at only half power, didn't I?" He had been impressed by her sensible practicality in the television interviews all of the women underwent the first day on the set of "Eligible Male." She had seemed so much more real than any of the others. Now she had all that approachability along with a hefty dose of passion, a vibrance of spirit. The combination proved damn potent.

She shrugged as the elevator slowed at the fourth floor. "Maybe. But I wasn't in the market for an eligible man anyway so I don't suppose it matters."

Stepping out onto the richly patterned Persian rug that carpeted the hallway, Francesca held one hand across the open doorway while Lucky hauled his garment bag from the elevator.

When she started down the hallway, presumably toward her room, Lucky followed.

"If you're not looking for a date, how did you wind up on America's latest answer to matchmaking?" He enjoyed the view from behind, her long, bare legs making slow time down the corridor in her gravity-defying boots. He'd locate his suite in a minute, after he made sure she found her room safely.

Finally she halted in front of the Vixen's Villa, one of many theme rooms in Club Paradise. Had she chosen the vixen suite with any naughty interludes in mind? The hotel was known for its decadent, sometimes erotically inclined accommodations. He wouldn't mind spending a few days with this woman in the Harem Haven or the Love Slave Suite.

"Purely by chance." She withdrew her room key from a miniscule patent leather purse and rolled the electronic card back and forth between two fingers, oblivious to the wayward turn his thoughts had taken. "My cousin Giselle is one of the part owners of the hotel and she's been trying to lure me down here for years but since I'm not quick to spend money on myself, I kept putting it off. Finally, she took it upon herself to enter me in every single 'Win a Florida Vacation' sweepstakes she could find and guess which I won?"

Vaguely, Lucky recalled hearing something about "Eligible Male" trolling for contestants by offering elaborate getaway packages. "But you must have agreed to do it at some point. They couldn't have dragged you on there kicking and screaming."

Maybe some stubborn part of him wanted to hear her admit she wasn't totally immune to the lure of an upstanding bachelor type like himself.

"Of course I agreed. Giselle would have gone on the warpath if I turned up my nose at the Florida trip she'd managed to finagle for me." She smiled with obvious fondness for the warmongering relation. "But believe me, I wasn't thrilled at the prospect of flaunting my dubious wares on national television." She looked down at the body most women would give their eyeteeth for. "Not a curve in sight. I told Giselle she needed to put me on a quiz show or something to do with brainpower instead of the 'Eligible Male' T&A fest, but what are you gonna do? It actually worked to my advantage to be voted off the first day because I've been able to romp all over South Beach while you and the rest of the bachelorettes have been working your butts off filming this week."

The action was taped during the day and broadcast

at night for viewers to watch then vote off the woman they felt undeserving. After Francesca had been cast off the island paradise, the viewers had eliminated the bachelorettes until he'd been left with Marley Sinclair.

Some dream woman. Marley was all about career and getting ahead in the world, seeing Lucky as more of a professional opportunity than a chance for romance. Somehow the television audience had overlooked the kind of woman that he *really* needed.

Flipping her key card into the slot, Francesca shouldered her way into the Vixen's Villa, effectively communicating her desire to drop the subject.

But Lucky wasn't nearly finished with this conversation yet.

"Then how about sharing some of your travel insights with me tomorrow? Maybe you could show me some of the finer points of South Beach." He levered the door open with his hand, not crossing the threshold into her room, but keeping her in his sights enough to talk to her.

Francesca pivoted to stare at him, her dark eyes wary. "According to your bio, you're a South Beach native. Why on earth would you need a tour guide?"

She made no effort to hide her skepticism. Lucky guessed she wouldn't be an easy woman to sweep off her feet, and oddly, he found himself thinking about making an attempt. When was the last time he'd taken a few days off just for fun? And now that he'd decided to leave his demanding career behind, he couldn't have asked for a better time to enjoy himself.

"I work all the time. It's not the same as coming here to play. You said it yourself—you've had time to find all the best places. Why not share one or two with me?" His gaze roamed her long legs and slender body silhouetted by a lush room furnished to resemble an open loggia overlooking the sea. A mural behind her took up the entire wall, a painted view of the Mediterranean, complete with white boats in the distance and a low stone wall in the foreground.

"What about Marley?" She folded her arms across her chest, tapping the floor impatiently with her toe. "Aren't you supposed to be squiring your dream date around town for the next few days?"

"I'm committed to one televised date. Definitely not a conflict." After making a career out of managing political campaigns, Lucky knew a thing or two about the fine art of gentle persuasion and he didn't mind employing it now if it would win him a date with Francesca. "Besides, why don't I get some say in who I want to be with in my private life? 'Eligible Male' might call the shots for what goes on in front of the cameras, but they sure as hell don't weigh in on who I spend time with in between takes. What do you say, Francesca? Will you show me a few sights?"

She shifted on her heels, her vinyl outfit squeaking just a little with the movement.

He didn't realize he'd held his breath until she nodded.

"As long as there's no Marley involved, I say be ready by nine." She bent to unzip the boots that came up to her knees and Lucky thought he'd never seen a more erotic gesture as she bared a few more inches of toned calf. A hint of a smile played at her lips as she looked up at him. "I've got a few sights in mind that you won't want to miss."

His mouth gone dry, Lucky agreed to meet her in the

lobby the next morning and let out a low whistle as he allowed the door to swing closed.

With the delectable image of Francesca Donzinetti starting to undress burned in his brain, he had the feeling his luck was about to change.

2

I'M GOING TO GET Lucky after all.

Francesca smiled at the thought as she blinked her way out of a delicious daydream early that evening. Unwilling to waste a whole day sleeping to make up for her late night out, she'd catnapped on and off between trips to the beach, the salon and the way-out-of-her-price-range Bal Harbour shops where she'd drooled over everything from handbags to home furnishings. This was her vacation after all—her first real holiday in ten years. She deserved to live it up.

And to get lucky.

Leveraging herself up on one elbow as she lounged on the coffee-colored leather divan, Fran dialed room service and ordered a slew of appetizers in place of dinner. She needed to keep herself grounded in real, obtainable pleasures and not pie-in-the-sky wishes like a romantic interlude with Lucky Adams. The sexy eligible male was sort of like the Bal Harbour shops—fun to look at but well out of her realm of possibility.

She checked her watch and hurried to brush her teeth, making it all the way to final gargle by the time a rhythmic knock sounded at the door to the Vixen's Villa. She wriggled her way into jean shorts and tank top then added a quick coat of lip gloss to complete her beautifying ritual before jogging over to the door.

"Hey, gorgeous," her cousin Giselle greeted her,

marching into the suite with a bottle of champagne in hand. "Ready for a night of dancing under the stars?" She twitched her hips with the innate grace she'd been born with—a delicate, curvy contrast to Fran's big, straight everything.

"Right after I try out a few more things from the appetizer menu." Fran reached for the champagne bottle and started peeling off the foil seal, reminding herself that time spent bonding with girlfriends was every bit as fun and important as getting lucky. Okay, maybe not quite as fun, but definitely as important. "You cook some mean food in that kitchen of yours, woman."

"Happily, I'm off tonight." As executive chef for Club Paradise, Giselle supervised all the food prep on site from catering commitments to running three different restaurants on the property. "If any of the food is off it's because my assistant is in charge, but I refuse to care since we are finally going to hit the town for girls night." She reached under the honeyed-maple wet bar in one corner of the living area and located two champagne glasses, which she presented with a flourish. "Have you thought about where we should go? I vote we hit whatever nightclub the eligible male patronizes with his date. Maybe we'll see them together and we can throw ice cubes at stuck-up Marley."

"Excuse me?" Fran halted in the middle of untwisting the wire holding down the cork. Had she missed something?

Setting the glasses on the bright, mosaic-topped coffee table, Giselle took the bottle out of her hands. "Haven't you heard? 'Eligible Male' is doing a live special featuring the highly anticipated Lucky and Marley date night. The network has been advertising it nonstop all day." Giselle popped the cork with swift efficiency and poured two glasses. "Of course, you know how I feel about Marley. All the kitchen staffers agree she seems to have a stick up her—"

"Agreed. But apparently plenty of people in America like her if she snagged enough votes to win the game." And the man.

Fran's stomach bottomed out at the thought of Lucky's big date night. What if it went really well? What if he called to cancel their sight-seeing gig from the comfort of Marley's bed tomorrow morning?

Eew.

"Well, I'll give her that much. She knows how to play the game." Switching on the television tucked inside a cypress armoire, Giselle flipped through the channels with a remote control until she landed on a closeup of Marley Sinclair's smiling face.

And—no kidding—she was already in bed with Lucky.

Fran bit back a gasp, heart sinking at a nosedive rate, while Giselle squealed out loud and tossed the champagne cork at the TV. After Fran had been gullible enough to be taken in by a hunky helper in her pizza shop who filched her secret sauce recipe and sold it to the competition, she'd been extra careful not to be duped so easily.

Not careful enough, obviously.

"Can they show this on network television?" Fran covered her eyes, already counting the ways she would tell Lucky to step off tomorrow.

"They're not really in bed. Those king-size mattresses are part of the décor at a lounge up the street," Giselle explained, tugging Fran's fingers off her eyes. "Honest. It's a restaurant by day and a club by night, and they serve all their food and drinks in those beds.

No doubt the network wants to capitalize on the steamy South Beach ambience to ratchet up their ratings."

"Really?" Fran braved another glance at the flickering screen, this time noticing a uniformed waiter handing Marley a cocktail complete with pink umbrella. "How...clever."

"Sex sells, girlfriend. The success of Club Paradise and all of its erotic theme rooms are banking on it. The Vixen's Villa is lightly sensual and very popular, but the really sexy accommodations like our bordello and harem suites are booked for a year in advance. Things were tight for the first few months, but they're really taking off now." Giselle handed her a champagne glass and reached for the remote just as Lucky and Marley leaned in for a kiss.

Fran's heart twisted in her chest at the image and was all too glad when Giselle stabbed the off button. Still, the vision lingered in her brain to mock her foolish hope of getting Lucky for herself. Hadn't she learned anything about deceitful men from the last guy who'd taken her for a ride? Forcing herself to focus on her cousin's words, she sipped her drink and tried to relax. "The hotel is gorgeous, Giselle. You're going to achieve huge success here."

"I hope so. But tonight I'd rather skip the decadent atmosphere and just go someplace where we can dance under the stars rather than lounge in bed." Giselle clinked her glass against Fran's. "Here's to having fun."

Swallowing the lump in her throat, Fran echoed the toast before she downed the rest of her bubbly drink. And although she didn't exactly feel like celebrating when the guy she'd been daydreaming about was out locking lips with another woman, she refused to allow her vacation to be ruined because of a self-important bachelor who probably charmed his way through life.

Besides, tomorrow would be soon enough to tell him exactly what she thought of him and his empty flirtation.

LUCKY HIT THE LOBBY at ten minutes to nine the next morning, determined to beat Francesca downstairs. He'd thought about her and her white vinyl go-go boots nonstop since yesterday morning. In fact, visions of her slipping out of those sexy boots had kept him from losing his cool twenty different times last night on his date from hell broadcast in five different languages.

Talk about torture. Marley Sinclair was driven and ambitious, focused solely on her career and how to further it. An attorney with political intentions, she viewed her connection to an up-and-coming king-maker like Lucky as a benefit to her professional goals. Therefore, she worked every conversation back around to their so-called mutual interests and what was happening in D.C. at any given moment. And while Lucky definitely cared about that, he'd been at the game long enough to know he didn't want to live and breathe politics.

He wanted something real in his day-to-day life, some area of his world that could remain grounded even when the bottom fell out of his professional realm. Which, in politics, happened with ulcer-inducing regularity. Maybe he'd give high finance a whirl. He'd always had a knack for the stock market.

Skimming the coffee shop news racks in search of a paper that didn't feature something about his staged date last night, Lucky kept one eye on the action in the lobby as he settled on a week-old magazine. Buying a

cup of coffee along with the travel magazine, he settled
into a small table that overlooked the Club Paradise re-
ception area.

Where he spied Francesca Donzinetti live and in person, breezing through the lobby wearing a white sundress printed with big yellow lemons. Her tan legs
walked with efficient strides, her espadrille sandals
making no noise on the tile floor as she slowed to a stop
and searched the morning crowd.

Standing, Lucky raised his arm to get her attention.
Only he didn't receive the smile he'd hoped for in return. Instead she barreled her way over like a woman
on a mission.

The surge of disappointment surprised him. He
hadn't realized how much he was counting on more
sparks to fly today until she pinned him with a cool
look as she arrived at his table.

"Morning." He gestured to the vacant chair opposite
him, ready to ply her with charm if that's what it took
to get her to relax. Now that he knew what a potent
punch she packed, Lucky wouldn't settle for Francesca
at half power again. "You look fantastic. Can I get you
some coffee?"

She didn't bother to sit, and now that he observed
her more closely, he realized her whole body brimmed
with pent-up energy. Her stiff shoulders seemed to
bristle.

"No thank you." She tossed a long lock of hair over
one shoulder. "But I would appreciate a little honesty.
What gives with playing tongue-tangle with Marley
twelve hours after you asked me out? And I'm surprised that you couldn't have been a little more specific
about the time frame for your date with the winning
bachelorette since I'd asked you about it specifically.

The network was advertising the big moment all day yesterday."

Her expressive hands went wild as she spoke, her gestures and her emphatic tone turning more than a few heads in the coffee shop.

"Believe me, the network knew when it would take place long before I did." And were advertising the news extensively, according to what he'd gathered after the fact. Damned if he intended to spend the rest of his career beholden to Nielsen ratings and public opinion polls. "I was already in the process of chartering a boat to check out the local fishing when I got the call to hightail it back to Club Paradise yesterday."

She didn't exactly appear placated. Color flushed her cheeks pink, her dark eyes glittering with an inner light. Lucky didn't have enough of a death wish to tell her she looked beautiful when she was angry, but he thought it just the same.

"And I suppose the television executives twisted your arm into taking her to bed and then forced you into kissing her, too?" Her arm jingled with an accompaniment of silver bracelets, a gentle note at odds with her in-your-face temper.

By now, she was definitely causing a scene. The college kids working behind the counter at the coffee shop were utterly engrossed, while a few tourists from the lobby slowed their morning hustle to watch the antics of the latest cast of "Eligible Male." And while he wasn't happy about being the center of attention again so soon after his week of hell on a reality TV show, he couldn't deny her wild antics turned him on, too. Did a little jealousy lurk under all that anger?

"As a matter of fact, the producers had indeed already set up the destination for our date, so the bed setting was very much decided for me." Her skeptical expression urged him on, made him want to find a way to make her believe him and keep their date today. "And as for the kiss, all I can say is that Marley originated it."

A little murmur went through the crowd at that bit of news. No doubt he and Francesca had created enough buzz to keep the gossip columnists busy for a week.

"Is that so?" She folded her arms across her chest, her tan skin a dark contrast to the white, lemon-covered dress. "Because it sure looked mutual to everyone in America tuned in to 'Eligible Male.' You know what I think, Lucky?"

Whether he said yea or nay, he knew damn well she was about to tell him. And from her raised eyebrows and her new hands-on-hips stance, he had the feeling he wasn't going to like it.

"What's that?"

"I think you are a total player without any sense of commitment. You're not the eligible male so much as the multi-eligible male, and I think you just took all your viewers for a ride." She tilted her chin up and cast him a hard look. "I think you are an absolute fraud."

Her words still smoking in the now still coffee shop, she pivoted on her heel and turned to walk away.

Normally, Lucky Adams was a behind-the-scenes guy who didn't take the spotlight on the tough one-on-one debates his clients often fielded. He preferred to steer the political candidates he managed from relative anonymity offstage. But that didn't mean he didn't know how to handle bad press.

For that matter, he had a thorough knowledge of playing out public scenes to one's own advantage and he'd never felt so utterly called to use that knowledge as he did while watching the most amazing legs on South Beach put far too much distance between them. And just because he didn't care to apply his skills in his chosen field as a campaign manager anymore, that didn't mean he couldn't use them to maneuver himself into a second chance with Francesca.

Because no way would he let this passionate woman slip away.

"If you're so all-fired sure of yourself, how about a little challenge?"

Fran froze as Lucky's words echoed in her ears, the mere mention of a challenge enough to halt any self-respecting Donzinetti in their tracks.

She was already at least five yards away and she had no damn obligation to turn around and stare into those whiskey-colored eyes of his again, but he'd chosen the one surefire strategy to capture her attention. Slowly, she spun about on the heel of one bright yellow espa-drille.

"A challenge?" She drew herself up to her full height as she stepped closer, unwilling and unable to let this man think her a coward. She'd started this little public drama because she couldn't control the nibble of jeal-ousy she felt whenever she thought about Lucky es-corting Miss White-Bread All-America around town. Granted, she realized he was as bound by his agree-ment with the producers as she was, but she knew damn well no one had forced him to kiss Marley.

Lucky stood still, refusing to meet her even halfway, damn him. He stuffed his fists into his pockets like a man who had all the time in the world to play games with her. "If I'm such a player, then I'd never be able to commit myself to one woman. But I'll bet you I can do exactly that for as long as you like." He took a step closer, flashing her a wicked grin that sent a heat wave from her neck to her toes and lingered at all the best places in between.

"Now that we're done with all the bogus hoops we needed to jump through for 'Eligible Male,' I propose we conduct a little private reality show of our own. Just you and me on the deserted isle of your choice. Give me five days to show you exactly how committed I can be and by Valentine's Day you get to make the call on whether or not this bachelor has won you over."

She shoved aside the excess of female hormones that her body seemed to generate every time the man was near to think about what he just said. Sure, the idea was giving her hot flashes, but that didn't mean she could spend five days in a secluded hideaway with Lucky Adams.

"I won't give up my whole vacation just because you want to prove something. I came to Florida to spend some time with my cousin who lives in South Beach." And she had sight-seeing to do. Soap operas to watch. Nails to file. She would do anything to get out of romantic seclusion with a tempting man who seemed to want her just because she presented a challenge more than any true desire to be with *her*.

After nearly losing her livelihood to the hottie who committed corporate espionage for the sake of her pizza sauce, she was damn well determined not to get mixed up with another slick player.

Lucky didn't look the least bit worried about her refusal, however. His grin widened. "Then we'll conduct our five-day reality experiment at Club Paradise and I'll only expect a few hours of your time every day. That's fair, right?"

He looked around the coffee shop as if seeking approval. The two college kids behind the counter were nodding along with a patron steadily forking in bites of key lime pie.

Damn.

It was all her own fault for a creating a scene. Mr. Slick had skillfully turned her weapon against her because there wasn't a chance she could walk away from a challenge with five generations of Sicilian and one generation of suburban Newark blood flowing through her veins.

"Fine. You're on." A murmur of approval rolled through the coffee shop as she closed the distance between them. "But don't forget, at the end of the week, it's still my decision." She leaned in to go nose-to-nose with Lucky. "And let me tell you, Adams, I'm a tough judge by anyone's standards."

He lowered his voice to a whisper for her ears only. "I'd be very disappointed if you weren't. What do you say to dinner tonight?"

Her heart thrummed an erratic beat in her chest. She was wading through dangerous terrain with this man.

But a girl had to eat, didn't she?

"You can pick me up at seven. Until then, I hope you'll excuse me as I made plans to do some sightseeing today."

Whirling on her heel, she left him there while she swaggered her way into the lobby and out the main doors of the hotel. And even though this week would no doubt wreak havoc with her self-control, she couldn't help but think at least her Donzinetti ancestors would have been damn proud.

3

A FEW HOURS before he was supposed to meet Francesca for dinner, Lucky rapped on the door of her suite. Loudly.

When he was certain she wasn't inside, he withdrew a duplicate key card her cousin Giselle had given him earlier in the day and let himself in the Vixen's Villa to prep for a decadent meal.

He'd found a willing co-conspirator in Giselle Cesare. Fortunately for him, she was fully supportive of his plans for seduction, agreeing to supply an assortment of tempting foods and erotic sweets for the dinner he'd planned.

Now, as he took stock of the Vixen's Villa and Francesca's few belongings scattered about the seductive Mediterranean setting, Lucky arranged for the finishing touches. He used his cell phone to call a local florist and ordered fifty white candles, three wrought-iron candelabra and ten pounds of assorted colored rose petals.

He scheduled a massage therapist and two representatives from the Club Paradise health spa to be at Francesca's beck and call from five-thirty to seven. To put her in the mood for self-indulgence, he also ordered a huge sampling of body lotions and potions to line the rim of her Roman tub. Giselle had promised to have a hotel staffer keep watch over the Villa while Fran was out so that the room could be accessed for setup, yet Fran wouldn't be unpleasantly surprised by any unwanted company when she returned from her sightseeing.

Finally he scrawled a note encouraging her to spoil herself and left it on the huge sleigh bed covered with brightly colored pillows, along with the key to her room.

Finished with his covert mission, Lucky lingered beside the bed, not quite ready to lose the scent of her. Her in-your-face wardrobe of vinyl skirts and fruit-covered dresses bulged from the closet in rainbow hues. A vague hint of her perfume teased his nose with citrus notes and something else that eluded him.

But even if the fragrance escaped him, the woman would not. He'd led enough successful campaigns in his business as a political manager to unlock a few secrets of winning.

He simply needed to stack the odds in his favor and appeal to her on as many levels as possible. Then he'd lodge a campaign she couldn't possibly refuse.

BARE TOES CRUSHING the soft rose petals beneath her feet, Fran nearly moaned with pleasure as she bit into yet another too decadent-for-words piece of chocolate. Yum.

She peered around her candlelit villa terrace and sighed with contentment. If Lucky Adams thought for a minute she wasn't going to indulge herself to the gills in this sensual paradise he'd created for her, he had another think coming. He might believe his generous gesture was buying his way to her heart—or, more likely, her bed—but Fran was simply too practical a woman to look a gift horse in the mouth. She'd rolled around in the thick carpet of rose petals the moment she'd walked into the room. Within minutes she was sipping sour-apple martinis and reveling in a massage to cure her every ache and pain from her first attempt at roller-blading around South Beach earlier today.

If Lucky wanted to spoil her, by God, she planned to soak it all up. Not in a million years would she have ever indulged herself this way. Of course, as the clock neared seven, she had to admit the nerve pangs were beginning to kick in. She'd been a starry-eyed romantic once before with a sexy stranger and she'd paid for it dearly when he used her on every conceivable level. Never again would she be so naive as to trust without question, to be swept off her feet by a man who was all seductive promises and no substance.

Still, some fanciful piece of her heart had always longed for *Romance* with a capital *R*, the kind of thoughtful sensitivity her father had always exercised with her mom. Could she help it if she was a sucker for rose petals on the floor?

The knock at her door made her jump, her heart-shaped chocolate lodging in her throat as she thought about the man behind that sharp rap. Although the man ranked every bit as delicious as the sweet confections Giselle hand-delivered to her suite earlier tonight, Fran reminded herself he was every inch the player she'd accused him of being. The lavish lengths he'd gone to only assured her he was hell-bent on winning this week's challenge purely for winning's sake. He'd probably never lost so much as a Monopoly game before.

Downing the last of her bright green martini in one gulp, she assured herself this was one game he wouldn't win. Neither her heart nor her body was up for grabs this week, especially not to game players like the latest eligible male.

The simple act of opening her door nearly made her change her mind. Lucky stood on her doorstep dressed in a lightweight silk suit favored by Florida business-men. His double-breasted, taupe-colored jacket had a purple handkerchief printed with palm trees stuffed into the pocket. His tie almost matched, but featured a lone palm tree silk-screened on the fabric and half hid-den by his buttoned jacket.

His dark hair was precisely cut, yet a rogue wavy lock threatened the neat line just above one temple. Whiskey eyes glittered back at her as she took in every scrumptious inch of him.

"May I come in?" His deep voice thrummed through her, swirling with the martini-induced warmth in her veins and making her a little weak-kneed.

Nodding, she opened the door wider and gestured to the candlelit paradise within. "You outdid yourself, Adams. It's beautiful. I won't pretend I didn't enjoy every facet of your plan to make me indulge myself."

Allowing the hotel door to swing shut behind Lucky, she watched him walk into the center of the room. He took in the mural along the exterior wall depicting a view from a Mediterranean terrace. But the real genius of the painting came into effect at night when the Feb-ruary Florida breezes allowed her to open the three huge windows wide. Reality blended with art as the painted seascape merged with a flawless ocean view outside. Salty air rode the wind to tickle her face and to scent the room with the rich fragrance of the shore.

Heavy wrought-iron candelabra stationed in the far corners of the room cast a flickering glow over the polished stone floors littered with hand-woven rugs and fluttering rose petals. The floral scent mingled with the ocean breeze and the jasmine body scrub the spa experts had slathered all over Francesca's body.

Her guest noted all of it, from the ocean view to the sideboard piled with fruit and cheese and chocolates. Finally his observant eye landed on her once again, his gaze absorbing her fuchsia sundress with skinny spaghetti straps and body-conscious shape. She'd worn it because the hem hit her just below the knee and therefore rated as her most tame outfit. But as Lucky's hungry eyes roved over her, her covered skin suddenly burned with a prickling desire to be seen by this man.

"I'm glad you enjoyed yourself. Does that mean I'm halfway home to convincing you I have an honorable side?" His teasing tone lured her in spite of herself. What would it be like to continue her evening of self-indulgence? To take her enjoyment right into his arms, or better yet, his bed? Her pulse picked up speed at the images she conjured. Thankfully, her mouth had years of practice at deflecting pleasure for simple pleasure's sake. Too risky.

"Hardly." She drifted over to the sideboard and popped a green grape in her mouth, savoring the sweet juice instead of the kisses she really wanted. "This decadent sensual display merely proves to me you are a bad boy used to having your own way and if you can't win by fair means, you're not above resorting to foul. But feel free to keep tempting me, handsome. I'm a new woman thanks to a massage and a seaweed wrap."

In truth, she was also a woman with frighteningly heightened senses thanks to that massage and seaweed wrap, but she didn't plan to share that with him. Even the ocean breeze drifting in the open window felt like a lover's caress.

Lucky stalked closer across the carpet of rose petals, the soft flowers muffling his steps. "Does that mean you can be bought, Ms. Donzinetti?"

He plucked a fat strawberry from the fruit board and took a bite, the red juice lingering on his lips. She could practically taste the seeds as she stared at his mouth.

"You are welcome to try." Her voice hit a husky note as she watched him polish off the berry. She'd bet her almost-famous pizza sauce recipe that he was a fantastic kisser.

And as she daydreamed in vivid detail about what his kiss might be like, Fran wondered why on earth she shouldn't simply find out for herself. Just because she indulged in a few kisses didn't mean he would win their bet. Surely she had enough sense to keep her feet on the ground even while she reached for this small, simple pleasure.

Her whole life had been about keeping her feet on the ground. Maybe this once she deserved to experience a little taste of heaven.

Just as soon as she enjoyed the thrill of being chased for a change.

Lucky couldn't begin to fathom the thoughts dancing in Francesca's dark eyes. She was a difficult woman to read, so different from any other female he'd ever known. He'd set the scene for seduction so thoroughly, he had thought she would have softened her stance just a little. But she hadn't given an inch yet.

Still, her words left him a very large loophole.

"I'm welcome to try? I hope you know I consider that an invitation." He reached behind the fruit and cheese board to the small sound system built into a wall cabinet. After punching a few buttons, a romantic fifties big band tune hummed over the room's hidden speakers. "If you're so willing to let me try, why not dance with me?"

He extended his hand as the blend of sultry strings and horns filled the air around them.

"I said you could try and buy me off, not coerce me into close encounters." She reproached him even as she put her hand in his. "But how much harm could there be in one dance?"

Her dark eyes glowed with mischief as he swept her deeper into the room in front of the open windows overlooking the ocean, the only spot in the luxury suite that had been left free of rose petals. But he didn't care what tricks she had up her sleeve. Or, in the case of her oh-so-delectable outfit, down her dress.

He just wanted an excuse to get next to her. To touch her.

"No harm at all." Only heat. His hand flexed on the small of her back, his fingers staying as low on her spine as he dared to go. Her slim-fitting dress allowed him delicious access to her sleek curves.

"But of course I'll still be keeping an eye on you." She toyed with his lapel before smiling up at him in the glow of flickering candlelight. "I have the feeling a woman can't be too careful around you."

"Funny you should mention that because I keep getting the feeling you are a woman who is usually far too careful." He spun them around the polished stone floor, their shoes shuffling a slow step in time with the bluesy tone of the next song. He wanted to find out more about her, to put his finger on what made Francesca Donzinetti tick. "I wasn't sure you'd accept my challenge this morning."

"I have a hard time walking away from a dare. It's partly an Italian thing, partly a Jersey girl thing." She shrugged, the movement nudging her breasts against his chest as they danced.

He caught a hint of her scent as the night air flitted in through the open window. The fragrance wafted, heady and exotic as it mingled with the soft smell of roses from the floor. Lucky found himself wanting to lean into Francesca's neck to sniff out the source of her perfume.

Damned if this whole seduction scenario wasn't doing a number on him more than her. Except for that one torturous graze of her breasts, she did an excellent job of keeping her distance.

"Is your whole family as quick to answer a challenge as you are?" He needed to remain focused on his goal of winning her, to learn more about her before he ended up trapped by his own scheme.

"They used to be." Her gaze cut to the open windows, lingering on the waves in the water for a moment. "I haven't seen them since they hauled tail out of Jersey three weeks after I turned eighteen to revisit their Sicilian roots. But last I knew, they were definitely always up for a dare."

Something in him stilled at her admission, but he wouldn't dream of halting the motion of their dance. He had a feeling Francesca was the type of woman who wouldn't take kindly to obvious interrogation, but he had to admit he was curious.

"Did you have other family to keep you company?" He twirled and dipped her, figuring it wouldn't hurt to keep her off balance while asking questions.

Cheeks flushed pink from the dip, she met his gaze

as she rose. "We cautious women don't need family to stay out of trouble."

"Fiercely independent. Now that's no surprise."

"Not unlike yourself, I'll bet. What's your story, Mr. Eligible Male? Raised from the cradle to be privileged and powerful? Or are you secretly more of a scrapper like me?" Although her body remained firmly in her own dance space, her tone invited confidences, sought answers. He wasn't normally the kind of man to give either, but he sensed he wouldn't make any headway without sharing something of himself, something that hadn't already been broadcast on "Eligible Male" for public dissection.

"A bit of both. My folks wanted a doctor but I found more affinity with people and numbers than biology and chemistry. But in my case it was me who hauled tail out of my suburban Tampa hometown to find my niche in Miami. I put myself through school so I could study what I wanted without a truckload of guilt." Not that he'd totally avoided his family's obvious disappointment, but he'd been determined to pursue his own goals and hadn't looked back since. Of course, now he needed to revisit those old ambitions and to figure out what he could do with his life besides manage political campaigns. "I figured I'd cash in all the alleged luck I was supposed to have, thanks to the nickname."

Fran's eyes glittered in the candlelight. "And just what is your real name? You guarded that secret like your life depended on it during the filming last week."

"I'm Lucas Adams the Fourth." Damn, but it had been a long time since he'd spoken as much aloud. "And the three other Lucas Adamses are all forces to be reckoned within the medical community where I grew up. When I decided to put a little distance between me and them, I latched onto the lifelong nickname since all the venerable Adamses are convinced I was born with the devil's own luck."

In fact, the Adams clan credited that luck for his success in whatever he undertook. That he might have been quick-witted or talented hadn't really occurred to them since they all agreed anyone with half a brain would have gone into the lucrative family medical practice.

More than ready to change the topic, he wondered what Francesca's mother and father thought of the spitfire they'd raised. Were they proud of her gritty determination? He twirled her around as their song ended. "It must have been strange seeing your parents leave."

"Strange but okay." She took a step backward as the notes faded, obviously no more willing to talk about her past than he'd been to discuss his. A breeze cooled the air between them, blowing a strand of dark hair across her cheek. "Challenges only make us stronger."

"I couldn't agree more. Aren't you glad you had me around on this vacation to up the ante for you?" He took a step closer, just enough to reach for the windblown lock.

He smoothed his thumb down the softness of her cheek while peeling away the silky strand. Her eyelashes fluttered for the briefest of instants at the contact.

"I would think you'd be equally grateful to me since I'm saving you from the monotony of eager women throwing themselves at your feet."

"Unlike *you*, who I needed to strong-arm into a date by tossing out a gauntlet in public." Having experienced the softness of her hair, the delicate cool skin of her cheek, his fingers itched to touch her more thoroughly. To tease her body into eager compliance with other, more explicit challenges running through his mind right now.

"What can I say? I've never been the type to throw myself at any man." Her chin tilted at a stubborn angle, her resolute expression at odds with her sexy-as-sin body silhouetted in close-fitting fuchsia silk.

Unable to resist the temptation of her almost bare shoulders, Lucky's hands settled there of their own accord. "What if a man threw himself at *your* feet?"

A slow smile spread across her features, igniting a hungry light in her eyes along the way. "You are certainly welcome to try."

Her voice caught on a hoarse note as his thumbs traced her delicate collarbone, finding every curve and hollow. As her eyelashes fluttered with the touch, he knew he'd found the right moment to press his suit, the perfect time to take this challenge to the next level.

Then his mouth touched hers and he forgot all about challenges and perfect timing. Her lips parted on contact, whether from surprise or invitation, he couldn't be sure, but he lost no time claiming new terrain. She sighed into him, her whole body succumbing to the lure of their mating mouths. Or, hell, maybe he had done a little falling into her, too.

She kissed like a goddess and he wouldn't be a bit surprised if he already was following wherever she led. He skimmed his palms down her shoulders to span her waist, her lean curves filling his hands. Steering her hips closer to his, he caught himself before he plastered her to him, forced himself to take his time. But in the split second of hesitation, Francesca beat him to the goal, solving his dilemma by wriggling closer, her breasts teasing his chest in that dress made of practically nothing.

Lucky swore he could feel the urgent press of taut nipples through the fabric. And even while he knew that sensation probably stemmed from wound-up male imagination, that didn't stop him from sliding a lone finger under one of the skinny straps holding up her dress.

She gripped his lapels in tight fists, her grasp so firm he worried he moved too far, too fast for this woman who seemed determined to deny their chemistry.

His noble instincts getting the better of him, he broke off the kiss, levered himself a few inches away so he could think. Speak.

"What's wrong?" His hands covered her white knuckles bunching the fabric of his jacket into endless wrinkles. "Are you okay with this?"

She took a long moment to pry open her eyes, her gaze unfocused even once she did. "What?"

Hoping like hell her senses were as scrambled as his right now, he squeezed her clenched fists. "You're squeezing the daylights out of the collar. I thought maybe things were moving too fast for you."

Dark eyes flicking down to her hands for a moment, she shook her head, a wry grin tugging the corner of her kiss-swollen lips. "No. That's not it at all." Carefully she relinquished her hold and took a step back. "I was just worried if I started touching you I might not ever stop."

4

AND SHE REALLY should stop.

She'd thought maybe she could simply enjoy a night of decadent kisses, but as her heart pounded with bold desire and foolish hopes, she remembered Lucky's motives. It would be different if he genuinely cared about her, but for him, this night overlooking the Atlantic disguised as the Mediterranean wasn't about romance.

It was all about winning.

Lucky's eyes seemed to soak up every nuance of her expression, and she wondered what he was thinking. Could he see all the things she secretly longed for? Did he know that she craved far more than a slick political manager could ever give?

He reached for her, stepping back into her personal space and automatically making her skin prickle with heightened awareness. "What makes you think we have to stop?" His hands landed on her shoulders, his thumbs grazing her collarbone. "There's definitely no time limit on touching."

The way his heated palms spoke to her body, she was almost willing to believe him. That small touch could be the start of so much more....

"But there is." She snapped out of it just in time, unwilling to give too much of herself to a man who monitored the "Eligible Male" voting results as carefully as he supervised election campaigns. Pulling away, she moved to the windows overlooking the ocean, desperate for a cool breeze to soothe her overheated body. "I don't dare get caught up in the chemistry when there are no emotions to back it up."

So what if that sounded hideously old-fashioned? At least she was being honest, which was more than she could say for most of the other scheming bachelorettes she'd met on the "Eligible Male" set.

"Emotions?" Lucky tested the word as if trying out a foreign language. "You mean like..." He trailed off, apparently waiting for her to provide him with answers. What was it with men today that they didn't have a clue about this stuff?

"Call it corny, Slick, but some women still appreciate a bit of emotional substance behind their romantic interludes. And let's face it—we hardly know each other."

The ocean breeze blew in off the water to cool her face. She sucked in long, steadying breaths until she felt Lucky's elbows beside hers on the deep windowsill. Her heart jumped, tap dancing lightly in her chest.

"Attraction doesn't count as an emotion?"

"That's just the chemistry part. All glitz and no substance." Totally unreliable in her book.

"Still, don't you think a lot of people find substance via attraction?" His gaze turned from the water to her. She didn't dare meet those whiskey-colored eyes in the candlelight for fear she would get sucked right back into those mind-drugging kisses. Focusing on a silhouetted couple frolicking on the dark beach, Fran wondered if she'd ever find romance like that. "Maybe some people initiate relationships that way, but I think attraction can be very deceptive. Isn't it better to know what you're getting into first before diving in head-long?"

"That sounds very...practical."

"Practical is not an obscene word, you know." She couldn't tear her eyes away when the couple on the shore fell into one another for a serious lip lock. "But I wouldn't simplify the act of getting to know someone as mere practicality, anyhow."

"Oh, no?" Lucky leaned closer to brush away a fallen lock of her hair, his thumb grazing her jaw. "What would you call it?"

Debating whether or not to risk a little bit of herself to Lucky Adams, Francesca found herself whispering the word like a cherished secret. "Romantic."

Romantic?

Lucky repeated the word in his mind, certain he must have missed something. What kind of woman thought it romantic to ignore undeniable attraction? He'd showered her with rose petals and chocolates and still he was getting it all wrong.

Valentine's Day—make that the whole month of February—was like the No Man's Land of the dating year. Women seemed to build these huge expectations for it and no matter what a guy did, it was never quite right.

Weren't roses and chocolates an automatic "in" with females?

His eyes raked over the wary seductress in front of him, his libido still hyperventilating from her kiss. He couldn't begin to reconcile his memory of her lips locked against his with the much more reserved message her mouth was sending now. "Anyone ever tell you that you have a rather unorthodox view of romance?"

"Just because I want to connect with someone mentally first?" She leaned down to scoop a handful of rose petals from the floor, then dumped them on the windowsill where she looked out over the ocean. "Plenty of generations before us used that method, and it worked just fine for them."

Lucky watched her arrange the rose petals in a line from the lightest pink the darkest red. The ocean breeze blowing through the open windows fluttered the petals, but failed to move them from where Francesca placed them.

"No wonder you rejected the whole high-speed dating world on 'Eligible Male.' Lucky stared, mesmerized by her light touch skating across the wooden sill on the delicate flowers. "I hear the episodes of the series that win the biggest ratings are when the bachelor sneaks a willing contestant into a cabana for a quickie."

"Well, I certainly don't have anything against a quickie when the situation calls for it." She flashed him a wink before steering the petals into a smiley face. "I just can't help but think there's some value in people getting to know each other first."

Do not think about quickies with Francesca.

Lucky repeated the phrase several times in his mind—all the while envisioning hot-and-heavy quickies with Francesca anyway—before he trusted himself to speak. "Getting to know someone first can be a good thing."

She shot him a skeptical look before her eyes strayed back to the beach and a lip-locked couple practically tearing one another's clothes off near the water. "Sorry if I find that hard to believe, Mr. Eligible Male. You said it yourself, the show is all about high-speed dating."

Lucky remembered she didn't know a damn thing about him. "Hey, wait a minute. I didn't want any part of being on that stupid show."

She wrenched her gaze from the touchy-feely couple on the beach, her finger pausing in the midst of shifting around a rose petal. "Don't tell me you won the trip to Florida sweepstakes, too." She rolled her eyes. "They don't pick just anyone to be their star for a week."

"No, but I had a hell of a lot less choice in the matter than you did." How could she have thought he was some pretty boy wannabe actor all this time? "I owed a favor to a television camera operator who made a campaign video for one of the first clients I ever managed. Now the guy is some higher-up executive producer on 'Eligible Male' and guess how he called in his damn favor?"

"And for once you couldn't fast talk your way out of it?" She nudged the flower petals aside to lean deeper into the window casing, resting her head in her hands.

"Not for lack of trying." He scooped up the petals and laid one on her arm. When she didn't protest, he positioned another and another alongside it, creating a design of his own on her body. "I tried every excuse I could think of, but for some reason the show is starved for real 'man on the street' type guys who aren't in it just for the television face time."

"Probably because real women don't want anything to do with the guys who are just in it for the face time." Francesca's eyes fluttered closed as he continued placing the soft bits of flower in a line up her arm.

As he balanced the last petal on her shoulder, he noticed the goose bumps all along her skin. Bingo. Maybe he was making more headway with the elusive Ms. Donzinetti than he thought.

He leaned closer, hoping he was starting to understand her better. "Does that mean there's a possibility I just won a few points in your book by being a real guy?"

A smile slid across her face a split second before she opened her eyes. Still, the vision of her smiling with her eyes closed would definitely haunt his imagination tonight. Then again, how many times had he told his clients that it was a good thing to be able to visualize your ultimate goal? Now at least he had something damn enticing to work toward.

"Maybe."

"Maybe?" He skimmed the last petal down the back of her shoulder along the skinny strap of her fuschia dress. "I just catapulted from the ranks of spotlight-seeking, overeager bachelor to your run-of-the-mill, normal guy. That has to give me a better dating profile."

He dipped beneath her hair to glide the soft pink petal along her bare back, relishing the way her skin shivered in response.

Now was the perfect chance to kiss her, to renew the heat that had flared between them earlier. But she'd been very clear about wanting to get to know one another first. Surely he could hold off. Ignore her lush red mouth. Her head tipped back ever so slightly. The slight catch in her breath.

He leaned forward, fighting a losing battle. Her lips hovered inches from his when a brisk knock sounded at the door.

"Room service!" Giselle Cesare's cheery voice called out from the corridor.

Lucky stifled the curse in his throat as Francesca

pulled away, gently brushing the rose petals from her skin. At this rate he was headed for the unluckiest night of his life.

FRANCESCA THANKED her lucky stars for the interruption or she would have been wrapped around her date with all the gentle reserve of a boa constrictor.

Now, two hours later as she lingered over her sambucca aperitif and stared at the bachelor bent on seduction in front of her, she wondered how she'd survive the rest of the evening without falling headlong into his arms again.

"So, what do you think?" Lucky dragged his chair closer to her side of the small round table, nudging aside their half-eaten, chocolate-cherry cheesecake dessert.

Caught off guard by his sudden nearness, Fran crossed her fingers he didn't have any more rose petals hidden up his sleeve. She didn't think she could withstand another sensual onslaught of delicate touches wrought by strong male hands. The contrast was too delicious to deny, even for a woman determined not to make any more mistakes where men were concerned.

She'd been so vulnerable after her parents had left for Italy, it had been only a matter of time before she'd ended up in a relationship. She'd even ignored a few warning signs that her boyfriend was up to no good, giving him the benefit of the doubt when she should have been on her toes. She'd wound up taking a major hit to her heart, her pride and her bottom line after he stole her secret sauce recipe.

"About what?" She set down her glass, suddenly wary of the relaxed inhibitions that often went hand in hand with alcohol. Sure, she'd only had a few sips, but Lucky Adams provided enough of an aphrodisiac on his own without Fran indulging any beverage that would make her let her guard down.

"What do you think about us now that we've had some time to talk?" He reached behind the temporary table that had been set up in the middle of their Vixen's Villa for their meal. Snatching up a notepad sporting the Club Paradise logo and the pen from beside the telephone, he slapped the paper on the white-linen tablecloth between them. "Over the course of dinner, we discovered one another's political leanings, pastimes and favorite baseball teams." He scribbled as he talked, then stared down at the paper. "And aside from you being a Mets fan, everything else is workable."

She waited for him to crack a smile, provide any indication he was joking.

He didn't.

"You can't be serious." Huffing with mild indignation, she peered over his shoulder to read what he'd written, ready to refute their compatibility—on paper and off.

Too bad the only thing he'd written on the notepad was "Please see me tomorrow."

She laughed in spite of herself. "I thought I had no choice but to be with you tomorrow. Isn't that part of the Lucky Adams challenge…to find out how long I can withstand all that charm before I cave?"

He shoved aside the paper and pen, the full force of his attention on her. It was a heady position to be in as he focused on her alone. "Don't do it because of the challenge. Only do it if you want to see me."

A little thrill tripped through her at the invitation, the persuasiveness of his voice. No wonder this man had an incredible track record for the campaigns he managed. Who could say no to him?

"I can't do it just for the sake of spending time with you." She rose, knowing the time had come to call an end to their date for the night. "I will fulfill our bargain because I won't walk away from a challenge, but you can't very well change the terms of our agreement now."

Lucky rose, his broad shoulders too close for her to think straight. "Why do I get the feeling you're going to use that damn bargain as an excuse to fight every ounce of the chemistry between us?"

She shrugged, reminding herself that she had her reasons for staying practical about this. "Chemistry or no, I'm not going to be wooed by a guy more interested in winning than dating."

Lucky's gaze narrowed. "Then by all means, let the courtship begin."

She had all sorts of arguments ready, all manner of verbal defenses prepared for whatever he might say. What she hadn't counted on was the sneak attack of his kiss.

His hands smoothed around her shoulders before she could even think about backing away. Her breath caught and seemed to halt altogether. Her limbs grew heavy with want as Lucky positioned her body in perfect alignment with his. He was strong and steely beneath that gorgeous silk suit he wore, his legs and abs almost as hard as the erection lying in wait for her.

Mmm.

She did that to him? Her body tingled at the thought that the ever practical, hard-nosed Francesca Donzinetti had inspired this sexy stud to lustful thoughts.

The time to pull away came and went, and still she

found herself glued to him, her fingertips dancing along the shoulders of his jacket—the only portion of her body that had sense enough to move away.

No, wait. As her hands skated down his back the muscled plane of his chest, Fran realized her greedy fingers were simply seeking out more terrain.

Her eyes fell shut to the candlelit paradise of the Vixen's Villa. Even though the scents of roses and ocean breezes blew around them, she sought out the starker scents of masculine soap and clean aftershave. Her lips followed her nose to his jaw as Lucky trailed kisses along her throat.

How long had it been since she'd followed her instincts and allowed a man take her to heady new heights? The only men she'd let get close in the past five years had been purely practical choices—men she knew wouldn't hurt her.

On the other hand, they'd never inspired a fire inside her the way Lucky could with the sweep of his tongue, the caress of his fingers, the burning imprint of his all-male body. She'd been missing out on so much by closing herself off from romance. And no matter how many times she had patted herself on the back over the past five years for distancing herself from the dangers of headlong attraction and delicious lust, here was Lucky turning her world on end again and making her rethink all her practical defenses.

Did she want to be the kind of woman who made the same mistakes over and over again? She forced her unwilling arms to push away from him, depriving herself of the sweet allure of Lucky's embrace.

"Game over." Her breath caught on the words, her blood pumping through her veins hard enough to make her sway on her feet. "I think we'd better call it a draw for today and say good-night."

Lucky squeezed his eyes shut for a long moment before dragging his hand through his hair and pinning her with a dark look. "This is no game, and we both know it's far from over. Do you think you're going to be able to handle round two tomorrow?"

Fran had to smile despite the sexual frustration gnawing at every inch of her body. Any Donzinetti would have to admire the way the guy went nose-to-nose with an opponent. "I'm not the one breathing so heavy my eyes are crossing." A blatant, bald-faced lie, but well worth it considering the way Lucky's brows knit together in a fierce, predatory glare. "Are you sure you're going to be able to handle it, Slick?"

"Hell, yes. And since this is so damn easy for you, how about we see how it goes for the whole day? None of this dinner-only crap." He reached to run the back of his hand down her cheek, the delicate brush of his knuckles softening his words. "I bet you can't go ten hours without touching me."

Her heart picked up speed at that simple caress. At this rate, she wouldn't go ten minutes without touching him. So it must have been some perverse inner demon that made her say, "You're on."

Lucky smiled as the full import of her rash words rolled over her. He leaned in to give her a fleeting good-night kiss on the cheek while she already made plans to keep them out on the town and busy every second of the day.

Because Lucky might be a smooth operator when it came to maneuvering her just where he wanted, but he hadn't seen her wily side yet. And when it came to protecting her heart, Francesca could be as crafty as any slick political manager, especially when she could already feel her traitorous body falling for him.

5

LUCKY HAULED HIMSELF out of the surf and up onto the beach just in time to see the last of the sunset. Muscles pleasantly aching from the rigorous workout of water-skiing, sunfish sailing and then windsurfing, he marveled that Francesca jogged out of the waves as if ready to run a marathon, her lean, toned legs glistening with water in the hazy purple light.

"I'm on to you," he called as she cruised by him, wringing out her wet hair. "Don't think your underhanded scheme has gone unnoticed."

She turned to look at him as he trudged across the soft white sand toward the deck chairs where they had piled their beach towels.

"And what scheme might that might be?"

"Your diabolical plot to keep me too busy to get close to you. You can't tell me you fill all your days with nonstop water sports." Lucky had been suspicious from the moment he'd met her in the hotel lobby at noon. She already had a schedule in hand, a carefully planned agenda that included more activities for the day than most people packed into a year.

Smiling, she reached for a towel and patted her face dry. She slung the length of terry cloth around her shoulders, a gesture that didn't even come close to hiding her half-naked body from view.

He deserved a damn medal for surviving this day of

torture—seven hours of seeing Francesca in a blue-and-silver bikini.

"You're the one who wanted to spend the whole day together. Can I help it if you can't keep up?"

She tossed him his towel and wrapped hers around her waist like a skirt.

Lucky might have been grateful for the respite for his eyes that had been glued to her body all day except that he could still see the shape of one tanned thigh through the slit in the material. He'd wrangled a chance to slather her entire body with sunscreen earlier that afternoon and the memory of her warm skin under his hands had fueled his imagination ever since.

"Who said I couldn't keep up?" He skimmed the towel over his face and tossed it back on the deck chair. "I just wanted you to be aware that you aren't fooling me for a minute."

"I gave you the option of going on the pontoon boat to search for alligators. You chose the beach." She dug through her bag and found a bright pink comb, then lowered herself onto the sand to work on untangling her long mass of dark hair.

"Some choice. Spend the day in a swamp staring at the mud for a hint of alligator eyes, or stare at you in a bathing suit. It seemed pretty clear cut to me this morning, but I guess I didn't realize how serious you were when you suggested water sports." Seeing a rare opportunity to get close to this dynamo in action, he snagged the comb from her hand and knelt behind her to take over the chore. "Let me. I'll do the work and you can tell me why you can't give me a break today."

"Admit it, Adams, you had fun." She stared out over the water as the sun slipped below the horizon, leaving only a red streak in the sky to color the Atlantic purple.

Starting at the bottom of her hair, Lucky combed the thick strands in sections, working his way up as he freed the tangles on the lower half. "You're right, I did. Before I had to take off this week to film the show, I can't remember the last time I took a vacation."

There was always a campaign that couldn't wait, or career development for his clients when it wasn't election time. Of course, his motto as a campaign manager had been that it was always election time.

Even though Francesca set a relentless pace for having fun, he had enjoyed every minute with her.

"Me neither. I guess since we're both workaholics that means we're very incompatible—two people who share that trait would never get to see each other."

"Yet put us together, and what do you know?" He smoothed a hand down her hair, straying onto her shoulder. "We relax."

"I don't know if this is so relaxing." As testament to her words, her body tensed beneath his hand.

"That's just sexual tension," he breathed in her ear, allowing the words to whisper lightly over her skin. "But I know how to make that go away, too."

"Mmm. I'll just bet you do." She closed her eyes, her head tilting back with another downward sweep of the comb. "Why do you put so much time in at work?"

At first Lucky thought maybe she asked the question just to distract him from his obvious provocative thoughts. But then he noticed her eyes were still closed, her body more relaxed than it had been all day. He continued to comb her hair as he stretched out on the sand alongside her.

"Commitment to what I do. I enjoy advancing politicians' careers to a point where their ideals can actually do some good. One of my clients, Jackson Taggart who just got elected to the Florida state legislature, is in the process of rezoning South Beach to help bring in some new businesses and still keep the locals happy. I'm damn proud of the initiative." In fact, Lucky had been damn proud of his whole career until the "Eligible Male" thing bit him in the butt. "Still, I'm looking at some new directions. Investments, maybe."

Which, although he'd always turned a nice profit for himself, making a career out of it didn't exactly sound exciting.

"Big mistake." Francesca opened her eyes and turned her deep brown eyes on him. "I can tell just by the tone of your voice where your passion lies. It's not many people who are blessed with a job they love." She pointed a finger at him as if to drive home her words.

"Just because I'm passionate about something, doesn't mean I can have what I want. Take you for example—"

"Nice try, Slick, but you're not fast talking your way out of this one. Why would you ever leave a job so obviously perfect for you?" She plucked the comb from his hand and dropped it back into her bag before digging through her purse in search of something else.

"Because getting trapped into doing the television show made me realize I don't want to spend my life paying back favors. In my line of work, I'm constantly asking for favors, jockeying for better media positioning, talking my way into what I want."

"And no doubt you're getting better and better at it. Maybe after this experience you'll be all the more careful not to back yourself into a corner." Apparently finding what she was looking for, Francesca withdrew one tortoiseshell comb decorated with a rhinestone swirl from her seemingly bottomless handbag. "And if you do—so what? You said yourself that you're having fun this week. Maybe you shouldn't be so quick to write off a little favor payback now and then. It could be good for a man who's used to getting everything he wants."

She pulled aside a section of her dark hair and jammed the jeweled comb into it, exposing more of her face.

Lucky stared back at her in the rapidly fading twilight, this woman who seemed so wise beyond her twenty-six years. His hand moved to stroke her damp hair. He intended to send her a message she couldn't run away from. "I only get what I want because I'm willing to work for it."

Francesca got the message loud and clear. Lucky wasn't giving up on her any time soon.

How would she survive the next three days of relentless campaigning? Just seven hours of close proximity to all those exposed male muscles had her so restless she didn't dare sit still for fear of flinging herself in his arms.

All her Jersey tough-girl bravado was only going to carry her so far when faced with the temptation of a scrumptious man determined to have her.

"It's good to know you're not afraid of a little hard work." She should stand up now and find some other rigorous activity to throw them into.

And not *that* rigorous activity, damn it. She didn't need to think about what all Lucky's strength and admirable stamina would mean for her if they ever hit the sheets.

Instead of standing, however, Fran found herself sitting totally still, paralyzed by the heat she spied in

Lucky's eyes. He hovered closer, his lips suddenly close enough to touch. To taste.

"I've found that hard work is usually rewarded." His words inspired a soft heat to spread through her limbs. "And that the prize is all the more sweet for the effort invested."

By now, her legs were so heavy with liquid desire she couldn't have moved if she'd tried.

She didn't.

Her eyes closed a split second before his mouth moved over hers, his lips claiming her with the slow thoroughness of a man intent on reaping his full reward. His tongue tangled with hers, flicking over her with soft insistence and making her long for that kiss all over her body.

The relentless swish of the waves hitting the shore mingled with the sounds of their ragged breathing. She reached for him to anchor herself against a tide of hot sensation all the more intense for having been denied.

His shoulders were steely and smooth beneath her touch, his muscles a warm wall of strength to her hands that trembled ever so slightly. She wanted to mold her whole quivering body to those hard masculine planes, to quiet the relentless hunger inside her with an all-night, all-day physical feast.

But as laughter and the raised voices of other nocturnal beach-goers floated on the ocean breeze, she recalled they were very much in public despite the intimacy of the dark. Pulling away, she bent her head to his coconut sunscreen-scented shoulder until the group of partiers past them.

"We could go dance under the stars." She forced herself to sit up, seizing upon the new idea. "There's a great outdoor bar with a band just up the street and—"

Lucky shushed her with a warm finger over her kiss-swollen lips. "Is that what you really want to do tonight?"

Of course not. And he had to know it from the way she'd just melted all over him like the cheese on one of her Jersey-famous pizzas.

"I think we both know what I want." Too bad acting on that desire would mean she'd lost Lucky's challenge and that she was setting herself up for potential hurt and disappointment. Then again, maybe the time had come where it hurt more to deny herself than to simply act on the need.

He flashed her a wicked grin, his white teeth a bright spot in the dark. "Then what if I challenged you to take what you want for a change?"

Her heart jumped with a dull thud against her chest. Heaven help her, she was honestly considering it. She wanted him with a fierceness she couldn't begin to deny. "I'd say that would be some very crafty maneuvering on your part."

"We both know you can't walk away from a challenge."

Shrugging helplessly, her heartbeat quickened even more. Could she do this and still protect her heart? Maybe if she went into it with no expectations for tomorrow. "How could I possibly walk away? Meeting any challenge *is* a proud family tradition."

Lucky turned to look at Club Paradise about a hundred yards away behind them. "You think we can make it back to your room without touching each other and setting off major fireworks between here and there?"

By now her blood swished through her with more force than the ocean waves on the beach. The sound roared in her ears while her skin burned with the need to get close to him. She'd never wanted a man so desperately. "Not a chance." She rose to her feet, shaking the sand off her legs as she scoped the terrain between them and the privacy of the Vixen's Villa. "My guess is we end up making it in a cabana before we get there."

Lucky's fingers flexed as he stood, his male body practically radiating sensual heat. A needy whimper escaped from the back of her throat as he slanted his mouth over hers, walking her backward across the beach while his tongue dueled with hers.

He paused long enough to retrieve his towel, draping the long length of terry cloth around his shoulders and still somehow managing to keep her locked to him.

"No way are we hitting the cabana," he warned between kisses. "I dreamed all last night about seeing you wearing nothing but rose petals."

She tugged away just as they reached a small footbridge across a patch of sea oats. "I dreamed about the rose petals, too."

She'd also smelled them all night, the scent invading her dreams and teasing her with vivid fantasies.

"Please say you didn't clean them up yet." They stuck to the shadows as they crossed the Club Paradise grounds dotted with torchlights, tiki hut minibars and bubbling hot tubs full of mingling singles. Lucky used his room key to open one of the side doors.

"Are you kidding?" She shivered as they entered the air-conditioned hotel, her bare feet padding over the cool terra-cotta tiles near the spa. She peered back at him over her shoulder as she pressed the elevator button. "I slept with them last night."

Could she help it if she took wicked delight in his hoarse growl?

"I hope you're enjoying tormenting me." He stood back to let her enter the elevator as the doors swished open. "Because payback is coming as soon as these doors close." He stepped in behind her, stalking her until she backed into the far corner of the small space.

"Oh, really?" Her pulse thrummed triple time at the intent look in his eyes. "Should I be worried?"

His hands bracketed her on either side, his palms flat against the wall behind her just as the doors closed and the car swept them upward.

"No." He breathed the word over her lips, the scent of coconut sunscreen intensifying from the heat of their bodies. "You should be very, very excited."

She closed her eyes, waiting for his kiss. When it didn't arrive, she pried open her lids just in time to see his finger slide down the small valley of her cleavage, her bikini top baring the tops of her breasts to his avid gaze.

Her nipples pebbled, pressing against the confines of her swimsuit. Heat swirled through her at that bold touch, her knees growing weak as he tugged at the knot between her breasts that held her top in place.

Breath catching in her throat, she arched back against the wall, ready and willing for whatever payback he had in mind. He bent to kiss her there, trailing his mouth over one exposed curve and stalling as he reached the spandex barrier of her bathing suit top.

Not that he let it stop him.

He flicked his tongue beneath the hem, grazing one taut nipple with damp heat. She moaned at the sensation, her soft cry mingling with the elevator bell sounding for her floor. She didn't know whether to weep with frustration or to cry out in relief.

"Please hold that thought." Lucky held his breath and hoped the sound of the elevator bell hadn't inadvertently brought Francesca to her senses. Damn it, he couldn't bear to see all that relentless practicality rain over the fiery spirit beneath.

But instead of coming to her senses, Francesca gripped the towel around his neck and tugged him out of the elevator. "I'm only going to be able to hold the thought for so long before I jump you, so unless you want to provide quite a spectacle for inhabitants of the fourth floor..."

Never one to take a woman's word lightly, he plucked her off her feet and hauled her over his shoulder. She squealed, but didn't protest, using the position to nip him on the back. He picked up his pace to the Vixen's Villa and accepted the key card she shoved into the waistband of his shorts. The woman was a spitfire.

He'd planned to take his time with her tonight, to woo her and to seduce her slowly so that they'd have something solid to build on if ever he could convince her to see him again. But once Francesca had made up her mind to go forward, *slow* didn't seem to be a word in her vocabulary. The moment he inserted the key in the lock and nudged the door to her room open, she started slithering her way down his body, her bare skin and skimpy bikini teasing him with the promise of what was to come.

He would have lit candles for her, romanced her in every way imaginable, but she backed him into the door like a woman on a mission. Catching her up in his arms, he couldn't deny he welcomed her enthusiasm after their rough start. Even though he'd wanted her from the moment she'd stumbled onto the set of "Eligible Male" with bleary eyes and refreshing honesty, he'd had to chase her all the way from their private island back to South Beach, ditch the man-eating woman America had chosen for him, then shower Francesca with roses, chocolates and rigorous water-sports outings to get her to come around to his way of thinking. Now, finally, she was wrapping her strong, slender arms around his neck and plastering her sexy body to his.

Francesca Donzinetti ranked as his best dream come true—grounded but spontaneous, tough enough to relish a challenge yet soft enough to sleep naked in rose petals.

Of course, he didn't know that she really slept *naked* with them. That part might have been lustful conjecture on his part, a vision brought on by the very real press of her half-exposed breasts against his bare chest.

Catching the heat of her impulsiveness, Lucky slipped his hands between them, untying the knot that held her swimsuit together. She helped him by wriggling out of the shoulder straps, sending the scrap of spandex to the floor and leaving him squinting to catch a glimpse of what they'd unveiled in the dark, rose-scented room.

Heat thick between them, he bent his head to kiss her and prayed he'd have enough restraint to give her the best night of her life. Because now more than ever, he needed this stubborn, determined woman to come back to him, to crave his touch and his kiss, again and again.

6

COOL AIR floated over Fran's bare skin for scant seconds before Lucky closed the gap between them, pulling her into his arms and slanting his mouth over hers. Warm honey flowed through her veins as her breasts crushed against the sinewy muscles of his chest.

Heaven.

She'd wanted to be romanced, to enjoy the thrill of being chased if only to assure herself she was a prize worthy of pursuit. If only she hadn't underestimated how badly she wanted to be caught by this man. Lucky's attentive seduction combined with his absolute compliance to her rules for their game had swayed her too soon, too completely.

Now, she was melting beneath the stroke of his tongue over hers, sighing into him with her whole body.

"I want to see you." His deep voice whispered against her mouth, his words a throaty plea.

She felt in the dark for the dimmer switch that controlled the suite's two small chandeliers. Rotating the dial just a fraction, she filled the room with a warm glow. "How's that?"

He pulled away just enough to stare down at her, her skin tingling with his slow perusal. "Perfect. Delicious."

She leaned closer, needing the feel of his body flush

up against hers again, but he sidestepped her approach and pulled her deeper into the room. She might have protested except that she had an amazing view of his bare, suntanned back while he navigated them toward the sitting area. Dark shadow and the golden glow of dim lighting played across the muscular plane, mesmerizing her.

When he paused behind the distressed-wood coffee table, she pointed to the doorway across the decadent room. "The bedroom's that way."

"I'm not interested in the bed so much as seeing you in these." He bent to scoop up a handful of rose petals and sprinkled them lightly over her shoulder.

The silky shower tingled her nerve endings and tickled her skin, making her long for a more substantial touch. His touch.

Her pulse leaped as he drew her down to the floor with him, their gentle fall cushioned by fragrant pink, red, peach and white petals.

"What if I don't want to wear roses?" She whispered the words as Lucky trailed kisses down her neck, over her collarbone and toward her aching, needy breasts. Flicking open the towel that had been wrapped around her hips, she slid out of the damp terry cloth.

"I'd say you're a woman who strives to make my whole life one big freaking challenge." His gruff words lacked any bite since he breathed them out over the delicate hollow at the base of her throat.

"Then what would you say if the only thing I'm interested in wearing right now is you?" Reaching for his swim trunks, she slid her hand over his abs and down to the tie at his waist before he halted her progress.

Still, he couldn't disguise the wave of need that

tripped through him. Muscles flexed in the most enticing places while his breath hitched in his throat.

"I'd say you don't have too long to wait, Ms. Impatient." Bracing himself up on his elbow, he removed her questing hand and placed it above her head. "What happened to romance and getting to know one another better? I'm not going to blow my chance with you by falling victim to overwhelming lust." His fingers skimmed down to trail over her hip, the warmth of his hand igniting a blaze deep in the pit of her belly.

Or was that actually a warm glow in the vicinity of her heart?

Fran blinked back the emotions she was already feeling too soon. Deliberately she arched her back to twitch her hips against his. "I would think overwhelming lust would be a good thing in this case."

Lucky's jaw flexed, his gaze flicking over her with intent, golden-brown eyes. "If I can be with you tomorrow, I guarantee I'll be all about lust. But just in case I only have this one chance, I'm going to make damn certain you know that this wasn't just about sex."

But it *had* to be just about sex.

Francesca thought it, but she couldn't say it since Lucky was already—finally—dipping his hand to smooth over the narrow band of blue-and-silvery fabric of her bikini bottoms. Her fears took flight as sensation tingled through her, thoughts of tomorrow fading in the sudden all-consuming need for the here and now.

Her back settled more deeply into the blanket of roses beneath them, the cool floral cushion so different from the hot, hard male above her. He traced idle circles around her nipples, his unhurried movements infusing her whole body with heat. Hunger.

Her skin tightened, her breasts cresting all the more from his touch until he lowered his lips to draw her into his mouth, one needy peak at a time.

Unable to keep her hands off him, her fingers found their way back to his chest, smoothing over hard pecs and square shoulders. He was sculpted perfection and every American woman's dream according to the promo spots for "Eligible Male" all last week. And for tonight he was hers alone.

She walked her fingertips south to the intriguing portion of him that nudged her hip and made her thighs twitch in restless anticipation. He sucked in a breath as she skated her touch over the crisp cotton of his shorts and around the hard length of him. Closing her fingers around him, she stroked her hand down him from tip to base and then slid back up, her whole body turning warm and liquid at the thought of him inside her.

"I don't stand a chance of taking my time tonight, do I?" His voice rasped over her shoulder as he molded the curve of her waist and then her hip with one hand.

"I've made it my personal challenge to test your willpower." Fran drew her thigh upward, gliding her bare skin along the outside of his leg.

"Then congratulations." Lucky gripped the waistband of her bikini bottoms and dragged the fabric down her thighs and off her bare feet. "You're succeeding with alarming speed."

Lucky cursed his lack of restraint even as he welcomed the satisfied smile on Francesca's face. He couldn't stop staring at her, touching her, devouring her with eyes and hands. Her long, dark hair spread out over the rainbow of rose petals, her cheeks flushed pink and her lips swollen from his kisses.

He shoved off his swim trunks and retrieved a condom from the tiny pocket normally reserved for a key. Thank God foil was waterproof.

Before he could rip open the packet, Francesca stole it from his hands and tore the foil, then took her time rolling the condom down over him. He understood her need to take some control tonight, recognized that she wanted to keep things on her terms, but he didn't know how much more of her teasing torment he could bear.

He wanted her now.

Nudging her thigh with his knee, he positioned himself over her. He leaned in to kiss her, long, slow and deep as he edged his way inside her. She was slick and warm and so damn snug he thought he'd lose his mind. Her nails sank into his shoulders as she kissed him, the scent of coconut sunscreen and the ocean still clinging to their skin. Sweat beaded on his brow as he eased in deeper, not wanting to rush.

Still, the restraint was killing him when all he wanted to do was to bury himself to the hilt. And just when he thought he'd have to withdraw and start all over again, Fran tilted her hips upward and arched her back to accept every aching inch of him.

Heat and steam clouded his brain, fogging his thoughts until he could only think about this moment, this sensation, this incredible joining. He reached between them to touch her, his finger settling on the throbbing center of her. She cried out at the soft pressure his thumb exerted, telling him through her sighs and moans exactly what she wanted.

Lucky obliged, timing deep thrusts of his hips with the gentle pressure of his fingers until her whole body tensed, stretched and then shuddered with the force of her orgasm. Her cry rent the air around him, her body squeezing his with electrifying little pulses until his release surged through him with more force than the South Beach surf.

He lay over her for long minutes, unable to move, let alone think or speak. No woman had ever bowled him over the way Francesca had from the moment she'd strut onto the set of "Eligible Male" with her blunt directness and no-time-for-games attitude.

She was the real deal, the kind of woman you didn't trifle with, and somehow he'd just slept with her even though his life was at a huge crossroads and he had no idea what tomorrow held for him professionally.

Damn.

Apparently his brain had recovered from sex long before his sated body.

Prying himself up on an elbow, he glanced into Francesca's eyes and realized she appeared even more worried than he felt. An utterly unacceptable consequence of their time together.

He lifted them up off the floor, recognizing the time had come to retreat to the bedroom. If she let him stay with her, that is.

"You look ready to boot me out at a moment's notice." He tugged her toward the doorway on the other side of the room, hoping he could ease her fears easier than he could address his own. "Yet I'm pretty damn sure you were feeling good a little while ago when we were...together. Why don't you at least let me tuck you in and talk to you before you do anything rash?"

She pushed open the door to a small bedroom painted with Mediterranean golds and bronzes. The walls were decorated with a wide assortment of black lingerie in glass frames, providing an element of naughtiness to an otherwise understated, elegant room. Francesca slid between the covers of the large sleigh bed and then held the corner of the bedspread out for him. "I'm just a wary sort. But you can join me for a little while if you want."

He wanted. In fact, it surprised him how much he wanted to crawl into bed with this woman just to sleep. To hold her.

The notion scared him to his toes when he had no clue what would come next once he left politics behind. Sliding in between smooth bronze sheets beside Francesca, however, he shook off his own concerns to quiz her about hers.

"You care to explain how the gutsy woman who put herself through college on the profit from her own pizza business ended up so cautious?"

Fran wondered for a split second how Lucky knew that about her, then remembered her bio on "Eligible Male" had highlighted her entrepreneurial spirit as one of her "defining qualities." As if people could be so pigeonholed by their work.

"It's easier to take risks in business than in my personal life." She drew the covers into her chest, needing just a little distance from this intriguing man she'd already allowed too close. "If you fail in business, you end up broke. Been there, done that and lived to tell the tale. But if you fail with another person in a—" God, but the word still stuck in her throat "—relationship, that seems more difficult to overcome."

Lucky threaded his fingers through her hair and tugged them down the length of the strands. She had to admit the man knew ways to touch her that made her feel special. Unhurried. So different from those one-dimensional men whose fluency in sensual language was limited to the missionary position.

"Can I translate that to mean you've coped with a broken heart at some point?" His attention seemed fixed on a sun-streaked strand of her dark hair, but Fran suspected he was paying close attention to her answer.

"A little bit of a broken heart," she admitted, settling the pillow more snugly beneath her head while she took in the details of Lucky's dark hairline, his five o'clock shadow visible even in a darkened room lit only by moonlight and the dim glow from the chandelier in the sitting room. "But also some broken pride, which can be almost as devastating when you're young and you think you're invincible." He didn't say anything, obviously waiting for her to continue. Couldn't he see that this was a story she didn't like to dish out to just anyone?

Unable to stand the silence, she pried herself up on her elbow. "He was the pizza dough tosser." She flung her arm above her head to demonstrate. "You know what I mean? He made dough for me and I fell for him. I gave him complete run over the kitchen for a few months and he ended up stealing my most lucrative asset—my sauce recipe. I wasn't just hurt, I was embarrassed. The whole shop knew what an idiot I'd been. For that matter, half of Newark knew since I make the best pies on the west side of town and I'm not exactly the secretive type."

"You mean half the town knew what an idiot *he'd* been, don't you?" He propped his pillow under his head and laced his fingers together where they rested on his chest.

She rolled her eyes even though his words soothed her. "But at the end of the day, it was me who got to stick around through all the pitying looks. Trust me, I felt every inch the moron for letting him get close to me."

"Good thing you know me better than that."

"Hello? I've know you for what—a week?"

"Ten days. Most of which were cram full of more information about me than any woman on earth probably cared to hear. Viewers across all of North America got to see photos of me at my high school prom, my college graduation, my first political campaign victory." He scraped an impatient hand across his forehead. "It was ridiculous. I think they even interviewed my third-grade teacher."

"Actually, it was your fourth-grade teacher." Fran smiled as she needled him, grateful to have someone else's life on display for a few minutes. "She said all the girls had crushes on you even then."

Lucky groaned, covering his eyes. "Enough. But at least you know I'm not some sticky-fingered chef."

She had to admit he had a point there. Thanks to "Eligible Male," she knew a lot about him. Enough to know she was safe spending a few more days in search of sensual uses for rose petals with him, anyway. And despite his determined pursuit, she knew he couldn't possibly have any expectations for a relationship between them. He lived in Florida and was pursuing a high-profile career—something she felt certain he'd stick with even if he was a little worried about his future right now.

She, on the other hand, would never leave New Jersey since she didn't have the wandering feet her parents had always possessed. And damn it, she liked making pizzas. It might not be a glamorous career, but her kick-butt pies made a lot of people happy.

Surely she could just indulge herself in a simple vacation fling for the week. Her time with Lucky could be the icing on the cake for her Florida vacation as long as she didn't grow too attached.

"Maybe you don't have sticky fingers," she whispered in his ear as she leaned closer, edging her thigh up against his in an unmistakable message. How hard could it be to steer a man into purely sensual terrain for a few days? "But I seem to recall you have very *greedy* fingers..."

THREE DAYS LATER, Lucky reached across the South Beach sand for the bottle of sangria tucked away in its own cooling sleeve.

"We're out," he called to Francesca, sprawled on a bright yellow beach blanket beside him. She was sketching a quick picture of her outfit for the "Eligible Male" post-production wrap party that night—Valentine's night—where the pressure would be on to either say goodbye forever or to figure out a way to keep her in his life despite his lack of career direction. "Want me to go get some more?"

They'd been spending all their free time together for three days straight—the days had been filled with every tourist activity available in southern Florida, while the nights had been unbelievable. Their time together had been special and Lucky knew it was about to run out if he couldn't get his head on straight.

She held one hand above her dark eyes to shield the sun, peering from the empty bottle to the busy deck area behind Club Paradise where party preparations were already under way.

"That's okay. I'd better switch to water if I want to be gorgeous later." She flipped her mini notebook in his direction to show him the simple drawing. "What do you think of my outfit?"

He tried not to do the cartoon double take, but he felt his eyes pop a few inches out of his head. "You're wearing this?"

The tiny jean shorts looked more suited for a roll in the hay than a schmoozy, fancy TV party, but who was he to talk? He'd kill to see that much of Fran's legs.

Of course, he'd like it even better if they could just skip the party altogether and stay in the Vixen's Villa for their last night on South Beach. He'd been racking his brain for three days straight on how to convince Fran to stay in Florida with him, but what did he have going for him right now that could ever make her change her mind? He was a man in the midst of a career crisis with no clear-cut professional prospects on the horizon. He simply knew he couldn't stay in a business where he would be continually beholden to other people for granting him favors. Wheeling and dealing great placement for his political candidates wasn't nearly as rewarding when the payback involved stints on reality TV shows.

Fran frowned down at her rough drawing. "Granted, I'm no artist, but the theme tonight is Redneck Romance as a nod to Valentine's Day. Don't you think Daisy Dukes are the perfect shorts for a redneck event?"

Daisy Dukes? He wouldn't even ask. "Sorry, I didn't know the network was going redneck. What does that mean—we're drinking moonshine instead of martinis?"

Fran stuffed her drawing into her beach bag and reclined on the towel. "Actually, I think you can order anything you like, but it all gets served in Mason jars.

Giselle said they're putting couches out on the deck along with a few refrigerators full of hors d'oeuvres. Should be a fun last night."

Lucky stared down at her as she soaked up the sun beneath multiple layers of sunblock he had taken tremendous pleasure in applying. Didn't she feel even a hint of regret that they'd be parting ways tomorrow?

No, because she had steeled herself up front for a short-term encounter. And thanks to the professional upheaval in his life right now, he hadn't done a damn thing to change her mind.

Scooping up the empty bottle of sangria, Lucky rose to his feet and waved a hand toward the tiki huts and minibars lining the Club Paradise property. "I'll go find us some water."

Francesca shaded her eyes with one hand, her fluorescent orange fingernails painted to match her latest bikini. "That's okay. I'm probably going back up to my room in a few minutes anyway. Why don't you go ahead and I'll see you at the party?"

Dismissed.

He could hear it in the forced lightness of her voice, see it in the tense muscles of her body. After three days of nonstop sun, fun and sex, she was giving him all the signs the party was over. But what good would it do to point out her polite withdrawal from him today—the most romantic damn day of the year?

He sought for an easy comeback, knowing she probably had the right idea by bowing out gracefully, but no words came to mind. He wasn't ready for this to end, damn it.

"Seven o'clock on the beach." He confirmed the time with a nod and stalked away, storm clouds gathering around him despite the relentless blue of the Florida sky. As his feet carried him off the beach and up onto the sprawling Club Paradise property, he told himself as long as he allowed his career to run his life he had no business getting serious with a woman like Francesca. She deserved a man with his head on straight, especially after another guy had taken her for a ride.

He needed a career that would keep him in the driver's seat at all times. He'd call the shots, not the candidates he managed, and not the hordes of business professionals who circulated in the political realm. Brushing past a series of sunken hot tubs filled with soaking hotel guests despite the warm weather, Lucky peered out over the hubbub of party preparation on the Club Paradise property in search of a bar and ended up locking gazes with Marley Sinclair instead. And not only did she see him, she also seemed to be actively flagging him down, waving one pale, gingham-clad arm in his direction.

Just what he didn't need right now.

"I've been looking for you everywhere," she chided, brow furrowed as if vaguely annoyed. She wore some sort of checkered dress that looked more hoedown than redneck to him, but what did he know about clothes? Her blond hair was tucked neatly into a blue ribbon, consistent with her all-American image that had captivated television viewers and catapulted her to the number-one bachelorette status. Lucky couldn't imagine how anyone could think he was better suited for her cool, cut-throat style of ambition than Francesca's fiery nature and blunt honesty.

"Fran and I have been on the beach." He turned back to look for Fran and her fluorescent orange swimsuit, but he didn't see any sign of her where he'd left her. "Did you need me for something?"

She flashed him the smile she usually reserved for the cameras and leaned closer. "Could we speak somewhere more private? I wanted to discuss my upcoming campaign with you. I'm ready to capitalize on the high profile the show has given me and announce my intention to run for Congress."

Could he help it if the word shot a little thrill through him? Conducting a campaign at that level was like moving up from the minors to the big leagues. And no matter what he thought of man-eating Marley on a personal level, she was exactly the kind of energetic candidate who would appeal to voters. Her "Eligible Male" stint might make a few skeptics sneer, but it would make many more people sit up and take notice.

Too bad he didn't want to be in politics anymore.

"I can't, Marley." He was going into high finance to make a killing on the stock market instead. So what if he grew bored out of his mind within a few weeks? He refused to be a slave to his ambitions taking on campaigns simply to further his career. "I'm getting out of the business."

"What?" She looked like she swallowed something uncomfortable and couldn't quite get it down. Her neck muscles grew taut as she stared up at him. "You can't just leave the business. The whole reason I lobbied for last week's episodes of 'Eligible Male' was so we could have a chance to work together."

"I can recommend some other campaign specialists. Do you have a pen?" He'd rarely turned down a potential client before—especially one that was on the verge of a big campaign—and it surprised him what a freeing experience it had been. Francesca hadn't understood how he could walk away from his work, but damn it, he was doing it so he wouldn't be perpetually obligated to the whims of whomever he happened to be managing.

"I don't want a pen." She bit the words out with crisp articulation, irritation etched in the pinched lines around her perfectly painted pink mouth. "I want you."

It occurred to Lucky that maybe if he changed his approach to his career, drew more boundaries and remembered to say no to the kinds of clients he wouldn't enjoy instead of operating purely on ambition, maybe he wouldn't find himself in the awkward position of having to payback favors he hadn't wanted to request in the first place. Maybe if he took a page out of Francesca's book and kept himself grounded, he wouldn't allow the career he thrived on to take over his whole life.

Damn but he needed to find a way to reach her before it was too late. The stakes were no longer as simple as winning some four-year political term for a client. This was about something that could last a lifetime and losing was *not* an option. He wouldn't be able to rely on slick speeches like in the past. Instead, he'd have to undertake something far more risky.

Straight talk from his heart.

Infused with a brand-new focus for tonight's party, Lucky edged away from the fuming bachelorette who never would be the right partner for him.

"Sorry, Marley. I'm already taken."

7

FRANCESCA SIPPED her Long Island Iced Tea from her Mason jar and wound her way though the "Eligible Male" bash while Lynyrd Skynard blasted across the Club Paradise grounds. Buxom pole dancers shimmied around the temporary poles erected for the event, their ripped T-shirts advertising local beers barely covering their cartoonish bodies.

"Don't you love the theme?" Giselle settled into step beside her at a few minutes before seven, looking more like a chic Guess girl than a redneck with her tight jean shorts, black bra half exposed beneath an open denim blouse and dark eyeliner surrounding her already exotic eyes. "Or are you too depressed about leaving tomorrow to enjoy the party tonight?"

"Who's depressed?" Fran had been telling herself for the past two hours that she'd be okay leaving Lucky behind. He had a flourishing career even if he didn't see it right now. And he probably had a zillion tempting offers for female companionship waiting on standby. Marley Sinclair certainly hadn't wasted any time moving in on him this afternoon when she thought Fran wasn't looking. She'd seen the whole encounter while she was heading back up to her room earlier.

Not that she was jealous. She knew Lucky well enough to recognize he didn't care about Marley. But somehow it hurt to think about all the greedy females waiting for Fran to relinquish him tomorrow.

"Well, I'm hardly Miss Insightful when it comes to affairs of the heart," Giselle huffed, leaning against the trunk of a dwarf palm tree at the edge of the festivities, "But I have the feeling that glum look you're sporting isn't because you'll be leaving your favorite cousin tomorrow. Why not just admit you fell head over heels for Lucky Adams this week?"

"Maybe because admitting it would mean I've once again failed to avoid heartache despite all my best precautions." Her heart tightened in her chest, the ache of leaving Lucky already taking hold. She set down her drink on a waiter's tray and bent to pluck a stiff palm leaf off the ground. Tearing it in thirds, she began braiding. "I think it has something to do with Valentine's Day. I told myself I had no expectations, but all of a sudden the whole Cupid syndrome hits and I turn into Miss Lovestruck. Totally nauseating."

"But it's not over yet," Giselle reminded her. "You could still bag the 'Eligible Male' and dethrone Marley from her position as reigning bachelorette. Lucky seems like a great guy, if you ask me. And believe me, after having been fooled by a player myself before, I'm definitely a tough critic."

Fran knew Giselle had been even more deeply wounded than her by a guy in the past. She'd slept with a married man who'd sworn he was single and now had the dubious pleasure of sharing part ownership in Club Paradise with the man's ex-wife.

"I don't know. I can't see myself relocating to Florida even if he was really serious about me, which I'm not convinced he is." Still, as she peered around the party and her eye snagged on a couple sharing a boxed pizza that served as one of many unorthodox food selections for the Redneck Romance theme party, Fran couldn't help a twinge of longing for what might have been. She sighed with envy as the guy sporting a T-shirt advertising a tractor pull caught a long strand of cheese his girlfriend tugged off the pizza with her teeth. Scooping up the mozzarella with one finger, the guy munched on one end of the cheese until his lips met hers for an oregano-flavored, romantic kiss Fran could almost taste.

What had she thrown away by allowing herself to keep things in the short term with such a great guy?

"He looks damn serious about you from where I'm standing," Giselle assured her, pushing herself away from the trunk of the palm tree. "Especially since he's carrying a big bouquet of daisies over here right now."

"Daisies?" She turned to see North America's current favorite bachelor clad in jeans and a T-shirt and strolling toward her with a fistful of flowers that looked like they could have been picked along the side of the New Jersey turnpike rather than purchased at a fancy Miami florist.

Heart skipping just a little at a gesture that swayed her more than a truckload of rose petals, she turned to Giselle for support and found herself all alone to face the biggest temptation of her life.

"Happy Valentine's Day, Francesca." Lucky slowed to a stop in front of her, offering up the bouquet tied with a wide white ribbon. "They're not roses, but they seemed in keeping with the theme for the night."

She reached for the daisies, ridiculously pleased at the simple gesture. How many times had she seen her father—the original Mr. Romance—bring her mother flowers he'd picked from alongside the highway or pilfered out of a neighbor's yard? The whole neighborhood grew extras because everyone knew how much Franco Donzinetti doted on his wife.

The memory was too special, too sweet, to think about now when Lucky had simply been thoughtful about their last night together. Francesca sniffed away thoughts of the kind of romantic man she'd always dreamed of and concentrated on getting through the night without turning to heartbroken mush.

"They're beautiful," she told him honestly. "Thank you." Leaning in to breathe in the scent of the bright white-and-yellow bouquet, Fran noticed a dark shadow buried among the green stems. "But there's something stuck in here."

She reached in among the stems to withdraw what looked like...a velvet box?

Her gaze whipped up to meet Lucky's. No way.

The small box in her hand simply could not be what she was thinking. Not after she'd known this amazing man for such a short amount of time.

"The florist seems to have left something personal in here," she murmured, forking over the box to Lucky before she made a complete jerk of herself and started searching for happily-ever-afters in daisy bouquets. "Maybe you'd better return it because it might be something important and—"

"I put it there." Lucky settled the box back into her slightly shaking palm. "And it's definitely something important."

Francesca knew she'd have a heart attack before she even opened the unbelievable black-velvet box. The suspense was killing her and was it her imagination, or was a small crowd gathering around them?

Giselle was back in view, drawing forward a couple

of her girlfriends who were also co-owners of the club. The tall concierge who had enjoyed a laugh at her expense when she'd ventured to the Vintage Vinyl party seemed to appear out of the woodwork with the spa employees who had given her a seaweed wrap. And— holy moly—the "Eligible Male" TV cameras were creeping forward on rolling dollies across the poured concrete surrounding the swimming pools.

"What are you doing?" She held Lucky's dark brown gaze, knowing she'd never recover if this velvet box she clutched contained a necklace with a sand dollar on it or some other Florida remembrance to commemorate their week together.

"I'm trying my best to woo you, Francesca, but never let it be said you make it easy." He took the daisies from her hand and set them on the waiter's tray near her discarded Long Island Iced Tea. "Why don't you see what's inside?"

Because she was scared spitless of being hurt, and Lucky hadn't given any indication he meant for things to be serious, and...

She pried open the box to peer inside.

"Oh. My. God." She stared down at the most fabulous diamond she'd ever seen. And in Trenton, New Jersey, she'd seen some pretty big, in-your-face rocks.

This blew them all away.

Not only was it huge, it was also colored yellow. An emerald-cut square set in platinum.

Lucky's voice whispered across the space between them while the crowd around them seemed to collectively hold their breaths. "I love you, Francesca. I know it's not necessarily practical to propose after two weeks, but—"

He might have been proposing to her at that moment, but all Fran kept hearing in her head was the *I love you* part.

It was all she needed to hear.

She screamed. Jumped up and down. Flung her arms around Lucky's neck and planted a kiss on his still speaking lips.

The "Eligible Male" cast cheered and toasted them in the flickering torchlight, the best moment of her life captured on film for all of North America to witness. The last-place Jersey girl contender had won first prize despite the fierce competition. And as Lucky twirled her around in his arms, crushing her to him as if he'd never let her go, Fran even spied Marley Sinclair raising a glass to their happiness.

The DJ spun a Bruce Springsteen tune in honor of Fran's roots and the crowd dissipated to dance and party—giving them enough room to talk without being followed by cameras.

Fran finally let go of Lucky. She slid down his deliciously hard body to stare into his whiskey-colored eyes.

"I love you back." She'd been so overwhelmed by his admission she hadn't thought to reciprocate the sentiment that had been growing in her heart ever since she'd walked into her suite covered in rose petals. "I was determined to deny it because I didn't want to hurt when I left Florida, but I realized tonight as I watched a couple sharing a pizza that it was stupid of me to be so damn practical as to miss out on the possibility of love just because I was scared."

Lucky had the feeling his ear-to-ear grin would be stuck on his mug all day. "You? Scared? Lady, you wouldn't have walked away from a challenge, scared or not."

He couldn't believe he'd won over the most grounded, no-time-for-games woman he'd ever met. He'd taken a huge gamble to buy her a ring and by the time he'd given it to her, he was so damn worried she might say no, his carefully planned words of proposal had vanished from his memory banks.

But no matter that he'd forgotten a few of his well-crafted arguments for why they should be together, she'd still said yes.

Hadn't she?

"There's no rush, Fran. But about the marriage thing... Can a guy interpret a scream and a high jump as a yes?"

She laughed, sliding the ring out of the box and depositing it on her finger. Ever helpful Giselle had struck again when he'd called her from the jewelry store earlier. She'd pilfered one of Francesca's rings while she was showering to measure it for him.

"That's definitely a yes. I wasn't sure I could ever leave Jersey, but Giselle is down here and so are you. And from what I've tasted while I've been down here, it's pretty obvious South Beach needs a good pizzeria."

"Who said anything about needing to move to Florida?" She'd been willing to do that for him? God, this woman was so much more than he deserved. "Trenton's a hundred and fifty miles from D.C. I figure that's close enough to let me take an occasional big league campaign but far enough away to help me make sure I stay grounded in real life without letting ambition run me over."

"So you finally figured out you should stay in politics." She nodded approvingly as if she'd known it all along. "Wise man. What made you realize you were right where you need to be in your professional life?"

Lucky stared down at the ring on her hand, the unconventional diamond so perfect for this unconventional woman. "Marley asked me to run her campaign for Congress and I said no."

"What are you—crazy?" She blinked up at him like he'd lost his mind. "As in the United States legislature? That's the big-time."

"Exactly. And that's always how I thought about my career in the past. I took the jobs that would catapult me higher and higher. But I already cut a decent paycheck for myself by keeping tabs on a few stocks. I got into politics because I believed in the people I was representing and because I thought I could make a difference. I need you to make sure I stick to that."

Fran patted her heart, her yellow diamond and fluorescent orange nails visible even in the dim light. "You do a woman's heart good, Slick. All that flowery romance and you're still grounded enough to make practical decisions."

Shrugging, he pulled her into his arms, ready to celebrate the best Valentine's Day of his life. "I told you I was willing to work for what I want. I think I'm finally getting this romance business right."

She peered around the throng of redneck romantics whooping it up by the light of a dozen flickering torches, then leaned close to whisper in his ear. "Actually, you're close, but you're not there quite yet."

"Oh, really?" Awareness fired through him at her husky tone.

"If we want to really ring in the holiday the right way, I think we need to indulge ourselves in our first official quickie."

Amazing how the mere mention of the word fired him up from the inside out. He gauged the distance to

the Vixen's Villa and wondered how he'd ever make it.
"You think we can get from here to there without setting off any major fireworks?"

She tugged him away from the hotel, closer to the
beach. "No. But there's this cabana I've been thinking
about..."

*   *   *   *   *

If you enjoyed these two stories,
you've got to check out...

Don't miss:

964 COVER ME
by Stephanie Bond

Available next month wherever
Harlequin books are sold.
Here's a preview...

1

"KENZIE," my best friend Jacki said, "if you're going to have a one-night stand, you have to know the ground rules."

"I'm not having a one-night stand," I insisted, shaking my head. Then I squinted. "There are ground rules?"

Jacki nodded. "You have to let a friend know who you'll be with."

"That's so if you're strangled, we'll be able to give the police a description," Cindy added solemnly.

"Ah."

"But don't worry—I could describe that guy across the bar who's interested in you with my eyes closed," Denise said, then closed her eyes. "Brown hair, chinos, T-shirt, cowboy hat." She opened her eyes. "How'd I do?"

"You got the T-shirt right," I offered.

Denise frowned and twisted for another steely observation. "Damn, why did I think he was wearing a cowboy hat?"

"Because he has that look," Jacki said. "Like he might lasso something." She looked at me. "Or some*one*."

I laughed. "This is not going to happen."

"Don't take him back to your place, and don't go to his," Cindy said.

"Right," Denise added. "It has to be somewhere safe and neutral—like a hotel room."

"That way he won't know where you live."

"Oh, and lie about where you work, in case he's a stalker."

"And don't give him your real last name."

"Or your real phone number."

I was dizzy from looking back and forth. "If a one-night stand is so much work, why bother?"

"Good sex," Jacki said.

"Great sex," Cindy said.

"Fabulous sex," Denise said. "It's very liberating to get down and dirty with someone you'll never see again."

"Right," Jacki said. "Sex with someone you love is the best, but sex with a stranger is right up there near the top of the list."

"It's kind of like being a man for one night," Cindy said. "Having great sex with no emotional attachment, no strings."

They were all nodding, and I felt ridiculously left out. A liberating experience might be just what I needed to make an unremarkable thirty-first birthday. I glanced toward the bar and the sandy-haired guy was still there, watching TV and sprawled loosely in his chair. Unbidden, I began to salivate.

Jacki glanced at her watch. "I have to take off. Cindy, Denise, want to share a cab?"

"Sure," they said in unison, and reached for their purses.

"I'm not staying here alone," I cried, scrambling to gather my birthday gifts and purse.

Jacki made a protesting noise. "Kenzie, he isn't

going to talk to you if we're in a huddle. Good*bye*." The girls waved and strode toward the door.

I glanced in the direction of the bar and the guy seemed to have noticed the commotion. He leaned forward slightly, as if he was trying to decide whether to make his move. I panicked and stood to follow my friends. But when I hit my feet, the tequila hit my adenoids and sent an air bubble to my brain. I grabbed for the table, and all my belongings fell to the floor. Something heavy hit my shoe, but I was too light-headed to do more than wince. Slowly the sparkly feeling subsided and I blinked him into view. If anything, he was even nicer-looking up close.

"Are you all right?" he asked in a warm, husky voice.

Thick hair the color of antique brass, wide cheekbones, sun-bleached eyebrows...and shiny brown bedroom eyes. The moisture evaporated from my mouth, and pure desire bolted through me. "I...yes."

He flashed that killer smile, and my knees turned to elastic. At the same time, we bent to gather my wayward items. When our fingers touched, my heart raced and my ears rang like wedding—er, *church* bells. Spending time with this man would be hazardous to my plan of finding a nice unsexy guy to settle down with. I was already half in love with him and I didn't even know his name.

While covering the words on the box, I stuffed the canisters inside and stood, trying to act as nonchalant as possible. "Thank you, um—"

"Sam," he said.

Nice name. "Thank you. Sam."

Desire gripped me and I mentally reviewed the ground rules for a one-night stand.

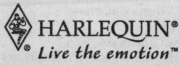

**Don't miss the exciting February 2004
Harlequin Temptation lineup!**

CUT TO THE CHASE by Julie Kistler
BACK IN THE BEDROOM by Jill Shalvis
LEGALLY MINE by Kate Hoffmann
COVER ME by Stephanie Bond

Save $1.00

off any February 2004, Harlequin Temptation title

5 65373 00076 2   (8100) 0 11118

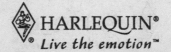

HARLEQUIN®
Live the emotion™

Visit us at www.eHarlequin.com

Don't miss the exciting February 2004 Harlequin Temptation lineup!

HARLEQUIN®

Temptation®

CUT TO THE CHASE by Julie Kistler
BACK IN THE BEDROOM by Jill Shalvis
LEGALLY MINE by Kate Hoffmann
COVER ME by Stephanie Bond

Save $1.00

off any February 2004, Harlequin Temptation title

52605677

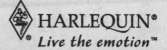

HARLEQUIN®
Live the emotion™

Visit us at www.eHarlequin.com